MR C. CHAMBERS

MR CHAMBERS

Tammy Bench

British Library Cataloguing in Publication Data.
A catalogue record for this book is available from the British Library.

ISBN-13: 9781517525248
ISBN-10: 1517525241

www.tammybench.com

For C, when going 'all out' is the best you can do.

PROLOGUE

August 2003

It was late. All the commotion of the day had slowly ebbed away leaving a steady calm and silent darkness, but Alice still couldn't sleep. Her beautiful lace wedding dress that she had cared so much for at the start of the day now lay crumpled in a ridiculously expensive ball on the hotel room floor. Her new husband slept soundlessly in the huge bed behind her and for the first time in a long time she felt that she had found her place in the world.

She sat on the sofa near to him, oddly hypnotised by his rhythmic breaths. An old leather-bound journal sat on her lap. Her name *'Alice Rutherford'* was embossed in antique gold lettering across the front. It was the keeper of her secrets and dreams – not a diary of the everyday – but the loyal, hard backed guardian of her most special days and the simple, magical and sometimes random moments that had moved her.

It was nearly full now and she wondered if its successor would have *'Alice Lyons'* printed on its cover in the same way? She didn't know if she would like that or not.

Opening it to the next blank page she prepared to tell to it of the day that every girl dreams about, her wedding day.

Alice's hand hovered delicately over the page fully prepared to begin, when an old habit, or had it now become a compulsive need, rushed at her suddenly.

She breathed out heavily.

She knew what her heart wanted. She resigned herself to the long standing ritual and the course of action that would be required to fulfil the feelings that it would stir.

She put down the pen beside her and flipped guiltily to a handful of pages she had read and re-read a hundred times before. These pages were worn thin at the bottom edge and her thumb and forefinger fit neatly into the frail indentations. Her own looping handwriting held her focus for a moment as the odd word jumped out at her, making her heart speed up a little, seducing her.

This was a story she knew so well. She didn't need to read it to be able to recite every single word that was written. But looking at those words she had once formed so lovingly during the heat of things, made the memory come to life. Made what happened back then so real.

'*Do you know hard it is to say no to you right now?*'

She could hear his voice talking to her in his enchanting Irish accent from beyond the lines she had quoted him. His laugh echoed around the intimate privacy of her bridal suite.

'*You are wanted. I do want you and I want no one else to have you.*'

God it felt like she was self-harming, like it was torture, but a beautiful torture though, one that she must endure to gain a release that would make him hers once more for a few short moments.

Then she found the date she was looking for.

Saturday November 25th 1995.

Two little hearts scrawled in blue pen to the side of the date. She read the first few lines to herself.

I arrived in the taxi as he had instructed me to. He's still so worried about people finding out about us. I got to the door and he pulled me inside, kissing me so passionately I would never get over it...

Alice cringed slightly at her seventeen-year-old self. Her stupid optimism and childlike description embarrassed her. But she couldn't deny that was how it had felt. She flicked forward a few pages and read on.

Sitting on the edge of his bed watching him as he took his t-shirt off – I almost ran from the room with nerves. Of course I wanted to do this but now there was just me and him. No other students or teachers around. No one to stop this but me... and I wasn't about to stop it. I was pretty sure Tom wasn't going to stop what was happening either. I can't begin to describe how amazing he looked tonight...

Alice sat back and closed her eyes. The dim light of his bedroom lamp had shone to the side of her young face. Her thick hair falling over her shoulders and when she glanced down at her own hands she noticed how they trembled with the realisation of this fantasy unfolding before her. There was a song playing, a country song. She had always meant to ask him what is was, but never did. Tom tossed his shirt onto the floor and made a joke about something, making her smile and blush. Then he had smiled too and her whole world had shifted.

Alice breathed away a tear that was threatening to fall. She opened her eyes, checked her husband was still sleeping and continued to read.

He pushed into me so hard this time, I could feel him inside me. I didn't want to cry out. I wanted him to think I was mature and cool with everything, but the noise escaped me before I could stop it. He froze and a look of sheer terror appeared on his handsome face. But I told him to carry on. I didn't want him to come to his senses and tell me this couldn't continue.

He made love to me for the first time tonight. He made love to me like I was his equal.

She remembered the feeling of him so well. The way he had started gentle... until it wasn't anymore, until it was unforgettable...

Before I went to sleep that night (in his bed!), I remember wishing that the way I felt right then was how I would feel every night of my life. I remember thinking as I looked over at him that this was the man I wanted forever. I wanted him to love me in spite of everything and because of everything.

Alice put her hand to her mouth and looked away as she read the last passage from memory.

What happened not only changed my life, but it changed me. This kind of thing doesn't happen every day. I finally lost my virginity and it was the most honest moment I think I will ever experience.

I actually had sex with Tom! There, I said it. I had sex with Mr Chambers! I'm totally in love with my teacher...

Alice slammed her book shut.

The hole that he had left within her soul, she thought, had almost disappeared. The years had done their job efficiently and softened the edges of a pain that had once ripped her to pieces. She had met a great guy. She was looking forward to her impending motherhood. A surprise that herself and Stuart had to keep a secret, however hard they were finding it, for another few weeks at least. So, today especially, Tom had felt as good as gone. He was a distant memory, ancient history and that had made her feel safe and happy.

But now, at 2.39am and the ink still wet on the marriage register. With her mind full of baby names, best man speeches and first dance nerves. Only hours after vowing to honour unto him as long as they both shall live and forsaking all others – she was back there again, in Tom's strong embrace wishing it all away and that truth made her utterly sick.

She promised herself then in that moment of self-awareness and loathing that she would never open the journal again. It would stay shut. For the sake of everything that was dear to her now. Her amazing new husband and precious baby on the way and for the hopes of a peaceful contented future, Tom, was staying well and truly within the pages of a book...

JOIN, MAYBE, DECLINE

July 2010

Tom hated Facebook. He didn't know why the hell he even bothered with it? He had set up a profile years ago, didn't add a picture and had never once posted a status. It was more of a voyeuristic tool that served him a purpose from time to time.

Today was different however.

He had received an email at about 10.30am. Just as the third bell had rung and his class noisily left the room. His smartphone had pinged.

'I want that coursework tomorrow, Jake,' he called after one of the boys.

'Sir,' he shouted back as he sauntered from the classroom.

He waited for the last pupil to exit the room before he snuck a quick look.

Facebook event invitation – wonderful! But just before he hit delete, which would have been his default response to all these emails, something in the subtext caught his eye... *Claude Bennett School.*

Tom quickly hit open.

'*Claude Bennett School Reunion*' – '*Sixth Form Class of 1997*'

Tom's mouth went dry and he sat forward in his chair.

Saturday July 31ˢᵗ 7.30pm All Students and Teachers Welcome.

He quickly looked at who had added him to the invitation list, Simon Harris, a PE teacher and friend of his at the time. Jesus, he had only been at the school a year and was sure no one would remember him, let alone find him on here without a damn picture.

But there it was.

Tom wanted to delete it but he didn't. Instead his thumb hovered over the list of people invited. He knew she'd be on it.

As he had mentioned Facebook was good for something and over the years that he had been a member on the world famous site he had – more times than he could remember – clicked on her name. She was Alice Lyons now, no longer Rutherford (that still got to him.) He would study her profile picture, the only public photo of her he could find and think of all they had done together. Of course he would never 'friend request' her, that would be the most inappropriate and distasteful thing he could think of. Even looking at her picture felt wrong and dirty somehow.

He clicked on the list.

Halfway down the page he saw her name and her response to the invitation. She was going. Six names below her name, his, Tom Chambers. Just seeing his name near to her own made him feel like the room was getting smaller. The collar on his shirt felt a little tighter and his stomach turned over with a mind of its own.

He pushed his hand through his hair, his fingers grabbing the thick ends. He looked at the clock. Break time. Thank goodness, he wasn't ready for more pupils yet – not like this.

Calm the fuck down.

'Coming to the staff room?' Ann Parris stuck her head round his open door and waggled a coffee cup at him making him jump.

'What? – Um no thanks Ann, I'm going to be in here for a bit… finishing up a few things,' his answer was skittish and he thought his voice sounded a little too high pitched. She looked at him with mild concern.

'You okay?' she asked.

'Good thanks. Just…'

'Worried about taking over as Head after the summer?' she smiled at him like she had got it in one. How further from the truth could she be?

'Is it that obvious?' Tom smiled at her through his lie. She blushed then, the way she always did when she talked to him.

'You'll be amazing, Tom,' she met his eye and her hand smoothed her hair, 'you always are… anyway I'll bring you a cup back,' she hurried out quickly.

'Thank you!' he called after her. He smiled as she raised her arm in a frantic wave but didn't look back at him.

Alice Rutherford was going.

Tom obviously wasn't going. He looked at the date. Two weeks from now. He would be on summer holidays from school at that time. His mind wondered for a moment or two as he started to form logical and genuine reasons why a trip across the Irish Sea would be a good idea. He could fly over and spend some time with Neil and his sister and many of his friends in England he hadn't seen in a few years?

Are you seriously considering this?

No. He was just cruelly teasing himself.

He had moved back to Ireland after they had ended and he had vowed to leave it all alone. Leave her alone. Let her have a normal life.

The eighteen months that had followed 'Alice' had been a living hell. He had bought a plane ticket on four separate occasions determined to win her back. Two of the times he got to the airport before he realised how much his actions would hurt her. Once he actually touched down at Gatwick before turning around in the arrivals lounge and flying straight back home. He had wanted her back more than he had ever wanted anything. But he had made the decision, he had broken both their hearts and she was better off without him.

You don't believe that...

None of it mattered anymore. It was fourteen years ago and an awful lot of water had flowed under both their bridges.

Alice was married with a daughter.

He had married. He had two children, twins, a boy and a girl. Unfortunately, the marriage didn't last and they were now divorced, but thank God still good friends.

He had loved his beautiful, gracious wife dearly but the ghosts from his past wouldn't stay hidden. Over the years they were together she had learnt little bits of what had happened. He would play it down to save her feelings. He had even changed Alice's age making her a few years older to take the edge off a little. When his wife would ask if he loved her more than he had loved Alice? He would laugh and say *'Are you seriously asking me that? Of course I love you more, you're my wife. Alice was just a crazy fling'* but unfortunately that wasn't the truth.

Time went on and slowly she saw past his façade. She knew he loved her but that wasn't enough. She needed and wanted more than he would ever be able to give her. He tried desperately to make it work, as had she... but in the end it hadn't.

You can only hide for so long.

Fourteen years ago, as a teacher he had done the worst thing imaginable, he had conducted a sexual relationship with a seventeen-year-old student. It was totally unforgivable and he had desperately spent the time from that day to this trying to be the best teacher, father and man he could be. Trying to make up for the despicable things he had done.

But also fourteen years ago he had found and deeply fallen in love with the one girl who had brought him to his knees, amazed him and belonged to him. He had spent the autumn and winter of 1995 locked in the most beautiful and briefest encounter with a woman he could never forget.

That truth was still as raw as ever.

On the 31st of July you know where she is going to be…

Tom shook his head. Picked up his phone and scrolled back to the top of the page. Tom Chambers – he read his options again. Join, maybe or decline?

He looked at the small thumbnail pictures. The faces of a class he had once taught. Some were bald, some had beards and a lot were pictured with their own children. Their faces pushed lovingly against that of their offspring smiling in a selfie. They were adults now with adult lives.

Then there was Alice. Still blonde, still a little pixie and still the loveliest thing he had ever seen.

He stared at the pictures for a long time, until the bell rang again indicating end of break.

Times up, Chambers?

He paused for a moment. Looked down at his phone and hit decline.

No way.

With an angry sadness he wasn't expecting he launched his phone towards his laptop, it hit the screen and ricocheted onto the floor, sliding to an abrupt stop at his foot.

No fucking way.

OLD HABITS DIE HARD

Alice was packing for everyone. Why did she always have to pack for everyone? She had enough to think about with arranging cover for the gallery and putting the dog in kennels. Making sure Hayley's favourite programmes were recording, cancelling the damn papers and doing a last minute clean and vacuum. She didn't have time to worry if Stuart would be happy with her choice of shirts for him or if he had enough boxers for the week. Why couldn't married men pack their own – excuse her French – shit?

'Mum, why do we have to go for ten whole days?' Hayley had been following her around all morning asking questions just for the sake of asking questions.

'Baby, it's the summer holidays we're going to see your cousins. Nannie and Pops and Auntie Steph are looking forward to seeing us.'

'Not Uncle Tony?' she asked suspiciously.

'Yes of course Uncle Tony, too. You should be itching to get out of here,' she ruffled her daughter's hair lightly.

'Itching? But I'm going to miss Zach's party. It's a dinosaur party... so not fair mummy,' she sulked.

'You don't even like dinosaurs.'

'Yes I do.'

'Since when?' Alice asked patiently.

'Since two hours ago when I saw some on the telly.'

Alice rolled her eyes, 'Hayley there are twenty-seven children in your class I don't think it will hurt you to miss one party, there's still twenty-six more you can attend.'

'Not a dinosaur party and not my best friend Zach's party,' Hayley crossed her arms and stared at her mother.

'I've heard you mention Zach three times in two years, he's not your best friend.'

The mum part of her felt guilty that Hayley would miss out on anything. But when did she ever do anything for herself these days? She needed this break.

'We became best friends last week actually.'

Actually!?

'Well he can come round and play when we get back, you have the big holidays now and also you can choose a nice present for him whilst we're at Nannie's house.'

'I don't want him to come and play,' she picked up her Barbie and added it to the pile of stuff Alice was yet to pack.

'I give up then, Hayley,' she wasn't going to win. 'Go and get your dad to help me – I don't know what he's doing?'

'Okay mummy, by the way Zach's not my best friend now actually.'

Alice turned on her monster face, roared at the top of her voice and chased Hayley round the side of the bed. Hayley squealed and ran out of the room laughing.

Alice was going home. She was kind of excited and kind of apprehensive. There was just so much to think about. She and Stuart loved getting away, but the art gallery and his sports physiotherapy took up so much of his time that they always felt like their world would implode or something if one of them wasn't there to keep a watchful eye over everything. Control freaks? Probably.

It's wasn't like they never saw their families, just not as much as they would like. It had become snatched weekends here and there as that's all they had been able to manage in the last few years. So it was going to be fabulous to kick back for a while without having to unpack on the Friday and re-pack on Sunday, rushing home for school the next day.

Stuart and Alice had moved away from her small home town in Oxfordshire to the beautiful rugged shores of Norfolk about five years ago, just after Hayley was born.

Stuart was working as a physiotherapist at the time and Alice was getting used to becoming the mother to a small baby with all the joys and pitfalls that entailed.

They had taken their first family holiday on the broads because they hadn't fancied braving a flight anywhere with a baby, so opted for a good old British break instead.

They had spent their third morning milling in and out of little shops trying desperately to get Hayley off to sleep, but in the end they had given up and stopped for coffee. She remembered how they had instantly loved the feel of the area. It was untouched and held a charm that appealed to them both.

It might have been because they were new parents and slightly worried about what the future had in store for them. Or maybe they had feared that their adventurous days were behind them because afterwards as they re-joined the cobbled street Stuart had wandered over to the window of an estate agents. In the business section a local hairdressers called 'Snips' was pictured, just below that two large warehouses. But then right at the bottom a card advertising a small art gallery and craft workshop in Holt had caught her eye, the picture was tiny but it looked interesting. She remembered how they had looked at each other. She had shrugged at him and he had smiled back. Then with Hayley strapped to his chest in a baby sling he had pushed opened the door and asked for a viewing that very same day.

That was one of the things she loved most about her husband, he was impulsive and unpredictable. But at the same time solid and unwavering in his choices.

Six weeks later they had moved. Not knowing what they were doing or why? Six years and a lot of hard work later, they had a business they were proud of.

Alice took care of Hayley and worked at the gallery around school hours. Stuart was full time, but still practiced physiotherapy on the weekends and evenings. He also swam three times a week to keep fit. He was the busiest man she knew but still made so much time for his family.

That's where they had met actually – in a swimming pool. Not the most romantic setting but these things rarely are.

It was her first year at university and his second. He was studying Sports Science and she was doing a Philosophy degree. She couldn't face taking English as she had planned, not after Tom.

Stuart was a part-time lifeguard at the university pool and Alice was trying to throw herself into college life by joining the swimming club, the running club and the events committee. Basically she was doing anything and everything that didn't remind her of Tom.

Stuart had said after they got together he had noticed her the first day she walked out of the ladies changing rooms. But Alice didn't believe him, she thought he was just trying to add weight to his claim that they were fated to be together or something? Anyway, she had observed the way the girls flocked around him.

With his cheeky good looks, dirty blonde hair and 6'4 swimmers physique who could blame them really?

She was swimming late one evening. The clocks had just gone back and it was dark by 6pm. The pool was almost empty and had a yellow dreamlike glow about it. She was doing lengths, over and over. Trying to push her body past where her mind wanted it to go. She was doing anything to keep Tom from her thoughts. It felt crazy that he still occupied so many of them.

On what could have been her twentieth lap she stopped to catch her breath at the shallow end. She lifted her goggles and noticed him sat with his legs dangling into the water, watching her. His hair was wet and he wasn't wearing a t-shirt, a whistle hung around his neck on a length of blue cord.

'Impressive. You're quick,' he spoke in a low hushed tone like it was their secret, but it could have just been the pool's vastness and the water in her ears.

'Thanks,' Alice replied pulling the goggles over her eyes again. She didn't want to stop and chat.

'Stuart Lyons,' he held out his hand before she could excuse herself. She paused and shook it once.

'Alice Rutherford.'

'Want to race?' he asked narrowing his eyes and smiling a crooked smile.

Alice looked at him for a moment. Then cocked her head to one side, 'sure, why not.'

He had won the race but she had always maintained that it was because she had already swum so much that evening and nothing at all to do with him being the stronger swimmer.

They started dating a week later, nothing serious at first just the odd drink now and again. She suspected he was still seeing other people and keeping his options open. But gradually over the next month or two he changed. Soon he seemed to always be available when she called. He would randomly buy her flowers or turn up at her room with takeaway food and a movie. He was silly and made her laugh. He made her think less and less about Tom.

The other thing she liked about him was that he was a contradiction. He looked like a British version of the all American boy. He was jock-like, handsome, blonde and very popular. But unlike the stereotype he wasn't mean or arrogant. He was kind to people, he liked to help and was rarely selfish or insensitive.

She fell for him – how could she not? And the rest was history.

So, as she was saying, she was going home.

She was also going to her school reunion. That little blast from the past had come quite out of the blue and to be honest Alice's first impulse was to say no to the invitation. But she had spoken to some of her old girlie mates and they were all going. They hounded her with texts, calls and emails until she had agreed.

None of them knew about Tom, if they had, she doubted they would have pushed so hard.

Alice had watched Facebook like a hawk after she had posted her response. She waited a week until someone had finally added Tom to the invite list, so tempted she had been to do it herself. Then, within a day he replied saying he wasn't able to attend.

Just to see that he had actually responded at all made her heart speed up... he was alive out there somewhere in the world and this was the first bit of communication, however tenuous and indirect she'd had with him in fourteen years.

First she felt relief that she could go to the party and not worry about seeing him. After relief came sadness and emptiness, then frustration and finally a raging anger. Anger that he could see she was going and within hours of his name appearing on the list, he had declined.

He had said no. No, he didn't want to see her. No, he didn't care anymore. It had taken him zero time at all to make his decision, where she had thought about him for seven long, painful and confusing days.

He had said without a shadow of a doubt, as if he was stood in front of her, 'Alice, I don't ever want to see you again.'

Get over it.

Alice wandered into the study and flipped on the computer. Why did she keep checking? She knew it as a pointless exercise. She logged on, waited and once more was smacked in the face by his complete disinterest.

'Alice?' Stuart rested a warm hand on her shoulder, 'you alright honey?'

'Yep fine, just seeing if there were any last minute changes to the plan for Saturday. Times or place?' she swallowed hard and looked up at him. He was still so boyishly handsome that when he frowned – like he was now – it seemed odd.

'He's not changed his fucking mind has he?' his harsh words didn't match his kind eyes. He was so worried about the whole thing.

'No. Don't worry. I wouldn't be going if he had,' she lied.

'Good. Alice, I'm not being possessive or freaky, but I couldn't stand it if you saw him.'

'I'm not going to see him. I don't even think he lives in the country, Stu,' she stroked his hand gently.

'I don't like it,' he half smiled at her.

'I want to go. I haven't seen the girls for ages and some of the others I haven't seen since we left. I've said you can come if you want to?'

'And be the only partner there? Looking like I'm some kind of 'sleeping with the enemy' husband or something?' he laughed swinging their office chair around to face him and kissing her.

'I love you, but please don't worry,' she whispered.

'You know there's part of me that wants to see him? I want to look him in the eye and tell him what I think of him. How disgusting he is. How dare he ever have touched my wife like that?'

Alice had made the mistake of telling Stuart about her relationship with Tom after a few years of being together. They had been out drinking, when they had got back to their flat they started chatting about their first times, the way we all do eventually. She hadn't given him all the details initially, but as time went on he had questioned her more on the subject and pieced bits together.

'I've told you so many times it was never like that. It was never disgusting or wrong to me. I didn't feel abused. I wasn't raped. I just fell for the wrong guy and vice versa. Please don't make it feel perverted,' she hated him talking about it. It was before his time and deep inside she didn't want his judgement on her actions or his judgement of Tom. If anyone had the right to be angry it was her alone.

'Sorry… am I forgiven? I don't want to upset you,' he kissed her again.

'You're always forgiven silly,' she kissed him back and turned off the computer monitor.

'I would love to flipping knock his block off though…'

'Leave it!' she shouted kindly and pushed him towards their room to sort his own packing.

THE PROBLEM WITH NEVER

T om wasn't considering this a secret mission or anything like that, but he was certainly keeping a low profile as he watched the baggage conveyor belt travel slowly around and around. He had watched the same hideous floral green suitcase go past him three times already and just as he was about to complain to lost luggage the machine spat out his old leather holdall. He grabbed it, slung it over his shoulder and headed for the exit.

He was here. His better judgment had lost out. As it always had where Alice was concerned and he had booked a last minute flight. He resisted all the way up to the wire. His confident 'no fucking way' had lasted an impressive thirteen days.

He still wasn't going, not to the actual reunion. He just wanted to be around, in the area. He wasn't about to make a grand entrance, he was pretty sure he would make no entrance at all, but he might just swing by and take a look at the old place.

Neil, his best friend and eternal bachelor was picking him up out front. He had agreed to let Tom stay with him on the condition that Tom promised not to go to the party at all.

'Tom Chambers, as I live and breathe,' Neil shouted as soon as he stepped outside, 'looking good!'

'Thanks man, you too,' he pulled him in for a hug. It felt good to see him again.

'Seriously Tom how do you look better every time I see you? You're practically an old man now and still…' Neil joked holding his arms out in mock amazement.

'Fuck you!' Tom pushed him and opened the car door.

'If I was that way inclined I would jump at that offer dude!'

'Tell me why I'm staying in a house with you again?' Tom shook his head and laughed.

'You can't keep your hands off me?' Neil blew him a kiss and Tom jumped up to catch it and tucked it away into his jeans pocket with a girly tap. They both cracked up laughing.

'How're the rug-rats?' Neil asked. He was Tom's children's godfather and doted on them.

'Grand. Not really rug-rats anymore. You need to come over at Christmas, they miss you,' Tom answered.

'I will, definitely.'

Neil started the engine of his impressive new company car and revved it a little louder than necessary for effect. Tom rolled his eyes. He still drove the same blue Peugeot 205 that had been his constant companion for the last sixteen years. He just couldn't get rid of it, even though the repairs had cost him way over the price of a new car in the last ten years. It was now considered 'old school cool' as his pupils informed him all the time. Some of the sixth form lads had even tried to buy it from him, or their daddy had. The downside of working at a private school was spoilt kids. Besides Tom definitely wasn't selling.

'So tell me again what you think you're doing here?' Neil asked on the drive to his house.

'Not seeing Alice Rutherford.'

'Ah correction, she is no longer a single gal, Tom. Alice… what was it, Lyons?' Neil glanced at him.

'It's Rutherford,' he gritted out.

'Think you'll find it isn't,' Neil whispered under his breath.

'I'm here to see you. To see the guys and if I catch a glimpse of her then at least I'll know she's alright.'

But you won't be.

'Do you have any idea what you are about to do to yourself?' Neil's face and tone changed from jovial to deadly serious.

'No.'

'Tom, I'm not being funny but do you remember the conversations we had on the phone after you left? Do you remember the total devastation?' Neil pulled the car over and flicked on the hazards.

'It was a long time ago. We've all moved on, changed. It's just curiosity,' he pushed his hand through his hair in frustration, 'a forty something guy doesn't go into this thinking that he gets a second chance,' Tom tried to assure him.

'And a thirty something guy doesn't risk everything for a relationship with a teenager at a crucial time in his career... or at all for that matter. But you did. So it's not as if we're talking about a normal guy here, are we? We're talking about a heart-on-sleeve wearing, crazy mother fucking loose cannon!'

Tom snickered, 'Maybe. But I've tried to bury him, remember?'

'Oh yeah I remember. Bloody reformed character,' he cocked his head towards his friend and smiled, 'don't think you're fooling anyone in this car by saying you just want to see if she's okay. You're not.'

'Neil, you're the most perceptive person I know. I wouldn't even try to pull the wool over your eyes. But this time you're wrong, I have no intention of confronting her. Really, I'm not that brave... I wish I were.'

He was sure the words that were coming out of his mouth were the truth.

'Then you must have buried the old Tom good and proper. Because I know for sure the Chambers I used to hang out with would take one look at her and try to kidnap her or something just as dumb,' Neil stated.

'Tempting,' Tom joked.

'Don't even say that, Tom. You sound like you're taking the piss, but I hear your cogs whirring.'

'She's a grown woman. She has a child. I'm not about to come crashing into her life and make trouble. She probably remembers me as a pervert now anyway. She certainly remembers me as a bastard, I made sure of that.'

'Ah don't beat yourself up, you did what you had to.'

'Did I?' Tom let his head fall back against the rest. It was heavy with old memories and new fears, 'Neil, I walked away from her. Why am I only fully realising the enormity of that decision now?'

Tom could remember every word they had said to each other the last time he had seen her. It was a Tuesday. It was raining. She had just found out he was leaving.

'How can you love me and see me reduced to this, Tom?'

'Alice, I will love you forever but this is wrong... I can't do this anymore. I'm not strong enough... and you're not strong enough for both of us.'

'I can't be anything without you.'

'You can be everything without me, in time you will realise that, baby... can't you see this is ripping my fucking heart out too?'

'You're right I shouldn't have come,' Tom turned to his friend and shrugged.

'Let's get back, mate. Have a beer and then maybe a couple more after that.'

Tom nodded, 'Sounds good.'

'Sounds like the good old days is what it sounds like,' Neil pulled off again, 'and if you're having trouble in the S.E.X department,' he spelt out the word discretely, 'and if anytime in the next week feel as if you're about to cash in all your chips for a certain blonde. I have plenty of women at work that would fall off their chairs to help a beef cake like you forget the past. If you know what I mean?'

'Beef cake!? I worry about you, I really do.' Tom shook his head and laughed, 'and I'm not so hard up yet that your sloppy seconds hold much appeal.'

'I've had yours on more than one occasion,' Neil said through his own laughter.

'Yeah that's because I'm better looking than you.'

'Still the same arrogant bastard.'

'The truth hurts,' Tom smiled and looked out of the window. Tomorrow would be alright. He wouldn't mess up.

'Oh tell me one thing… you didn't bring the photos did you?' he asked narrowing his stare at Tom.

Tom had kept two photo booth pictures of himself and Alice from back then. He kept them in his car and if he was being honest he looked at them almost every day. At first it was a need to see her smile, to prove that what they had shared was real. As the years went by it had become habit. Now it was a temptation. In the last two weeks he had thought about little else but that temptation.

'No, I didn't bring the damn photos, don't worry man I'm not that obsessed.'

He had brought the photos.

"TONIGHT IS YOUR NIGHT BRO"

Saturday July 31ˢᵗ

Alice stood in her parents' en-suite shower and let the water flow over her already sensitised body. She was on edge and inconclusively excited. The water was hot but it did little to chase the goosebumps from her skin. She was stepping back in time tonight and she was feeling good about it.

"…looking from the window above, this is the story of love… can you hear me?" Alice sang her favourite song by Yazoo.

It's funny how your voice doesn't sound exactly like your own when taking a shower. It always makes you a slightly better singer, she thought absentmindedly.

"Came back only yesterday, moving farther away…"

That sounds really sexy.

'Tom.'

A massive rush of nerves hit her stomach as she said his name out loud.

Why say that?

'Tom,' she said again and bit her lip. Her voice was outside of her body. She could hear it, but it was disconnected.

'Tom Chambers…' arousal shot into her temples and spread down her cheeks. It made the corners of her lips twitch of their own accord.

'Mr Chambers.'

Stop it!

The memory of him giving her an antique bracelet with the little ceramic teapot charm, blazed across her mind. He had called her his *Alice in Wonderland.*

'I'm not trying to buy you...' he whispered.

'If you were, I'd sell...' she had replied.

Enough, this was silly and expected. Of course being in this house again and knowing she was going back to the old school this evening would bring back memories. It would remind her of everything that had happened. She shouldn't dwell on it. She needed to treat tonight as a fantastic opportunity to see old friends and have some much needed and long overdue 'me' time and leave it at that.

She had to stop hoping he was going to be there.

Stuart popped his head around the door a few minutes later, 'Hun, I've ironed your dress for you it's on the bed and Stephanie has just got here. She's on her own and she said she wants to give you a 'pep talk' before you leave?'

'You didn't have to do that, Stu, thanks. Tell her I'll see her in my room in about twenty minutes. It's an old ritual – don't ask!' she shouted back kindly.

'Okay.'

Alice found her dress where Stuart had left it. They were sleeping in her parents' room during their visit so they could have the room with the en-suite and enough space for the camp bed. Hayley still got nervous about sleeping in different houses so for transitional ease she bunked in with them.

Alice blasted her hair with the dryer and combed it into place. She carefully applied mascara, lip gloss and a little blusher. Slipped the navy dress over her head and spritzed with perfume. Finally, she pulled on her knee length boots and checked herself in the mirror. She thought she looked alright, maybe even quite nice.

'Tonight is your night bro…' Stephanie smiled as soon as Alice entered her old bedroom.

'That again?' Alice smiled back cheekily.

The room was no longer a teenage haven filled with the thousand things a girl had amassed over her childhood. It didn't house her jar of shells or her sixty-four Troll figures with brightly coloured tufts of hair. Her complete works of Shakespeare had been evicted from the pine bookshelves and the neat pile of *Smash Hits* magazine had long since been recycled. But her old *Commodore 64* PC still sat at her now clutter-free desk. The humongous cream coloured dinosaur probably hadn't even been switched on since she left. She recalled hours spent at that computer writing and re-writing essays and coursework. She had no idea why her parents still kept it as they both had laptops?

Her bedroom had evolved into a small tasteful lilac inspired guestroom. With dried flowers on the window sill and too many scatter cushions on the bed. If Alice had any criticism at all, it would be that it felt a bit too circa 1992 for her taste. But then, her mother had anything but a minimalistic eye for design.

'Tonight is your night bro,' Steph sang again.

When they were teenagers they had started this little routine. Whenever one of them was going out on a date or some other significant venture, the other would sing those words. She was sure it had come from the Arnold Schwarzenegger film *Twins*. Danny De Vito sings it to Arnie just before he goes to get laid for the first time – that's how she remembered it anyway.

'Nervous?' she asked.

'A bit. It's going to be weird seeing some of those guys. I hope I haven't aged the worst.' She sat down beside Stephanie on her old bed.

'You've aged into a fox, chill out.'

'Well at least my sister has my corner. Did you bring me a glass of that?' Steph nodded and pointed to the bedside cabinet.

'Cheers,' Alice sipped the wine and the fledgling mouthful served some way to centre her growing apprehension.

'I know what you're thinking.'

'Oh?' Alice asked looking away.

'Why isn't he going, right?' Her sister was the only person aside from Stuart that she had told about Tom, 'He's not going because he doesn't want to mess with your head.'

'Well by not going he has already done that,' she replied, 'but I didn't want to see him anyway. I just wanted him to want to see me. How conceited is that?'

'Put yourself in his shoes. If you had fucked a student repeatedly whilst teaching at the school you had just received a reunion invitation from, if you had told this girl you loved her, if you had then ran away from her and broke her heart, would you show up?' She looked at Alice and shook her head slowly.

'No, probably not. But I'm not Tom. Tom would show up... I know he would... at least I thought he would.'

'Stop talking seventeen. He wouldn't. Only an idiot would go tonight.'

'He's not so it doesn't matter either way.'

'Listen I know it matters to you. This is a tough night and I'm not sure why you even agreed to go? You're brave, Alice. Because this is truly going to be closure and I'm not convinced that's what you want?'

'It is,' she sighed.

The truth was Alice wasn't sure if she was ready to say goodbye to all the stuff that still clung to the sides of her heart. Her sister was right. She was dancing with the devil.

'If that's the truth then good, go have a cracking night, get pissed and dance and don't look back.'

'I will.' Alice nodded and got up. She tipped the rest of her wine into Stephanie's glass.

'Here's looking at you kid.' Stephanie raised her glass and smiled.

Alice picked up her best bag and headed for the door, 'Thank you.'

'What for this time?' she joked and rolled her eyes.

'Always being the angel on my shoulder,' Alice winked at her sister.

THE REUNION

Claude Bennett School – a cliché – but it was so much smaller than she remembered.

Alice walked slowly from the car park towards the lecture theatre. She wanted to breathe in the feel and spirit of the place. She wanted to take her time to remember the way things had been.

She wished she could spin around like Wonder Woman and magically change into a grey skirt and itchy blue blazer. Pull her hair into a scruffy ponytail in the toilets and idly wander to her next lesson without a care in the world.

She walked past the dinner hall. The light green eggshell coloured paint still chipped away on the thin doors. She put her hands up to the window to shield her gaze from the evening sun. She peered in, the stack of brown wood effect melamine dinner trays looked like they hadn't been changed since she had left. Alice remembered the way she and her friends would sit and chat at the corner table near the door and watch as more students poured past the till point and into the already rammed-full dining area.

Tom often bought a sandwich from the canteen and took it back to the staff room or his classroom and before they had started

24

a relationship the simple thrill of what he was having for lunch would make her day and often she would buy the same thing.

Alice turned and walked on. She looked up at the English block, situated on the second floor above the Languages department. Tom's room was on the other side the building and it looked out over a sports field. When she didn't have him for a lesson she would daydream about what he was doing, imagining him talking to a different class capturing their minds and awakening innocent first years to Shakespeare or Keats. He was nothing if he wasn't a fantastic teacher.

As much as Alice loved her life, being back here now was making her wish that she was a child again. A time when all you had to worry about was being told off by a teacher hanging out of their classroom window not to cut the corners of the green patch of grass they called 'The Quad'. That maybe there was homework that you had forgotten to do? Or fretting about whether your parents would buy you the latest pair of 'Kickers' so you could look the same as every other kid.

Alice reached the door to the lecture theatre. A colourful hand-painted sign welcomed her to the 'Class of 1997' reunion. Whoever was organising this event had gone to considerable trouble with the details. There was a large pin-board just inside with lots of photos of her year group and she spent a few moments looking at them.

Smiling, she felt a bittersweet sadness that couldn't be avoided when you're confronted with memories of people and a time that you had loved and lost. Through no fault of your own, you eventually lose all these little things. As you grow into an adult you have less and less opportunity to remain the person that smiled a goofy smile for the yearbook picture and signed the back page with an open hearted, 'Friends forever' or the world changing, 'Stay cool' or her personal favourite, 'You better keep in touch or else…'

Alice took one last nervous breath and pushed the door open.

He still might be here…

She knew he wasn't.

The music was loud but not too loud, they were in their thirties now after all. *Breakfast at Tiffany's* blasted out and she smiled again. Someone had even worked on the perfect playlist.

"And I hate when things are over and so much is left undone…"

Alice walked in and looked around. The room was nearly full. Lots of people seemed to be hanging out at the makeshift bar near the centre of the room. A small dance floor had been taken over by a group of ladies she didn't recognise and prayed she wasn't the same age as or she was seriously living in denial about the state of her own wrinkles.

Someone grabbed her arm and she turned.

'Why didn't you bloody text, I would have come out to meet you?' Cara said smiling.

One of her closest friends from school and one of a handful of girls she had kept in touch with. Cara was a sweetheart and surprisingly still with the same guy she was with back then, but now with four sons to boot.

'Hey. That's alright I wanted to soak it up a bit, you know what I'm like about school days,' Alice giggled, 'so who's here?'

'Loads of us, come and I'll re-acquaint you with a few people,' she said.

The next few hours passed quickly. Drinks flowed freely and what at the start had felt odd, after a short time seemed wonderful. The faces of kids you once knew didn't seem all that different. The boys had got tall and become men. The girls were either wives or mothers like her or still living the single life and enjoyed a bit too much to drink. The teachers she recognised were mostly aging or retired.

But the bond was still there. The time they had shared when they were free and not always sure who they were, was very real.

It felt safe and nostalgic. Like leftover roast beef sandwiches and *Birds of a feather* on a Sunday evening before school on Monday. One classic old school tune bled into the next and she felt content.

At about ten-thirty she was in conversation with a group of girls from her Drama class. Sarah, a girl she was quite close to back then started talking in a hushed voice. She glanced over guiltily to where some of the teachers were congregated.

'How old did Davidson get?' she whispered.

'He was old when we were kids, what did you expect?' Jenna, her friend replied.

'Don't know really? It's just... they seem so different,' she continued, 'hey, does anyone remember that really hot English teacher we had for A-levels? He was an Irish guy... oh, what was his name again?' Sarah asked.

Alice's heart picked up and her face, she was sure, turned red.

'Mr Chambers,' someone offered.

'Yes! Mr Chambers, that's right. He was so handsome. I would have loved one of his detentions,' Sarah laughed.

'You and he were quite close Alice, he always talked to you?' Jenna turned to her.

Alice smiled a little, 'he was nice, he helped me a lot with my coursework when I was struggling.'

'Teacher's pet,' she laughed kindly.

Alice shrugged her shoulders and smiled again.

'I would have happily been his pet,' Sarah flashed her eyes at the group.

Alice wanted to slap her. He wasn't something that should be joked about – he was her first love and not remotely, anything to do with this girl.

She remembered his body moving inside of her, sweat gathering on his back and his harsh words as he lost control. Sarah could have never handled a detention with him.

Where's your head at?

Alice knew her thoughts were irrational and pushed the childish jealousy to the back of her mind. It had been a great evening, an evening of craziness and probably too many drinks. But definitely one she would remember. All too soon she found herself kissing scores of people goodnight, swapping numbers and promising they wouldn't wait as long to catch up next time. Her good friends she would see again before she went back home. But as for most of the others who knew when their paths would cross again?

Fittingly the last song she heard before Stuart appeared in the doorway, smiling and ready to drive her home was *Wonderwall*. She blinked back a few tears she hadn't expected to shed and headed towards him. She took one last look behind her and smiled.

'Goodbye a younger me, goodbye the days I miss so much… it was really good to see you again,' she whispered.

"I don't believe that anybody feels the way I do, about you now…"

STAKEOUT?

'For the hundredth time Neil, this is not a stakeout,' Tom dropped his head into his hands.

'This *is* a stakeout mate and I'm quite excited. So if, in your head, this isn't a stakeout don't shatter my illusion. I am a computer geek by day and you're an English teacher – this is great!'

Tom sighed.

'Come on man don't ruin it. If it wasn't Alice we were looking for, you would be right up for this. So as I was saying I'm Axel and you're Billy okay?' Neil was practically jumping up and down in his seat.

He had stopped at the all night shop for drinks, crisps and two huge bars of chocolate. He had even borrowed a pair of night vision goggles from his next but one neighbour who Tom referred to as Creepy Colin. Tom was more than a little concerned as to why he would have a pair of night vision goggles in the first place? And how Neil knew about them was a question he didn't want the answer to either.

'You wouldn't be Axel,' Tom corrected him.

'Okay you be Axel. As long as you play,' Neil replied.

'Play?' Tom started laughing and it made his head wring with all the beers of the previous night.

He had tried to convince Neil it was a good idea to let him go alone tonight. But he had failed. Neil was his self-appointed chaperone and now it would seem, his stakeout partner.

They had parked in the school's brand new car park, near to the back and behind a collection of cars at about 8. 30pm. They wanted to get there after most of the guests had gone in and catch people leaving or just milling around outside when it was darker and it allowed them better cover.

It was gone eleven now and they hadn't seen Alice yet.

'You might not recognise her,' Neil offered unhelpfully.

'She hasn't changed. I've seen her bloody Facebook picture.'

'Facebook can tell you fibs dude. For example, your Facebook tells me you're a boring bastard.'

'I don't like the fucking thing,' Tom looked towards the school hall again, '...do you really think it makes me look boring?'

'Afraid so, that or like you think you're too cool.'

'I am,' Tom smiled at him.

Maybe it was a good thing that his friend was here? It was taking his mind off what he was doing. If all he could hear was Neil's voice or Neil's chewing tonight that was fine by him. If he had been alone for all he knew he might have been in there now, on his knees telling her he was wrong.

He paused, why the hell wasn't he?

Man up and go tell her then...

In a moment of madness Tom opened the car door and put one foot on the freshly laid tarmac. This was the last place he had seen Alice. He had left her crying in the rain on the field to his right. He had walked away from her. Got into his car and drove out of her life. That wasn't okay. The years didn't matter...

'What the hell are you doing?' Neil tried to pull his arm back in. Tom was already out.

Neil jumped out of the car and ran around to face him, 'No way!'

Tom pushed him out of the way and started walking towards the school. She was potentially only metres away from him. Why had he been wasting time in a car?

'Don't do it, Tom. You fucked her up. Don't do it again. I'm telling you the truth man,' Neil pulled his shoulder, his voice panicked, 'Tom, after you left I saw her. I never told you. From time to time I actually saw her. She was walking around town with her friends and once on a bus to Oxford. She was bad. She looked like hell, skinny, pale and withdrawn. She looked lost...'

Tom stared at him hard and he could feel his body shaking, his hands making fists at his sides. He wanted to hurt something. Neil's admission came at him like a punch in the stomach.

'I couldn't tell you, not with how you felt too. But you messed her up and if she's at all happy now, please just leave it. For God's sake leave her be...' Neil backed away from him slowly and walked towards his car shaking his head.

Tom heard the door slam. He couldn't move. His legs felt rooted to the ground.

Why was he so shocked and upset by that? Just because she was younger than him why did he think she would have so easily got over and forgot the connection they had shared? When he himself had found it so damn hard?

It was self-preservation. If he convinced himself that she was okay after he left then he would have been able to go on, move on and have a relatively normal life. But if he had let himself believe that she had been as scarred as he by their parting, then his whole life would be dominated by that guilt.

Someone walked past him – a man heading towards the school hall – he still didn't move. He just let the darkness engulf his thoughts.

Moments passed.

The view in front of him offered him no solace. The school that had changed him was still trussed together by the same bricks and mortar. The classrooms that had their own heartbeat looked down on him. The shadows called out to him with a mocking, vivid reminiscence of their affair.

'Did you have a good time?' He heard a man ask as he stepped outside again, the same man from a few moments ago. Someone else was leaving. There had been a steady flow of half-drunk revellers for the last twenty minutes.

'Yeah, it was fun.'

Tom's head shot to the side. A ghostly hand ran up his spine.

Alice.

He'd know that voice anywhere.

He turned on his heal and sprinted back to the car. Jumped inside and shrunk down out of view.

'It's her,' he looked over at Neil who also slumped down quickly.

'You're sure?' Neil whispered.

Tom shot him a look.

'Okay, got it.'

Tom lifted his head the smallest amount. Just to see their backs disappearing into an Audi Q7 a few rows in front of them.

Alice. Her hair was shorter just brushing her shoulders. But it was the same rich blonde colour. She was still tiny. Next to the tall man she was with it only made her shorter still. He willed her to turn around. He needed to see her face.

'That's definitely her?' Neil whispered again.

'Yes,' Tom replied never taking his eyes from the other car. Their lights turned on and their engine started, 'They're going – follow them,' Tom looked over at Neil, 'What the fuck?'

Neil was sat ducked down. Now donning the night vision goggles and fiddling with the buttons on the side. Tom grabbed the goggles off his head, 'Drive.'

'Okay, drive,' Neil confirmed his instruction.

They pulled out behind the large 4x4 and tried to keep their heads low.

You're tailing a married woman – to what end?

What had he been thinking? This was a crazy idea. She was in the car in front with her husband. This wasn't some game that he still had a stake in. It wasn't a film where the hero (him?) saves his long lost love from a drug lord husband or abusive lover. He wasn't Gabriel Oak or Mr Darcy. He didn't own her anymore… he never did. He wiped his hand over his face and sighed, letting his head fall back against the headrest. He wasn't doing this.

'When we get to the main road turn in the direction they don't,' Tom said sombrely.

Neil looked over at him but he was already looking out of the passenger window.

'Good call, Tom. It's the only call,' Neil patted his leg lightly.

'Yeah, I know.'

'Did you see that guy she's with now?' Neil tried to lighten the mood, 'sweatpants and everything – what a…'

'It's alright, man. I'm alright.'

They pulled up behind the Audi at the junction. Its right hand blinker started flashing. Neil turned on his left. They were waiting for a gap in the traffic. Suddenly the passenger side door of the Audi opened and the interior light shot on.

'Shit,' Tom whispered in the darkness of the car.

Alice jumped out and hurried to the back of the car and the boot popped open.

She was in front of them, a bonnets length away from him. He needed to hide but couldn't look away. He couldn't breathe, think or move. All he could do was watch it unfold in front of him.

She pushed open the boot with her slender arms and reached inside. She took out a warm looking coat and slipped it on quickly. Her profile was so beautiful. She was her, the same, and he loved her.

'Shit. This time we're screwed. Quick put the night-vision goggles on they're big enough she won't see your face behind them,' Neil suggested, 'actually scrap that you'll look like a serial killer.'

Tom wasn't listening.

I love you.

Alice reached up to the handle, it was a stretch and closed the boot with a gentle slam. The red brake lights illuminated her body now and he could really see her. For the first time in fourteen years she was physical again.

She turned towards their car and put up her hand to them and with a small smile mouthed the words 'thank you,' and turned away. With that tiny pull at the corners of her lips his life started once more.

But Alice stopped dead.

Nearly five seconds past. Tom was counting, his stomach was in knots. He could hear his own breathing, heavy and laboured like he had just ran for miles. The tension within their own car was palpable and urgent. Neil's hands gripped the wheel tighter and Tom pushed his feet harder into the foot well.

Look at me...

She lifted one hand to steady herself on her own car. She faltered momentarily but slowly turned back to face him.

'You're going to hell in a hand cart, my friend,' Neil whispered.

Her eyes were full of tears and her expression was vacant. She blinked... once... twice, then she lifted her hand to her mouth and her legs gave way a little. She caught herself quickly and stood upright again.

Tom grabbed the door handle.

IN HIS IMAGE

Saturday July 31st

Alice huddled closer to Stuart and he turned the heating up. She had had a wonderful night, it had been funny and odd and at times pretty sad actually. But she felt okay now. It all felt okay.

'Jump out and grab my coat from the boot. Actually thinking about it, your North Face jacket might be in there too from last Sunday. I'm not surprised you're shivering though that dress is a wee bit flimsy.'

'You bought it for me,' she smiled.

'I know,' he grinned. 'Are you sure you want me to drop you at Stephanie's place? You could call her and cancel? Come home with me and let me take it off you?' he flashed his eyes at her.

'Tempting. But I told her I would stay. Post-match analysis and all that…'

'You two are mad. Still bloody teenagers,' he joked.

'Can we rain-check and you *rip* it off tomorrow night instead?'

'I'll think about it,' he kissed her hand, 'quickly grab that coat while we're stopped.'

They pulled up to the junction and Alice jumped out. Stuart popped the boot and she grabbed her coat. Turning she thanked the car behind for waiting patiently and not beeping them or anything.

She froze.

It's just not possible...

Alice felt the blood rush to her woozy head.

It can't be him...

Helplessness flooded her senses. If she turned around again and it wasn't him she felt like she would die.

In that split second through the tinted windscreen of the car behind her had she seen an untruthful vision? Was she that messed up that he was now some kind of mystical desert mirage appearing for her to cling to when all hope of him being there tonight was lost?

She couldn't stand it. This road was the last place she had seen him. She had watched his little blue car vanish from this very spot, transporting with it her oasis.

She was going to cry. Her husband was waiting to drive away and she was stood at the back of their car waiting for the world to change. She touched the smooth metal and its coolness under her fingertips kicked her into action.

Get it together... it's not him.

Not knowing what she would see, she turned back. In the shadowed interior of the car behind her what she saw was him.

Tom.

Her eyes locked with his and her mouth fell open.

It was Tom.

He was here. She felt her knees weaken and her heart quicken past any point it ever had before. The drinks that she had consumed over the evening did nothing to take the edge off the utter shock she felt. She sensed her lips tremble and the blood in her arms run cold.

Tom moved for the door. He opened it and began to rise from the car.

Panic replaced shock.

She had to do something. It couldn't happen like this. She raised her hand and shook her head once. Tom stopped. She breathed in and out trying to control her tears, trying to control her mind.

Stuart.

Alice wiped her eyes and wrapped the coat around her body and scurried back to the passenger side door and got in. Her eyes glued to the wing mirror as she slammed the door shut. Tom fell back into the car and she watched his head drop into his hands.

No…

'Alright, babe?' said Stuart.

'Fine – let's go.'

Alice wanted the dim car interior to swallow her whole. She searched for any thought or memory in her head that might prevent her from screaming out loud. Anything happy or joyous that was a million miles away from the crystal blue oceanic stare of Mr Chambers.

Don't look at me, she willed her husband to keep driving. Don't try to engage me in conversation. Ask me no questions, I'm not capable.

She watched the orange street lights rush past her. She felt other worldly. She felt like a twelve-year-old child being driven home from youth club after spending an evening staring at the boy of her dreams. Not being able to talk to her parents for fear of losing the image of their face from her consciousness. Needing that picture of schoolboy perfection to still be with her when she ran up the stairs to bed that night, a thousand teenage fantasies waiting for her to dream of when she closed her eyes. She was crazy…

In a minute Stuart was going to expect a loving goodbye. He would hug her and kiss her and she would have the thought of Tom emanating from every part of her body.

How fucked up was that?

She took her phone from her bag and began franticly typing a text message to Steph:

11.15pm
Something's come up, be a bit later than I said. Don't worry, explain when I get there. Leave key out just in case – love you xxxx

She hit send.

As they neared their destination Alice dared to look over at her husband. He looked relaxed. He was clearly happy to have his wife back safe and unharmed after a night that had worried him for weeks. The chance that your spouse would run into her first love was a weight that had hung heavily around his neck. He had laughed it off but Alice knew it had bugged the hell out of him.

So what are you doing now?

They pulled up outside her sister's house.

'You sure you want to leave me?' he asked turning to her.

In a performance that would have left Meryl Streep standing, she kissed him. With everything she had felt in the last ten minutes existing within that kiss. She worried he would feel it and pulled back after only a few seconds.

'I'm never leaving you,' she sniffed.

'You're a soppy so and so at times,' he said smiling at her sudden emotion.

Her phone pinged interrupting them.

11.23pm
Intrigued??? See you later xx

I bet you are…

Alice kissed him again quickly.

'Kiss Hayley for me and tell her I love her,' she requested tucking her hair behind her ear. She wanted to scream again just thinking about her daughter now.

Stephanie had taken Alice's overnight bag home with her earlier, so she grabbed her handbag and shut the door. She watched him drive away and around the corner of her sister's road.

As soon as he was out of view she walked as fast as she could away from the house. When she was safely in the next street she grabbed her phone from her bag and called a cab.

The man on the other end of the line had confidently advised her it would be with her in five minutes. She hung up and sat on the cold kerb to wait. Because in taxi-firm speak five minutes meant twenty minutes. But that was alright she needed some thinking time.

Okay. So Tom was here. Was she shocked? No, not really. Surprised and caught off guard? Definitely.

She had spent most of the night watching the door of the school hall half expecting him to walk through it. She had no idea how he had changed, if he had at all? So there were a few times she had to do a double take just to make sure the person she was staring at wasn't in fact him.

And then she saw him.

Was he watching her? Was it coincidence? No, she knew it wasn't that. He was waiting. The moment their eyes locked she was certain he was there for her.

How do you feel about that?

The fear that if she ever saw him again he would be different had played on her mind over the years. That she would see him, and he would just appear to her adult self as some older, creepy guy that should never have wanted a seventeen-year-old girl and she shouldn't have ever wanted him – it had scared the hell out of her. That's the problem with distance and perspective. What was wonderful then may now seem grotesque.

But he was the same. Unless it was the darkness and the Amaretto, he was the same.

Beautiful.

Alice closed her eyes. She remembered standing in front of him. It was November and absolutely freezing, but about the same time of night as now. A school trip... she could see it so clearly. She and Tom had gone to fetch blankets for the girls back at the dormitory, but couldn't remember how they had ended up with that task alone. They stumbled through wooded parkland in the pitch black darkness. Tom was leading and she followed.

She recalled how she had become obsessed with him in the months previous to this. How all she could think about was his voice when he spoke in class, his rich accent and amazingly beautiful face. How he held his coffee cup in one hand, but not by the handle. How his thick brown hair looked when he was bent down marking books at his desk. She would have followed him anywhere.

'You're shivering you must be cold?' he had asked her in the darkness.

'It's not the cold... you know it's not...' she had replied with a confidence she didn't know she possessed.

Ten minutes after she had said those words to him, against his initial shock and protestations of how it was wrong to talk like that. Letting it slip that he might feel the same but it was out of his control. She had found his breaking point and he had pushed his strong body against her own, he towered above her and she had felt so small, but so protected. Her fingertips traced his arms and shoulders. She gripped onto him like her life had depended on it and he had kissed her.

'Alright love, Alice is it?' A bald jolly looking man was talking to her, 'You order a taxi?'

'Yes please. Sorry, I was in another world,' Alice got into the cab. The heating was on full whack and only then did she realise how cold she felt.

'Where to my love?'

'Um, 64 Oak Moor Rise, please,' she said.

'Nice,' he replied and the meter started ticking.

It was a guess. She knew the man that was with him was Neil. She had never met him but Tom had talked about him a lot whilst they had been together.

After Tom had ended it she had frantically found out everything she could about Tom's life. She had watched Neil's house for a week after he left her, hoping to catch him before he left for Ireland. Praying she could change his mind.

But she hadn't seen him – just Neil.

It was a long shot. He had more than likely moved. She saw the car he was driving now and at least if it wasn't there she could go home and try to leave it alone. Hopefully tomorrow would offer her a different and sobering light on her predicament?

Here tonight she was wired and she was angry, probably with good reason. Alice needed to see him and there was very little that would stop her right now.

It wasn't on.

How arrogant was this guy anyway? Getting out of the car like he didn't have a care in the world? Happily risking a broken nose and at the same time her marriage.

You keep telling yourself that's why you want to see him.

The cab turned into a leafy suburbia. The typical home that appealed to wealthy professionals wanting a more rural and affordable idyll, but still requiring the essential short train commute to

London. The large detached properties she had to admit were impressive. Their perfectly manicured front gardens even looked good in the dark.

The cab slowed to a stop in front of one of them.

Not as far down the road as she remembered. But then she was on foot last time she was here.

'This is it,' the man consulted his meter, 'call it six pounds.'

Alice looked out. In the driveway was a large black BMW. It was Neil's car.

Alice slowly handed the driver the money and it was on the tip off her tongue to tell him to take her back... but she didn't.

'Thank you.'

No more thinking. This was it. Alice wrapped the coat around her a little more, breathed deeply and headed up the path. Her high-heeled boots, she was sure announced her arrival even before she had pressed the doorbell.

Ready?

It's 'Mrs Bouquet' sounding chimes really didn't fit well with the owner of this house. She doubted he had a gold carriage clock ticking away on the mantel or a large collection of well used Tupperware in the kitchen. He probably didn't own a West Highland Terrier and insisted that all his food come from the M&S foodhall. It was funny how a simple sound did that – stereo-typed by a doorbell – weird?

She held her breath.

Seconds later she saw an arm on the other side of the frosted glass reach for the deadlock.

The door opened and Neil stared at her in obvious surprise.

'Um... I... hi?'

'Hi,' she shifted her weight onto her left leg and fiddled with her hair.

'Alice… isn't it?' he stumbled over the words but what else could he say?

'Yes. Nice to meet you finally,' her tone was clipped and she could tell he was on the back foot so pressed on with added confidence, '…is he here?'

She watched the colour drain from his face a little more, but he smiled anyway.

He was a handsome man, just not in the same way Tom was. He was quirky and what many women would describe as 'cute.' He still had jet black hair despite thinning a bit on top. He was lanky, but she could tell there was a strange strength about him. He looked his age, but it didn't look bad on him.

'Yeah, he is,' he stepped aside and she walked in, 'do you think this is a good idea though?' he asked.

'Did he?' she answered flicking her head to one side and widening her stare.

Neil shrugged, 'I don't know what he was bloody thinking?'

It was an honest answer at least.

'Where is he?' she cleared her throat quietly, suddenly her mouth felt so dry.

'The lounge,' Neil pointed to the second door to his left. It was closed.

'I'm sorry to barge in like this but may I speak with him?' she asked.

Where was this bravado coming from?

'Be my guest,' Neil took a coat from the hat-stand, another thing that seemed out of place, and slipped it on. 'Will you be okay on your own with him? I'll pop out for a walk for a few minutes if you like?'

'I think I'll be fine.'

'Are you sure?' he asked again before opening the door.

'I'm a *big* girl now.'

'Yep, got it,' he nodded, 'I'd say go easy on him but I guess it's not my place...'

He closed the door silently behind him and she watched his silhouetted outline walk away from the house.

Alice looked around her. A large impressive hallway of cream coloured nothingness. It badly needed a woman's touch – had he never married? She felt woozy but at the same time stone cold sober. Her thoughts were clear one minute and clouded the next. She was in the same house as Tom... shit, she really was.

She tip-toed towards the lounge door and on the other side she could hear a television. She put her ear to it. It sounded like it was motor racing of some kind. He had never struck her as a TV watcher before, but then she had never really known the man wholly. Just the man he was when he was with her and of course the teacher.

She counted to ten slowly. Her hands were shaking as she pushed down on the door handle, closed her eyes and stepped into the room.

There was a Tiffany style lamp on in the corner of the room. Loud supercars raced each other around the large screen and a man was sat on the sofa in front of her, his broad back facing her.

Tom Chambers.

She stared at his head for a moment. All her senses were going into overdrive just millimetres below her skin. But on the outside she had somehow maintained an air of calm and tranquillity.

'How long does it take to get a beer, man?'

She jumped when he spoke. Her hand darted to her mouth. Every dream she'd had about him since he left, they were never as real as those few words uttered in the lamplight. His voice, that was always so much of a lure was one of the losses she felt cut her the deepest.

And on hearing it now, what she feared the most had happened… she was that girl again.

She breathed in.

He raised the remote control towards the screen and paused the cars mid-race.

Her body felt alive, but not at all like her own. All thoughts of her everyday life were mere background noise now. Even though she wanted to yell at him and hurt him the way he had hurt her, it would just be a polished performance of a well-rehearsed part. Reading lines from a script that no longer held her interest. She didn't want revenge or apologies… she just wanted him to speak again.

The truest fact was now staring her in the face no matter how much she wished it wasn't so. She had finally come into contact once again with her potent drug of choice and the perilous force at which its effects hit her bloodstream was almost irrefutable.

She breathed out.

'About fourteen years…' she whispered.

FALLING DOWN...

Sunday 1ˢᵗ August

What in the world had made him think that this inconceivably bad idea had at some point in his warped mind been a good one?

Yeah let's go on a fucking stakeout, let's track her down and watch her fall at my feet?!

He had seen her and she had said no. As if it ever could have been any different?

Just as he was about to turn around and lay into Neil for no reason other than he was presently co-habiting in Tom's wrong time and wrong place and he was angry at himself…

'About fourteen years.'

Tom sprang to his feet, turned and stumbled back slightly.

What the fuck?

He looked at her.

'Fucking hell, Alice,' he breathed.

She was small, beautiful and even sexier than he remembered. She was a woman now. Her face was more defined and her lips a little less full. Her large emerald green eyes still dominated her features and her hair framed them in a golden coloured halo of tousled waves.

My bewitching little pixie…

She looked back at him unmoving.

'Nice to know your language is still as blue as ever.'

He stumbled forward and she took a small step backwards.

'I'm sorry about… Alice… about earlier. We were going to leave it and drive away, but you got out and…' he rubbed his hand over his face quickly trying to wake himself up and get with it.

And that's what you choose to say to her? – Impressive.

'Were you even going to come in?' her voice had that same airiness to it, a breathy quality that was so damn feminine he was finding it hard to concentrate.

He moved from one foot to the other, while she just stood and waited with perfect serenity. He was never worthy of her and now he saw that. He also fully understood the fool he had been.

'No, I don't think so,' he replied honestly.

'So you just wanted to look? Allowing that level of insight and judgment for yourself but not for me?' she whispered.

What was the right answer to that question?

Tom swallowed hard, 'Alice.'

'Yes?' she watched him.

'It wasn't like that. I didn't want to rock any boats. I just wanted to…' he stopped. Saying what he was about to say would certainly rock boats.

'What did you want?' she snapped, tucking her hair behind her right ear and crossing her arms over her chest. He could see she was angry. What could he do? He was finding it hard enough excepting she was in the same room as him.

He waited a moment, 'I just wanted to see you,' he looked away, shook his head and cursed under his breath.

'Well, now you see me. Did you really think I would just drive off and not want to talk to you or anything? Did you think it would be better to spy on me? Possibly let my husband see you? Chase our car down, was that the plan?' her shoulders slumped a little and he saw the raw sadness in her eyes, 'I haven't seen or heard from you in fourteen years and now this?'

'Alice, I'm shocked you would want to ever talk to me again? I wasn't spying... there was no plan,' thank God he hadn't put on the night vision googles, 'I just didn't think you would want to see me. A lot happened...'

'It was a long time ago, Tom,' she'd said his name, 'but yes, I would have wanted to see you. Of course I would. Just to see how you were doing? Put to bed old ghosts, be able to forget it,' she bit her lip and stopped.

She hadn't forgotten.

Tom pulled his back a little straighter. He needed to man up. Get his head in it quickly. He needed this to go right, otherwise she would walk out of here and never look back, with the knowledge that he was pathetic and weak. Part of him wanted her to be able to do that. The other part wanted her to remember and miss everything they had ever felt because that might be the only place that he still existed to her.

'Have you got time now?' he asked awkwardly.

It was a clumsy shot and soon as he said it he felt like a desperate school boy. What was that he was saying about manning up?

Alice frowned.

'What for a cuppa and a chat?' she backed away a little more.

'Answers I suppose or questions, a drink, why not?'

Idiot!!!

'Coming here was a mistake.'

'No it wasn't,' he stared at her.

'It was – how can I sit down with you and have a drink? That would be like cheating, I'm married you know?'

He watched her pull her coat around her body.

'I know.'

'Don't you care?'

She was scared.

'No,' he didn't care that she was married he only cared that she was here.

'I'm going – goodbye Tom,' she turned towards the door, 'I'm glad I got to see you,' she choked.

Goodbye?

Like hell that was it. Like hell she would come in here say a handful of meaningless words to him and then leave? If she thought that was going to cut it, she was wrong. Why was she trying to run away after just two minutes in his company?

Work it out you fool…

It had all meant something to her. The same as it meant to him. The years hadn't eased any of that. They hadn't taken the pain away. They had only placed new things on top of it until it was hardly visible anymore. She stepped in here probably without thinking and now she wanted a quick exit from the can of worms they had both been instrumental in opening. She cared enough to find him tonight and whatever else she wanted to hide from him, she couldn't hide that.

'Don't go Alice, please,' he said moving towards her.

Alice turned to face him. He stood a few feet away from her now. He could feel her energy. He wanted to touch her so desperately.

'Don't try to see me again. I can't do this with you. This is it. We're done. You can't spy on someone and make them feel… weird, okay?' she looked away from him quickly.

Neil's idea of kidnap was now seeming like a good one.

'Weird?' he smiled.

She turned her body away from him, 'just leave it.'

He watched her struggle to open the living room door, her fingers clumsily pushing at it instead of pulling. He knew in a moment of perfect certainty that he would try to see her again. They weren't done. At least he wasn't, not by any means.

He stepped closer and put his hand out towards the door.

She turned to him sharply, 'What're you doing?'

'Helping you,' Tom pushed down on the handle, pulled it to and opened the door for her.

'Thanks' she walked past him into the hall.

'My god, Alice,' he sighed.

'Please don't, Tom.'

'You look beautiful.'

'Don't,' she didn't meet his eyes.

'You do,' Tom stepped out into the hallway too.

'Thanks. The years have been good to you also,' her voice softened a little and she looked up at him again.

'So they tell me,' he winked at her.

Alice smiled in spite of herself. It was the same wide radiant smile. Then she laughed.

Don't touch her.

God, his hands were twitching.

'I'm so sorry,' he whispered solemnly as her eyes met his.

She stopped suddenly and shook her head slowly, 'Tom,' her voice was a warning.

Don't.

She had looked up at him with the same eyes he had dreamt about forever. But she clearly didn't want to go there again. He on the other hand was ready to pounce, but he did everything in his power not to grab her. Instead he rooted his feet to the ground and began talking.

'I'm sorry, Alice, I can't change the decision I made, but believe me I have wanted to a thousand times. If it at all helps you understand how much what we had meant to me then let me tell you, please…'

Alice lifted her hand to stop him, 'Tom, don't say anything else. I'm trying so hard just to stand here and be strong. Please I can't hear anything else that's nostalgic or sad or even honest about us. I can't take much more memory lane tonight.'

'I need you to know. I can't let you leave with it unsaid,' he pleaded.

He stared at her expression, waiting.

'I can't know, Tom. I really can't,' she answered.

THE RABBIT HOLE

Sunday 1ˢᵗ August

Tom, don't smile at me. Don't make a joke. Don't be alive in front of me. Don't say the things that you want to say to me. I'm not the same girl, don't you dare make me wish I were.

'I need you to know. I can't let you leave with it unsaid,' he urged looking into her eyes.

He was close to her now. They were maybe a foot apart. She could have reached out the smallest amount and her fingertips would have brushed his body and she had spent the last five minutes trying not to look at that body.

But she had looked at him. Probably more than she thought, and she hoped it wasn't too obvious.

He didn't appear smaller or pathetic or less awe inspiringly handsome as she had always convinced herself he would. She hadn't remembered him as an impressive adult through her teenage rose tinted spectacles. She had remembered him exactly how he was.

Tom Chambers.

He *was* impressive.

If she could wolf-whistle she would have.

His face was older looking – a bit less school teacher and a bit more rugged huntsman. The strong jaw and angular cheek bones still made him appear arrogant. But he had a light stubble now which suited him. He messed with his thick chocolate coloured hair the same as he always had. His full lips still made him dangerous and that cool blue stare still danced over the face and dared her to jump right in.

If she had an ounce of sanity she wouldn't be in this conversation with him. The grown up, married woman that she was now wouldn't be thinking all these terrible betraying things, regarding him in the same silly way she used to.

The worst part was that despite every bloody thing he had ever made her feel and all the tears she had cried for him. Her stupid eyes looked into his stupid eyes and managed to forget it all. Did the small slither of a person inside of her that was still just Alice – the selfish and lustful, carefree and breathing part of her – seriously want to go there?

He still cares for you.

Alice told herself to shut up. He doesn't. He just wants to make it right.

He wants you still…

Why would he? For the same reasons she thought herself unworthy of him when she was a teenager. Those reasons were ever present and still very obvious. She was her and he was beautiful.

She needed to leave. Being here was a dangerous game if the last few minutes of craziness were anything to go by.

'I can't know, Tom, I really can't,' she whispered.

Tom narrowed his eyes at her.

'Just being here is bad enough. I'm married, happily. Standing here talking to you isn't fair on Stuart. He wouldn't like it,' she continued.

Tom frowned, 'Wouldn't he?'

'No Tom, he wouldn't. He definitely wouldn't want me in a house alone with you – that's for damn sure.'

'You're your own person, you chose to be here,' he reached out his hand. It hovered near her cheek.

Touch me…

Was she still that brain-washed she was encouraging her unmistakable and untimely fall down the obligatory rabbit hole and into a whole world of scary? Despite her body feeling electrically charged with a mind of its own she pulled back a little from his hand.

His face looked hurt, 'Okay, if you have to go, I understand,' he picked up a strand of her hair and carefully tucked it behind her ear without making contact with her skin.

I don't have to go.

'I really do need to go,' she breathed.

Tom nodded.

'I'll walk you out. It was really something seeing you again,' he looked deflated but he was doing well to hide it, 'and I'm so sorry about Neil and the car and the… spying,' he grinned a little.

As Alice walked next to him towards the door she looked down at their legs moving side by side. She felt panicked. It was a hot/cold kind of panic that she had never experienced before. Every step they took towards the door was a step closer to the goodbye she didn't want.

Even though everything she was saying was exactly what she should be saying in this situation. All the right words in the right order. The problem was it wasn't what she felt. It wasn't the truth. They were simply playing at being grown-ups dealing with a sticky situation.

'Um… do you still live in Ireland?' she asked polity as they reached the door.

'Yes. Just outside Dublin. I moved up there about six years ago.'

'Do you have children?' she wanted the whole picture before she left or was she just stalling?

Tom smiled. The dimples in his cheeks appeared and his eyes shone so beautifully.

God, she loved his smile.

'Twins, James and Abbie, they're nine. I'm not with their mam anymore we divorced about five years ago.'

'I'm sorry. That must be hard?'

'It can be. But I see them both loads. Estelle and I are good friends,' he pushed his hands into his pockets in a boyish way and it made his shoulders look even broader.

Alice looked away, she had to.

'I suppose if these things have to happen you have to hope they turn out well like that.'

'Are you happy, Alice? Did it turn out well for you?'

'Yes, I have the loveliest daughter,' she smiled.

Tom looked at the floor, 'I bet she's beautiful.'

'She is.'

He breathed out heavily.

'Listen, you better go before I get all…' he stopped and shook his head, 'forget it.'

The cold hallway sent a chill through her body.

Why did going feel like it would end her life prematurely? Like stepping out of the front door would somehow close her time limited portal to a dimension in which Tom Chambers is tangible. A dimension in which he says new things and smiles new smiles, not just the things she had entrusted to memory.

Don't think like that.

How can someone feel this way when everything in her life was perfect and happy? She felt so far removed from him now that she could have been a different person when they had been together. How could she want to jeopardise her perfect bubble for this moment?

Because this is what you would have chosen.

'Get all what?' she enquired helplessly. She was stupidly clinging to his every word.

Tom grinned again, 'stupid, crazy and Irish.'

He looked at the door and then to his feet.

'Tom?'

He looked up, 'Yes?'

The space between them filled up with a scintillating awkwardness. Had the instant mood change been fuelled by his statement or the way she had said his name? Was it her fault or his? She wasn't sure, but for a split second she rode high on it. The alcohol in her bloodstream helped too.

'I liked crazy, remember?'

What???!!!

He smiled, 'I do remember.'

She had lost it. What on earth made her think she could say that? She needed to cover it quickly, 'Maybe I'll see you in the future sometime?'

I liked crazy, remember?!

She couldn't get over herself.

'A man can dream,' he laughed.

She stared at him and he stopped suddenly.

'Tom, don't say...'

He cut her off, 'Alice, if I thought it would make a shadow of a difference to anything, I would get down on my knees and beg you to forgive me,' he spoke quickly, 'but as it stands you're happy and me doing that would be just another thing to feel foolish about when you walk out that door. Sorry, I...'

Alice could feel herself breaking inside. She had asked not to know how he felt and this was why.

She nodded slowly, 'Goodbye Tom,' she bit her bottom lip to stop the tears coming and opened the door, 'and thank you.'

The cool night surrounded her as she stepped outside and down the little slope onto the block-paved pathway.

She turned to face him and Tom's brow furrowed.

'What for?' he asked.

She felt braver in the moonlight.

'Thanks for convincing me that what I did when I was seventeen wasn't in fact the biggest mistake of my life. That maybe we weren't all that wrong. That you weren't some strange guy I would regret if I ever saw him again.'

She walked a couple more feet away from the door.

'So, you don't regret me then?' she could tell he was smiling.

Alice laughed lightly, 'careful Tom this is starting to sound like flirting.'

'Starting? And I thought I was being obvious,' he joked.

'You were.'

'Alice?' his voice sounded strained, she didn't want to turn around and look at him. She was barely holding it together now.

'Yes?' she called without turning.

'...I don't know? Ignore me.'

She smiled to herself sadly. He was feeling the same way.

A thought hit her suddenly and she just had to ask him. It was the last chance she would get and she needed the information to complete her most cherished memory of them.

'What was that song?' she didn't look back at him. She was almost at the end of the path, near to Neil's car. Her heart was in her throat.

'Song?' his accent was so much stronger than she remembered. It could have been because he lived back home or had she really forgotten its strength and impact on her senses?

'It's silly really, but in your room that night, you know? When we first... I always wondered what it was but I could never remember it?' she waited.

She didn't expect him to remember. It was so long ago. She suddenly heard a small noise, a whooshing sound and then felt a warm breath next to her right ear. He was behind her.

She jumped to face him, 'Um why...'

'Give me your phone, Alice,' his blue gaze bore down on her.

'Why?' she squeaked.

'Give me your phone,' he ordered.

'You can't talk to me like that anymore,' she looked up at him and he stared back at her, his chest rising and falling he was so close to her body now.

'Phone,' his voice gravelly and serious.

Alice yanked her bag from her shoulder and pulled out her phone. She looked up at him and placed it into his hand. Her own hands were shaking. She snatched them back quickly.

Tom began typing a number into her contacts. She watched as his commanding fingers travelled swiftly over the keys.

She remembered those strong hands...

Her heartbeat quickened and she let her eyes drift closed.

'Here,' he held the phone up to her and she opened her eyes, 'this is my number. You'll probably never need it or want to use it. But I'll never change it.'

She glanced at the screen, 'Edward?' he had listed his number under a different name.

'Rochester,' he smiled a little.

She smiled back. The first time they had ever really felt a mutual connection with one another was when they had read aloud to his class an extract from *Jane Eyre*.

'Like you said – crazy,' she tried to lighten the mood that had turned intense and popped her phone back in her bag, but it was suddenly her most treasured possession.

'No, this is crazy,' he whispered.

Tom grabbed her under her arms and swung her around towards Neil's car. He pushed her up against it. His body weighing down against her, his strong grasp felt so warm through her thick coat.

'Tom, get off me!' she shouted more in surprise than meaning.

He looked at her. His own breathing was fast and he felt like he was fighting against himself to stay in control. He shook his head.

She froze. If she moved even the smallest amount to meet him he would drag her back into the house within seconds and she would go… willingly.

Tom's face moved towards her own, 'don't,' she whispered, 'please don't make this any harder.'

He looked away and cursed. His profile, his harsh words and pained expression left her wanting him so vehemently, but still she didn't move. The small band of gold on her left hand wouldn't let her.

He lifted one hand and traced the edges of her cold cheek with his palm. She shivered and he pushed her hair away from her face and gripped it firmly between his persuasive hands.

'Are you ready for stupid?' he asked. His voice had the imperious tone it takes on sometimes. She felt scared of her own response.

She shook her head quickly, but she wanted to nod.

He gently wiped the tears that had begun to fall away from her eyes with his two thumbs, while still holding the sides of her face.

Why was she crying?

'Alice, I'm not going to kiss you. I know you're happy and believe me when I say that makes me happy,' he brushed his finger across her bottom lip and she trembled, 'so that means what I'm about to say sounds all the more stupid and wrong. I can't believe these words are going to come out... but fuck...' he paused and looked to the night sky then back at her, 'I'm going try you know? I'm going to try and win you back. I'm gonna try and keep you.'

'Oh, Tom,' she mouthed.

'Don't say anything else,' he placed his finger to her lips, 'you don't know how this ends. So don't pretend you do.'

He pushed away from the car. The sudden loss of his body was almost unbearable. She stared at his back as he paced towards the house.

"*The Closer You Get*," he shouted, 'that's the name of the song, Alice. I'd never forget that or any other part of that night.'

TOM VS. ALICE

'Shit, Tom I just saw you! Don't pretend you didn't do it. You were practically dry humping the girl,' Neil bellowed.

He had been back from his walk for about ten minutes and had been like this since he walked in the door. Neil had seen Tom grab her. That meant a lecture on doing the right thing and how a better man would walk away.

Tom was half listening and mostly agreeing because in any other situation he would always try to do what's right and honourable. But logic and good manners really didn't play a part in this one.

'I told you she wanted me to do it...' Tom cringed, 'okay that was slightly arrogant.'

'Slightly? You think?' he collapsed onto the sofa, 'Your trouble is you just can't toe the line. She gets upset and you think she doesn't want to leave you. So you step over that line, when you should be pulling back. She's married and confused and you have used her feelings to your advantage,' he shook his head.

On. The. Money.

Tom did feel ashamed.

'You have to remember she's not seventeen now. She's thirty-one. She's also not as weak and pathetic as you make her out to be.

If she had a problem she would have let me know it. I don't want to justify this to you – you weren't there.'

'Tom, I know how you feel about her, but really?'

'It's done now,' Tom sighed.

'I hate judging you...' Neil picked up the remote and started flicking, 'and God only knows she's fit...'

'Don't even start with the 'she's fit' comments. I don't want to know if you think she's fit. I don't even like the word 'fit' to describe any woman and certainly not her.'

Neil rolled his eyes, 'Oh here we go Mr English teacher is going to crack open the 'to be or not to be' romantic clap-trap dictionary. Let's all write a thousand-word description of her skin in the moonlight, or her smile on my pillow blah!'

Tom laughed, 'shut up.'

'Are you going to give it up?' he wanted a straight answer.

'She's gone. Home to her husband, do you really think she'll give it a second thought when she gets there? So, yes it's given up. Because I can't afford to hope it would be any different.'

'Tom, seriously what the hell has Alice got?' he looked at him, 'over any other woman you have ever had?'

'My heart you dickhead.'

Neil said nothing. He switched the television onto a repeat of *Man vs. Food*, 'Have you seen this one?'

'No,' Tom replied.

Lecture over.

By the second half of the programme with the host just about to chow down on 6lbs of tender Texan brisket, smothered in a secret dry rub of barbeque spices, slow cooked for twelve hours, topped with American melted cheese and home fries on the side. Tom decided he was tired and unavoidably hungry.

Bed or eat?

Eat.

He asked Neil if he wanted anything. Having not gotten an answer he got up to look, discovering Neil fast asleep in the dark with his mouth wide open. Tom pressed pause on the TV and wandered to the kitchen.

Now, what were the chances of there being some steak in here? A quick scan of the fridge told him negative. He found some ham and pickle instead and made a sandwich.

He looked in the freezer... Microwave chips. Not exactly home fries but still better than nothing.

Tom placed them in the microwave and set it for two minutes. The quiet hum of the oven as it spun gracefully around was nothing like the vintage example he had at home that sounded like a freight train. To make matters worse he had lost the special glass plate years ago and now used a dinner plate as its ailing substitute.

What did you do tonight?

He shook his head.

The microwave came to a stop and pinged twice. He was just about to open the door when he heard a third and fourth pinging sound. Tom bent down a little to look at the clock. Then realised it was his phone.

A text message at 1.20am on a Sunday – it meant one thing. He was sure of it. He dashed into the lounge. Neil was still asleep. He picked up his phone. Before he turned it over he screwed his eyes tight and counted to ten.

Please be her...

Quickly he realised how lame he had just acted about getting a text he could have quoted Jeremy Kyle.

"Why don't you grow a pair?"

Bloody summer holidays, too much time to get hooked on programmes that you love to hate.

"Get off my stage you useless excuse for a human being..."
Tom turned the phone over and pressed the round button next to his thumb. The screen lit up. The number didn't have a name. He opened the message:

1.21am
Hey Tom, it's me, Alice. I don't really know what to say about what happened tonight? It was so unexpected I can't get my head around it. I was glad to see you... but I think it's always going to be complicated – Isn't it?

I keep thinking about what you said and it's not fair to you if I leave it open like that. I'm married and I have a family, I can't and won't jeopardise that. I can't see you again and I hope you can respect that?

Wrong time, wrong place... I think that will forever be our Achilles heel x

Tom shook his head fiercely and started typing:

1.27am
If I were a less selfish man I would say sorry for what happened tonight Alice, but I'm not. If I said that seeing you again had somehow kick-started my old feelings for you I would be lying – because I don't think I ever stopped feeling them.

Time and place may well be a problem, but I think fear is a bigger one.

I know that this message sounds like I'm an insensitive bastard. Before tonight I was convinced that I would never get a second chance to even look at you again. You say that you don't want to give me false hope – you haven't. What you've given me is a shot, now if that was intentional or not, the damage has already been done.

I know it's the wrong thing to do, but how can I walk away from something like you twice?

He hit send.

Tactful.

Was there any way you could cancel a message once it had been sent?

No?

He didn't think so.

Tom was about to grab his food when he received another message – too quick, not a good sign. Why did he always act before thinking?

1.29am

Tom, you're making this hard for me. I'm surprised that you still feel like this after so long. You need to forget about me. I'm married – maybe some gentlemanly behaviour in this situation would help?

Gentlemanly behaviour? Did she really want that? It didn't feel that way this evening.

She was running scared and he had just fucked his chances. She was trying to pretend that she didn't feel the smallest thing for him. She was trying to erase the looks they had shared tonight, trying to disguise her increased heart rate when he had held her.

Back off Chambers.

1.31am

Sorry. I owe you more than that, a lot more.

If tonight was it? Then okay. I'll be here for a while longer; you know where to find me if you want to talk.

I hope you get everything you ever wish for baby xx

He never wanted to upset her. Even though everything within him wanted to type something else, he wouldn't. He couldn't picture her sat on a bed somewhere worrying, wondering if he would swoop in and ruin her life again.

He badly wanted to keep pressuring her. Telling her how she made him feel. These crazy feelings that within twenty minutes of being with her again were consuming his every sense. He had never stopped loving her and however dormant that love was over the years, it was always poised and ready to jump out and screw him up.

Stepping back Neil, stepping back…

If she was ever going to come to him again, see him again or even talk to him, it had to be her choice alone.

YOU HANG UP FIRST

Baby…

He was the only man that had ever called her baby and didn't make it sound contrived or silly.

He had sent her the message she needed. The message that she should have wanted…

She was itching to reply again but didn't know what to say? She should just leave it surely?

She stared at her phone and took another sip of tea. Her sister was asleep when she arrived home and in a way she was glad of that. At least this gave her the rest of the night to decide whether to tell her about Tom or not.

It was half past one in the morning she really needed to sleep too. But she knew as soon as she closed her eyes his face would appear hovering above her. She would construct intricate scenarios in which they could accidently see each other again. Her fantasies of being with him would run riot and she would wake in the morning more confused and frustrated than she was feeling now.

Why are your fingers moving?

1.43am

Thank you. You have my number now – so let's not be strangers x

Tears ran down her face. Circumstance and loyalty didn't allow her to say any more than that. She deleted the messages and all trace of their secret communication.

Then,

1.45am

We could never be strangers, Alice.

She smiled. He was still going to push and despite it all being impossible she loved that he tried.

1.46am

You're right. We couldn't.

Send.

1.48am

Alice, please see me again before I go home? I can't leave it like this, I won't.

She sighed. God, she wanted to see him again. But that was because she was sat in a kitchen that wasn't hers. The children dreaming in their beds weren't hers. The man snoring upstairs wasn't hers. If she were with Hayley and Stuart right now would she really be thinking of meeting up with Tom for round two?

No chance. This was make-believe. Tonight was crazy and she had felt like a teenager again. Tomorrow she would see her child and Mr Chambers would be a distant memory, as much as that fact hurt her.

1.52am
Tom, I heard what you said tonight very clearly. You said you were going to try and get me back. How can I meet you again knowing that? It would be too weird. I'm sorry.

Three minutes ticked by.

1.56am
I never was any good at keeping my mouth shut. I shouldn't have said anything.

But I can't take it back. I meant it. I can't begin to tell you the way I felt when I turned round and you were there tonight… it was incredible.

I felt like I was that guy again.

That fourteen years had just slipped away, like a coin, they fell down the sides of the sofa that separated us. I would have grabbed you then and there if you hadn't backed away.

Baby, there is no way I can pretend that I don't feel for you – I always have. I just wish I could say this to you face to face.

I don't want to wreck your head or your life. But I can't go the rest of my life knowing that I fucking walked away from you again, no man would do that, and I certainly won't.

And there I go again – not keeping my mouth shut. I could delete all my ramblings before I send this message to you, but as you already know, I won't x

Oh Tom. Don't do this to me.

Alice finished her tea and flicked the kettle on again.

The blood coursed through her veins a little faster and her skin felt the nip in the air a little sharper. Every time he spoke it made her feel like this, and reading his words felt as good as hearing him say them to her and if it's possible they pushed a little deeper. But meeting him again was as good as cheating, she knew that.

2.07am

What do you want Tom? Just tell me straight? What do you hope to gain from us seeing each other again? It will just complicate things further.

She sent the message.

2.09am

To talk more I suppose. I don't know… just for this not to be it.

Alice scowled at her phone. Talk? No, that's not what he wants. She started typing, not really understanding why she was angry suddenly.

2.11am

Do you expect me to leave my husband? Drop everything and come running back into your arms?

Or do you just want to have some sort of 'for old time's sake' sex?

When I saw you, I'm not going to lie, I felt something, but that's natural. I loved you more than my own life for years.

But that was then and this is now. Why should we prolong the inevitable parting? And do more to hurt each other in the process.

Should she send this? Probably not, but it had the questions she needed answering. She shouldn't be bending like this. She shouldn't be entertaining his fraternisation. Moments later her phone beeped. His answer:

2.16am
Okay, this is the truth. I want you anyway I can get you.

You're not naive and impressionable anymore and I think I can be honest. I want to see you again. What we do is up to you? I will happily sit on my hands, tied to a chair and just talk with you, if that's all you want?

If it's prolonging the inevitable and going to hurt me, I'll take my chances.

As for your question about sex, the answer is I would kill to fuck you again, but not for anything as pathetic as old time's sake.

Leave your husband? That's not going to happen and we both know it.

Run into my arms? Nothing ever sounded so good x

Arousal charged at her like a Spartan army, effectively moving as one unit to conquer their enemy. First taking hold of her head and torso, then filtering down her arms and legs. Her brain, that she had been trying to keep firmly in check up until now, pretty much told her to piss off, as it jumped head first into a vision of Tom pushing her against the car and taking it so much further than he had.

He had said he wanted to sleep with her... No, he had said fuck her and that made it ten times worse. He was being himself, the version of him that wasn't censored or scared, that just said what he thought and didn't apologise for it.

She held her phone. She was writing before her head could catch up and before she could stop herself it was too late.

Send.

2.18am
I'll think about it. No pressure. No expectations. No sex.

She had just stepped over the line. She was deceiving her husband for the thrill of being around Tom again and it had shamelessly taken less than three hours. All he had to do was say he wanted to see her again and she was falling over herself to accommodate him? What the hell was the matter with her?

Twenty seconds later.

2.19am
Absolutely. Tell me when and where?

Here, now, whenever you say...

2.21am
I'll be in touch. Night Tom x

She needed out of this conversation. Anymore of it and her half-drunk self would be actually typing these disgusting thoughts.

2.22am
Goodnight, Alice x

PREPARATIONS

Monday 2ⁿᵈ August

Alice handed Hayley the third bag of shopping that seemed reasonably light from the open boot. It was full to bursting with her mother's list of 'just a few bits while you're there'.

'Oh this one's quite heavy. Do you think you can carry it to Nannie in the kitchen?' Alice joked, pretending to struggle with the carrier bag.

'Mummy, you're so silly. Even daddy could carry this one,' Hayley rolled her eyes and stomped off to the front door.

'Yeah Mummy, you're so silly,' Stuart mimicked, grabbing her waist playfully.

Alice didn't think she flinched. It wasn't a flinch? It felt more like an unnoticeable recoil. He didn't seem to notice anyway. But Alice had.

She frowned.

She didn't feel any differently towards her husband. She loved him as much as ever. The events of the weekend hadn't tarnished those precious things. But her body, just then, had reacted of its own accord. Had it pulled back from her lover's touch?

They walked into the house and deposited the shopping in the kitchen.

Alice's mind raced.

'Are you still having a drink with Anthony tonight?' she asked. Anthony was Stephanie's husband. He and Stuart got on well, both having a love of all things sport.

'Yes, if you're cool with it? We were thinking of having a knock around on the courts first.'

Sport…

'That's fine, Stu. Mum's taking Hayley out to the cinema later and I said I might catch up with Emily tonight. So whatever works? But be careful I think Tony's been working out. Steph says he's been doing that *Insanity* DVD thing?!' she smiled and raised her eyebrows.

'He's no match for me – not on the tennis court,' Stuart laughed.

Alice headed upstairs 'I'm going to have a quick bath,' she leaned over the bannister and shouted, 'Hayley, no more chocolate buttons. You've already had a packet, and Mum don't you give in to her!'

She looked at herself in the mirror as the hot water filled the tub. Her lips trembled a little. Was she really going to do this?

She picked up her phone.

Why did that sound like the stupidest question ever? When all she could tell herself was how could she *not* do this?

She needed to see him again.

She had thought of little else for the past thirty-six hours. Her fingers were twitching every time she held her phone but she had tried to wait as long as she could. She needed this feeling to go away. Her head was full of Tom and now her body was acting strangely towards Stuart, none of it was right.

Closure had to come. She had to talk about what happened between them in past, she had to have the answers that had haunted her and she had to once and for all tell him goodbye, or he would always be the third person in her marriage.

However good it felt to know he still had feelings for her, however much it massaged her ego to know that he wanted her, it had to mean more to have the chance to put it to bed.

3.25pm
Tom, I can see you tonight. Can you make it?

Alice turned off the hot tap and started running some cold. Her phone announced his answer just moments later.

3.27pm
Yes. Do you want to come here again? I'm assuming you don't want to be seen?

Alice nodded.

3.30pm
No, I don't. Will Neil mind?

3.32pm
Probably, but I'll try and smooth him over.

3.33pm
Irish charm?

3.35pm
Something like that. About 8pm?

Really doing this then?

3.39pm
Perfect x

There seemed little else to say. It felt like a guilty woman's last attempt to remain proper and somewhat formal. To make arrangements as if he were just a fellow frazzled mum needing a Starbucks and some adult company.

Alice sank into the bath. She grabbed the razor and started shaving her legs. Even the routine removal of unwanted body hair felt like she was committing adultery.

She wasn't going to sleep with him – so what was the big deal? She was absolutely one hundred percent sure on that. Talking wasn't cheating and she was telling only a small lie to protect Stuart's feelings about where she was going tonight.

A nervous shiver ran over her body – just thinking about Tom in that way made her feel irrational. She could close her eyes and pretty much pretend that she was a girl again getting ready to meet him.

It was just like the way it used to be, a secret, illicit meeting between a teacher and student. A place where she knew she would get to see the most amazingly beautiful man. He would be naked and real. He would kiss her, undress her and then lay her down and hopefully forget she was delicate, young and inexperienced. She would pray he would give her everything she needed without worrying about the consequences.

That was the past.

Alice dunked her head under the hot water.

She thought about a line that *Tinker Bell* said in one of Hayley's movies *Hook*, "*You know that place between sleep and awake, where you can still remember dreaming? That's where I'll always love you, Peter Pan. That's where I'll be waiting...*" That's where Tom was to her, that's where she had been waiting – without ever acknowledging it – she had been waiting all this time to see him again.

You're going to end this tonight and not make it worse.

Was she? Her brain let itself play devil's advocate for a moment, flirting with the idea of Tom and slowly excitement replaced nerves and it danced over her face and shoulders mixing with the warm water that surrounded her. Thinking about what he had said to her was scary but clearly not enough to send her running from him. It was pulling her towards him if anything.

But she was not going to sleep with him. It wasn't an option. She wasn't going to be the woman that falls before the man that broke her heart. She was grown up Alice now and fully in control of her own fate.

RED SKY AT NIGHT

Monday 2nd August

'Neil, it's nearly eight, you said you'd go out,' Tom was begging now, he had been asking nicely all afternoon.

Alice was coming here tonight. He couldn't quite get his head to believe it. Neil on the other hand believed it just fine and was disgusted with the whole set up. Tom had assured him nothing funny was going on. He had shown him the text that had said 'No sex' but he still wasn't happy.

'*I* will answer the door when she gets here,' he stated getting madder.

'What do you hope to gain from opening the door and being here?' Tom snapped a little harsher than he had intended.

'Nothing really, I just want to.'

'You drive me fucking crazy. Why am I the bad guy in this?' Tom asked checking his hair quickly in the living room mirror.

'You're not. But I know you Tom and you know how she felt about you,' Neil got up and closed the window. It was August but there had definitely been a chill in the air the last few nights and it felt like an early autumn was coming their way.

Tom bristled at his use of the word 'felt' in past tense.

'I won't push her,' Tom promised.

Keep calm.

'You don't know how not to push her, Tom.'

'I'm not going to fuck up this time. Please mate...'

'Screw it! Alright, alright I'm gone,' Neil threw his hands up in surrender and Tom smiled.

'Thank you – I love you,' he winked at him.

'Sick. Why am I getting so wound up anyway? If you get laid, we all have a quieter life.'

Tom couldn't even entertain the idea of anything like that happening. If he did, then he would go into tonight with that on his mind and it would only cloud and influence everything he said and did. His sole focus would be on getting her into bed. As good as that sounded, he knew he couldn't play it like that.

'Good luck,' Neil held out his hand and Tom shook it.

'You're still the best Neil and don't you dare let anyone tell you differently,' Tom slapped him on the shoulder and laughed sarcastically.

'Call me when the coast is clear. I'll be at a friend's,' Neil winked, 'watching DVD's,' he nudged Tom in the ribs.

Tom shook his head 'another booty call?'

'Says the man entertaining his old flame who so obviously wants you to fuck her one last time,' Neil grabbed his coat and car keys.

'She doesn't. She just wants to talk about stuff that happened I think?' Tom assured him.

'Well you keep telling yourself that when she's laid out beneath you and you're reliving your school girl fantasy.'

Tom's jaw clenched and he stared at Neil hard.

'Okay sorry – touchy subject!' Neil almost went on, but stopped, 'see you later.'

'Yeah,' Tom slammed the door shut and breathed deeply.

Tonight was theirs. Only two people could determine how this would go – Alice and himself.

Would she even turn up?

Was he even ready?

Tom straightened his shirt and for one of the few times in his life he found himself worrying about what she saw when she looked at him. He was older now – and he felt it. Yes, he had kept himself fit. People said he didn't look his age and woman still seemed to find him attractive. But Alice hadn't really changed. She had aged in a way, but not in a way that meant anything, she was still just as she was when they had been together.

It didn't really matter he supposed. Tonight wasn't as Neil had insisted. It wasn't a 'date' of any sorts. He had to put all thoughts of romance, sex and seducing her in a box and concentrate on just being around her again.

Time ticked by.

At half past eight Tom picked up his phone. She still hadn't arrived and he had received no message. He knew he couldn't text her. He just had to wait.

He was jumpy now. Not for the thought of seeing her. But the chance she might not come.

Tom walked to the kitchen and grabbed a cold beer from the fridge. He had resisted up until now but he really needed something to do with his hands.

His phone beeped.

8.34pm

Tom, I've been outside in my car for the last twenty-five minutes… I don't know about this???

Tom slung his bottle on the side and sprinted to the front door, nearly knocking over Neil's hat-stand in the process.

The evening was still quite bright, but chilly, the red sky promising a warmer morning to come. Tom was hit by a memory of childhood as he stepped outside.

He remembered the evenings he would walk on Brittas Bay with his father. The beautiful powdery sand dunes would sparkle and wink at him in the distance. The sky was very much like this one, it enchanted a young boy's imagination as his father told him tales of brave Irish knights fighting dragons and pirates that were intent on taking control of their wondrous isle.

He missed his dad. He had died five years ago leaving Tom and his family broken. He had a heart that beat for his kin. He was the best man Tom had ever known and at times like this, when a moment hits him, Tom wondered if he would ever be at peace with the fact that his father was gone?

He jogged to the end of the driveway and looked right, then left. Her car was parked a few feet away and the engine was running.

Tom breathed in and out slowly as he walked towards the car he half expected her to see him and speed off.

When he reached the window she was already looking out at him. A shy half-smile on her face told him she was scared. He smiled back and shrugged his shoulders. She turned away from him casting her gaze to the steering wheel and then out of the windscreen.

She looked so beautiful. Her hair was scooped up on her head and pinned messily. She wore a pair of blue jeans, a tight white t-shirt and a light grey cardigan over the top.

She looked back at him, her emerald eyes held his stare for a moment longer and she opened the door.

Tom stepped back. He watched her grab her tan leather bag from the passenger seat and join him on the pavement.

'This doesn't feel at all strange, does it?' she asked him sarcastically.

'Are you alright?' he replied closing her door for her. She pressed the key fob, locking the car.

'Yes, I think so. Let's get inside.'

Alice started walking ahead of him. He lingered just long enough to recall the way she would walk into his classroom after a lunch break, gliding past his desk and her small fingers skimming its hard surface. Most days she had appeared confident yet shy. Open, but complicated. To him she was always the same heady cocktail of sexy and innocent... that was *his* Alice.

'Is this okay with you... here I mean?' she asked.

'Definitely. It's more than okay,' he replied.

'Did Neil mind too much?' she said as they neared the front door.

'He wasn't impressed, but more with me and the situation than him actually having to go out.'

'He worries about you?' she looked up at him.

'I think he worries about you.'

Alice laughed, 'I guess he still sees me as a child.'

'Yep, and me a weirdo,' he joked, 'after you,' he held the door open as she stepped over the threshold.

'I bet it's as strange for you as it is for me... all this? Talking to each other and feeling like different people but with the same history,' she cocked her head to one side, 'I don't even know what we're doing here. Do you?'

Tom paused for a moment. He had so many things to say to her. But if he was being honest he had no idea what they were going to do either or why? All he knew was he had to be around her and if he couldn't he felt like he would wither and die.

'Go through. You know the way. Drink?' he asked avoiding the question.

'What're you having?'

'Beer,' he replied.

She smiled, 'same old Tom. I'll have one too. You were right it does grow on you.'

Tom walked into the kitchen. He shook his head. The conversation they'd had the night they first made love. Alice had tried some of his beer and he had commented that it was an acquired taste, because the look on her face had told him what she had thought of it.

He removed the top from a second beer and carried his own back to the living room.

He was already feeling it, the pull. The insane attraction that had been alive in him since Saturday night had slowly built to this moment of absolute clarity.

I want her at any cost.

'Grow the fuck up,' he whispered under his breath before entering the room.

AFTER EIGHT

A lice sat and waited.
Was she being sophisticated enough?

She thought she was. She prayed her emotions weren't too obvious and her voice didn't sound nervous.

How could she be here with him again?

Tom Chambers. She had missed this man for hundreds of nights, but only now did she understand how hollow that loss had left her. He was here and whatever he had taken from her all those years ago, he had kept safe and was now letting her see and touch it again. As if it were a toy she had loved as a child or a hairstyle she missed when it had gone out of fashion.

The door pushed open and he walked back in. She had perched herself on the edge of the large leather sofa opposite the fireplace.

Look at him…

He strolled confidently forwards and held out the chilled bottle.

'Here you go.'

Look at him…

He was standing in front of her. She glanced up at him and took the drink he offered.

'Thanks.'

He wore dark blue jeans with a fitted black shirt that was tucked in at the waist. The sleeves were rolled up to the elbow and she could see the light sprinkling of hair on his forearm. His thick brown hair was messy, but cropped a little shorter on the sides now. He still had the five o' clock shadow so she guessed it was his new look.

It was hard to put into words the way he looked, smelt and moved – and what it did to her.

He was intoxicating.

His age was irrelevant. She thought it wouldn't be, but it was. He must be nearly forty-five but would have still passed for mid-thirties. His face still harshly chiselled and with the bluest eyes she had ever seen.

'Do you mind if I sit?' Tom motioned to the other end of the sofa she was sat on.

'Sure.'

'Did you want me to get some rope?' he grinned.

'Rope, what for?' she asked suddenly unsure of herself.

'To tie me to the chair,' he took a drink from his bottle.

Alice felt her face redden.

'At the moment, no, but I'll play it by ear if you don't mind?'

'Your call,' he smiled, 'but don't say I didn't give you the option.'

She looked around the room. She hadn't seen it in the light before. This room was nicer than the hall. It felt warmer, more intimate. But you could still tell it was a man's house by the hi-tech gadgetry and sound system that took up almost a whole wall and the random scattering of X-box games near the television.

'Neil has a lovely home,' she said awkwardly.

Tom looked at her and she looked down at her lap. Every time their eyes met she felt a reckless surge of lust take hold of her.

'He has. Computer programmer by day and by night he still spends hours on these shoot 'um ups,' he gestured towards the games, 'I've tried to get him to read a book… do you still read much?'

'Yes I do. Do you still teach?' she asked not making eye contact.

'I do. I actually take over as Head when I get back after summer break.'

'Wow that's brilliant, well done,' she sipped her beer again.

'What do you do? Besides being a mother I mean, you know what I mean…' he turned to face her, lifting one knee up onto the sofa, 'not that being a mother isn't job enough mind.'

'We have an art gallery. We run it together.'

She didn't know where to look now. Not at his face, and looking down meant looking at his strong and so familiar legs.

'Well I would have never guessed at that. I always thought you would become a teacher too or a writer, something like that.'

'I couldn't take English at university.'

'Couldn't?' he sounded confused?

'It was still too raw for me.'

Why admit that?

Tom stared at her.

'Fuck Alice, I'm so sorry… I never meant to screw up your education,' he grabbed at his hair in frustration.

'It doesn't matter anyway. I was a young girl and took everything to heart then. I wallowed in my self-pity for too long. Then I met Stuart and things got better,' she said honestly.

'I'm glad.'

She watched him swig his beer a little more aggressively.

'No, you're not,' she shook her head.

Tom laughed, 'okay, I'm not. Do you really think I want to imagine the girl that I loved getting over me with another man?'

'You did the same, Tom.'

'I tried.'

'You married and had children.'

Tom finished his beer.

'Exactly – I tried. It didn't work out in the long run, as it has for you. My marriage ended because I wasn't over you.'

Silence.

'Tom I…' she started but stopped again abruptly.

'Sorry. But I did warn you the other night. I'm going to push my luck,' he smiled sheepishly.

'Could you get that rope now?'

Tom laughed, 'I've got some handcuffs for taking you prisoner later – will they do?'

Alice felt her cheeks go red and a sharp spike of something dangerously close to sexual need rippled through her body.

'It's alright I was joking,' he said looking at her face.

'I know that,' she smiled and sipped some more beer needing to distract herself, 'this is so weird,' she mumbled.

'Thank you for coming,' he turned his body towards her a little more.

'I guess I had to come. I can't say for sure why though?'

'Because I was an absolute fool and you want to show me what I'm missing?'

'Yes, that was it,' she said smiling.

'Don't worry Alice I see it.'

'Tom, don't be an idiot it doesn't suit you. You're not missing anything,' she said kindly.

'That's a matter of opinion,' he laughed again, 'another drink?'

Alice looked at her bottle. Had she nearly drunk it already?

'Okay thanks. But I can't get drunk, I'm driving remember.'

'That's a shame because I was banking on it,' he got up and headed for the kitchen.

Alice rolled her eyes at him.

It was strange how quickly over a decade of vacant space can just kind of vanish between two people. Just sitting and chatting with him again felt like they were rapidly expunging the time that they had been separated.

He didn't seem to want to talk about Stuart at all and that was fine. To be honest she didn't want to talk about him either, because if she did it would just feel like an even bigger betrayal. He didn't know where she was tonight. She had never lied to him like this before and she wasn't comfortable with it. So he was better off left out of any conversation they may have this evening.

'Am I permitted to tell you how beautiful you look?'

Tom was back. He placed another drink in front of her.

'No, and you already did the other night.'

'My bad,' he grinned. It was the only time he looked anything but totally alpha male. His smile was his best feature. It made him look young and carefree. The dimples that appeared in his cheeks just added to the overall effect.

'I searched for that song. You were right, it was the one you said,' she had found and downloaded it the moment she had got back to her sister's on Saturday.

Tom sat down on the floor near to her and rested his back against the sofa. His long legs stretched out in front of him, one folded over the other.

'You don't have to sound so surprised.'

'No, it's just that I didn't expect you to remember. It's not really a boy thing, is it?'

He looked up at her and shrugged, 'maybe not.'

'It's not like it was your first time? It's the kind of thing you don't forget being a teenage girl...' her words faded towards the end of the sentence.

'It was my first time with you.'

Her stomach clenched and she fidgeted in her seat.

Why had she forgotten that about him? The way the smallest thing he would say could leave her head spinning.

'Yes, it was. But we don't need to talk about it...' she was flustered.

'You bought it up.'

'Yes, I did. *My bad.* Let's change the subject?' she said taking another nervous sip.

'I like the subject fine.'

'Of course you do,' she drank a little more.

'It was one of the best nights of my life.'

Mine too.

'Well it was certainly memorable,' she tried to draw it to a close.

'You could say that,' he paused, 'it's the night I fell in love with you,' Tom leaned his head back on to the seat and turned his face to her. His thick lashes made him look sleepy.

She didn't know what to say to him? She didn't want to stare back at him for this long but all his magnificent features screwed with her mind and let her think crazy things.

'I know,' she whispered.

She did know.

'So, what was the best night of your life?' he asked quietly. His accent playing havoc with her composure.

'The night my daughter was born. I had an emergency C-section at about one in the morning. I was so out of it at the time I don't actually remember much, just a lot of people in blue scrubs rushing in and out of theatre. Tubes were crudely sticking out of my hands. Machines were beeping and kind nurses talking to me like I was a child.' Alice wiped the condensation from the side of her bottle and continued, 'But I did remember the sun coming up hours later and realising my life was no longer just mine. Every decision I made from that moment on, I made for two of us. It was odd because suddenly everything mattered and nothing mattered. I never felt so scared and yet so fierce.'

'I know that feeling I think,' he smiled.

'I've had a few good nights,' she confirmed.

'Any of them 'us' nights?' he fished for information jokingly.

'Yeah, I think so,' she watched him smile again and continued, 'aside from the night you and I...' she paused and tried not to squirm.

'Fucked?' he offered cheekily.

'Made love,' she corrected him, 'I remember that late night on the school trip when we walked through the woods in the pitch black dark, it was freezing,' she hadn't forgotten any of the nights they were together but didn't want to tell him that, 'I told you how I felt.'

'Oh my God I forgot that was the start of it. Seriously after I kissed you in that shed I was so disgusted with myself. I had kissed a student. I couldn't believe it. After I walked you back to the dorm I drank half a bottle of whiskey and passed out – and I was supposed to be supervising the damn trip. If anyone had caught me I would have been sacked for sure.'

'That was more than a kiss.'

'Thanks... I was trying to block out the shadier parts of that night.'

Alice grinned at him, 'You know what I mean. It was a kiss that meant more.'

'It certainly was,' he nodded.

Alice pushed herself back onto the sofa a little more and dared to stare at him for a few seconds. He was looking down at his beer and deep in thought.

'Does your husband know you're with me tonight?' he asked out of the blue.

'No.'

'Does he know about us, what happened, our relationship?'

'Yes, some – not all. But he does know you were my teacher,' she felt herself frown thinking about him.

'Bet he thinks I'm a bastard?'

'Yes.'

Tom laughed.

'It figures. I'd feel the same.'

She watched him drink.

'How long are you staying over here for?' Alice asked.

'Till Saturday night I think. Essie is dropping the kids off to me on Sunday afternoon for a few days. So I will have to be back by then.'

'Uh huh,' hearing him shorten his ex-wife's name made her jealous. She didn't want to imagine the years he had spent with her and his own children. She liked it like this, where he only wanted to be with her again. She didn't want any other woman to even talk to him.

She knew how that sounded.

Insane.

There she was, married. No intention of changing that. Yet she wanted to keep Tom for herself. The more she thought about it the more jealous she felt.

'People were talking about you the other night at the party. Saying how hot you were at school' she grinned.

'Really?' Tom acted like he was interested, 'was she pretty?'

Alice pulled a face at him.

'I'm single and it seems you don't want me so I'll have to keep my options open,' he joked.

'I'll get her number for you and then you can leave me alone,' she laughed.

'You're not even going to give me a sporting chance then?'

'Sorry.'

'We'll see,' he shrugged again, 'want some music on?'

'Setting a scene are we?' her eyes narrowing.

'Your seduction,' he stated bluntly.

He was clearly joking but the words hit her like a potent aphrodisiac.

'You know I'm here to say goodbye?'

'I know why you're here, Alice, yes.'

'Good,' she whispered.

Tom picked up the remote control from the coffee table and aimed it at the cluster of electronic equipment, instantly chilled out club music started playing a little too loudly. Tom made a discontented face at the music choice, 'This is Neil's.'

'Its fine – I like it.'

They sat and listened to a couple of tracks. After Tom had adjusted the volume, the music felt much more relaxing and mellow. But the verbal silence that passed between them only heightened the feeling that they both wanted to talk, to fill the void. But talking might mean the evening ending sooner than either of them wanted. Would they stumble onto a subject that didn't feel right? Would he say something too scary? Would she be forced to leave? She needed answers tonight too, she just didn't know how to ask the questions.

Tom looked at her again, 'Baby…'

'Don't call me that please its distracting.'

'Is it?' he smiled.

'Yes. You shouldn't call me anything like that and you know it,' she scolded him.

'Force of habit, even after all this time.'

'It just reminds me of… everything,' she bit her lip and looked down at her lap.

'You remind me of everything.'

'God, Tom I'm married, stop it,' she sighed.

'It's hard.'

'Try,' she insisted. Why was she pretending that she wasn't enjoying him? That everything he was saying wasn't affecting her and pushing her further towards his attention.

'I miss you,' he turned his body and leaned against the side of the sofa.

'And I missed you,' she said.

'Missed or still miss?' he flashed his eyes at her playfully.

Miss.

'I used to think about you lots. Where you were? If you were alive, happy? I missed not knowing those things,' Alice replied.

'Alice, did you ever think of what I did, what we did, as wrong in the years that followed? I always worried that I might have scarred you or damaged you? Did you ever feel taken advantage of?' he reached up and brushed the sofa with has hand.

'Tom, do you really have to ask that?' she stared at him hard this time.

'I don't know? At the time I thought what we were doing was crazy, but we both wanted it as much as the other. Then when I left and as the years went on I started to really question my actions and wonder if I was truly a monster or something?' he blinked and his jaw tensed, she was watching him so intently as he spoke, 'but you're here and you haven't hit me and you don't seem scared so I hope you didn't feel that way?'

'No, Tom. I wanted and pushed you for what we had, if you remember it right?' she tried to reassure him.

'I remember it.'

'You didn't abuse me,' she said solemnly.

'You're sure?' he stared at her.

'Positive,' she vowed.

'Did I hurt you?' he watched her still.

'Not physically.'

'But you were a virgin. It's the worst part and the bit that feels the most perverted,' he rubbed his hand over his face, 'I can't believe I'm getting the chance to ask you these things that have been running around in my thoughts forever.'

'I was a virgin, but that doesn't...' she looked at him then not really knowing what to say.

'I just think of my own daughter...' he started.

'Don't compare what you're thinking, to what we did. It is a million miles away from that. You are not that guy, Tom. Honestly.'

'I look at the girls I teach now and I wouldn't ever dream of thinking about them in that way. So why was it okay with you?'

'Because you're not into young girls,' she said.

'I know that. I'm just into you,' he turned his gaze to her and smiled ruthlessly while trying to lighten the mood.

'I wouldn't have wanted it to be with anyone else but you.'

'Thank you.'

This was getting dangerous. She should think about leaving, but first she had to ask him something too.

'Tom?'

'Yes?'

'Before I go...'

Tom cut in, 'you're not going.'

It wasn't a question.

'Tom,' she frowned at him.

'What? You're not,' he half smiled.

'Tom, you're being an arse. I'll be going soon. I can't stay too long, you know why...' she sighed.

Please don't think I want to leave though...

'You won't, but go on?' he smiled again.

Why was his self-confidence always so attractive to her?

'I'm very strong you know?' he winked.

She looked at his arms and then back to her drink quickly, 'I do.'

'I might not let you go. I might just keep you here.'

She breathed out and felt a small shiver run over her shoulders.

'I'm stronger than I look. I could kick your arse.' Pure heat rushed to her head as she spoke.

'Care to try? I'm very happy to get physical.'

Alice rolled her eyes.

'I have a semi serious question I have to ask too?' she said then.

'Please ask? Anything you need to ask, I'll answer if I can,' he said.

'I just wanted to know for my own peace of mind,' she stopped and gathered strength for the next few words, 'the night we split... was it always going to be over?'

Alice looked away and prayed she wouldn't cry in front of him. She had said so much hurtful crap to him the night she had found out he was moving back to Ireland. Some of it probably responsible for his last question and his worry about being a pervert.

He had said he wanted to put distance between them and have a break until she finished her A-levels. She pushed him into walking away – but would he have done it anyway, if she hadn't?

'Did I push you away, Tom?'

Could her life have been so different?

Would she have wanted it to be?

Tom's expression turned serious. His crystal blue eyes clouded a little and he drained the last of his drink. He shook his head.

'Alice, that's such a hard question to answer. Everything I said about giving us some space, I meant. But if I'm honest part of my brain was telling me it had to be over for your sake. But if it hadn't ended the way it had, and we had parted on better terms? I know the way I felt when I left you – I would have been begging you to take me back within months,' he pushed his hand through his hair, 'but what we said to each other in the heat of things made it harder to go back. The amount of hurt that we both felt scared me into thinking that we wouldn't be able to tough out the bad times to come. There definitely would have been a few of those when we started telling people about us.'

Alice was close to tears, 'I know that. But did you walk away because of the things I said?'

Tom breathed heavily.

'No, Alice. Nothing you said to me pushed me away from you. What you said was close to the truth even. I was shocked. I was disgusted with myself. But nothing you could have ever said would have kept me away from you if I had not been so fucking scared of the consequences. I walked because I was young, idiotic and blind.'

'We both were,' she whispered.

'No. You knew your heart. You were steadfast in what you wanted. And because of that you were able to move on eventually and be happy. Because I ran like a fucking coward at the first sign of trouble I couldn't and I've had to live with that regret.'

So he blamed himself and not her? How messed up was that? They had both spent the last fourteen years blaming themselves for something that just simply was.

She looked at her phone, nine forty-five and it was dark now. She hadn't wanted it to get so deep tonight. But if this was the last time she would see him, she had to ask the thing that had eaten her up all this time. And now she had her answer.

'We all have regrets Tom, it's what makes us human,' she tried to change the subject again, 'take *Jane Eyre* for heaven's sake?'

Tom nodded slowly.

'True enough, that novel is full of them,' he paused, grinned and rubbed his chin, 'remind me again what happens at the end of that book though?'

Alice raised an eyebrow at him and he continued.

'Oh that's right, Jane comes back to Rochester and they live happily – as much as those two can – ever after.'

'Yes, but you're overlooking Rochester's shady past, his wife in the attic and illegitimate child? Also you fail to mention Jane's handsome young suitor, St John, and her ongoing reservations about Edward. In the end she returns to him out of love *and* loyalty. She also returns a young vivacious woman and he sadly is an aging, broken man,' she joked pushing Tom's arm.

'Such is life…' he started laughing too.

'The truth hurts old man!' she joked.

'Look at me now! Oh when I think of my glory days. How fit, how handsome, how modest…' he said in his best dramatic voice.

Alice watched him playing. Her heart fluttering like a stupid child and her pulse racing like she had never seen a more perfect man.

Oh God why did you take him from me?

'Look at you now…' she whispered to herself and turned away.

Tom stopped laughing.

'What did you say?' he asked.

'Nothing.'

'Tell me what you see now, Alice? Please, I want to know.'

Tom lifted himself on to the seat next to her and placed his bottle on the coffee table. He grabbed her shoulders lightly and turned her to face him. When she met his eyes he let her arms go. 'Tell me,' he ordered.

Alice swallowed hard. She knew he meant what she saw between them? If she still felt it too? Not a bit about his appearance.

'I see you, Tom. The way you are and the way you were. There is no major difference. You're an incredibly good looking man and I still can't believe that you ever wanted to be with me,' she tried to steer him off the subject.

'Are you fucking kidding me?' he looked annoyed.

'No.'

'You think that you were beneath me? That you were lucky I ever looked at you?'

'Yes.'

'You've got to be joking? I didn't deserve to even breathe the same air as you, Alice – I still don't.'

'Then we will have to agree to differ,' she insisted.

'I'm going to tell you what I see. Because I know you won't. Even though I know you understood what I meant when I asked you that question.'

She tucked her hair behind one ear and waited, her heart rate increasing with every second that passed.

'I see what we could have been and it's fucking killing me,' his jaw tensed. He reached over and took the beer from her hand and placed it next to his empty one on the table.

Her hands were shaking. He sat in front of her. Maybe five inches apart. His eyes locked with hers and he silently dared her to try and look away.

'I see you, the woman that should have been my wife...'

'Tom, don't,' she reached out and touched his hand without thinking.

He looked down at her fingers on his skin.

Touching him felt warm and safe. But it was wrong.

What kind of a woman was she?

'It's true. A handful of moments with you and…'

'Don't say anymore,' she cut him off, 'please don't say things that'll make me want this.'

She watched Tom's face change from emotional to something more dangerous. It had been so long since she had seen the hunger in him. His breathing quickened, she could see his chest rising and falling. His body was tense she could feel it under her fingertips.

'I've got to go…' she said in sudden panic.

'No,' he demanded.

'I have to. You know I can't let this carry on.'

'Please.'

'I have to go, Tom.' Her eyes pleading with him.

'Alice?'

'I know,' she breathed, 'but I'm not that sort of girl.'

'You're making it sound like it would be a mistake or wrong? You know it wouldn't be,' he locked her in his stare.

'Whatever it would mean to me is irrelevant, it's what it would mean to my family that matters.'

She moved her hand away. Tom grabbed her fingers with his.

'Don't leave,' he pleaded.

Her whole body was screaming in protest at her intent to walk away from him. She was at war with herself. If heart and head were ever truer she'd never known it.

'I don't have a choice,' she wiped her face with her free hand.

'You do have a choice,' he moved his left hand to her outer thigh and brushed his palm over the material.

She breathed deeply and looked up at him, 'What's my choice, Tom?'

'You know exactly what I'm saying.'

'You're saying I have a choice between leaving to go home to my husband and staying here with you and doing...' she paused, she just couldn't say it, 'If you were the married one and I was single you'd understand how hard this is...'

'If you were single and I was married we wouldn't be here right now – we'd be in bed.'

Alice felt her tummy turn over. She bit her lip to stop them from trembling.

'I'm losing my mind here because I can feel what you're feeling and I know you're just doing your best to push it away. I can't hold this back like you can,' he snapped.

She was walking the line here. She knew Tom when she had been a teenager. He had control around her, respect and patience. She also knew on occasion that control had slipped and a more dominant man had emerged, but he had pushed it back to protect her. Now that line seemed thinner. He was unapologetic about it what he wanted. Her marital status wasn't acting as any kind of barrier that was going to dissuade him. She wasn't an innocent anymore and he wasn't as he said, holding back.

'You can't put me in this position. You understood and accepted the terms of my being here tonight,' she stated.

'Screw that, be honest with yourself,' he was a potent mixture of angry and hot.

'I'm going,' she said but didn't move.

'If I let you leave this house I'll never see you again,' he whispered.

'Yes, you will.'

'No. You'll go home and be so scared about this thing that we still have between us, this obvious thing that you won't acknowledge and you will vow to stay away from me.' Tom stroked the side of her face lightly with his free hand.

She looked into his eyes and knew he was right. She would run and run and never look back, because the risk of falling for him again was far too great. So with every deceitful bone she had in her body she prepared herself for her lie.

'...there is nothing between us anymore,' she looked away from his face and bit the inside of her cheek hard enough she almost drew blood.

'Like fuck there isn't,' Tom roared.

He moved suddenly and hoisted her backwards onto the sofa. His arms holding his weight, he stared down at her.

Alice sat frozen.

He looked at her face, then to his left. He muttered something inaudible and Irish. Looked back at her, then with harsh resolve he shouted.

'Go!'

'What?' she didn't understand.

'Go, Alice. I can't do this. God knows I get that you're scared and loyal. You don't want to hurt anyone I understand that. But I can't pretend I don't need you – I fucking do. I need you so bad I'm close to breaking. I can't look into your eyes and see something true only for your lips to speak a lie.'

'Tom?' she didn't want to go like this.

'In about ten seconds I'm going to start pulling the clothes from your body. Right or wrong I won't stop. I'm giving you fair warning. I will touch you and worship you until you submit to this thing we have... so, please go now,' he cursed.

'Tom, why does it have to be like this? Why can't we just be friends and leave it at that?'

As she said it she knew the words were meaningless.

His face moved closer to hers. She could smell him. She could feel his body warm against her own, not yet touching, but its heat was present and so mesmerising.

'Friends?' he grabbed her hand and pressed her palm against his groin. Through his jeans she felt just how much he wanted her.

She gasped and stared at him.

'This isn't right, Tom,' she breathed rapidly and pulled her hand away, 'don't push me to a place where all I can do is follow you. This isn't real life. It's just acting on a memory of something we think we miss.'

'If this isn't real, Alice, then what the hell is?'

'We are. But not together, together it's just a dream,' she could smell the beer on his lips and wanted to lean forward and lick the nectar from them.

'Are you going?' his face moved closer to hers.

'I'm not going to let this happen,' she whispered.

'Are you leaving?' he said again.

'I'm not going to have sex with...'

Tom cut in, 'So stop me.'

CONTROL

God, her eyes amazed him. Did she have any idea how much they told him?

What are you doing you crazy bastard?

He had lost it. Without any doubt he had lost his mind.

But he couldn't stand to hear it any longer, that's no excuse for man-handling a married woman, he knew that. But Alice was his. As fucked up as that sounded he believed it was the truth. As arrogant as it seemed Tom was sure she wanted him too.

She was beneath him just as Neil had warned. He cursed himself for that too. He was weaker than he thought and his feelings too close to the surface to conceal. When she said she had to go he had been backed into a corner and right or wrong he had come out fighting. He was too fucking old and too much in love not to lay it all down for this one chance.

Alice started speaking.

'Stop you? I'm not even going to credit that with a response,' she said fidgeting.

He loved this woman. He had loved her since she was little more than a child. He would give her the world and his life willingly, but he wouldn't back down. For if he backed down now he would lose her all over again. Weakness here would show her he hadn't changed, that he still had the capacity to run from her.

'I want you,' he leaned down and rested his forehead against hers.

'You're confusing me...' she whispered.

You're confusing me.

'Shush...' Tom pressed his lips against her cheek and felt her body shudder.

'If you keep going you will hurt us both and when it's time to land back on earth we'll mourn the loss all over again,' she whispered into his cheek.

'I'm not losing you again.'

She didn't respond. He felt her face turn towards him. Her soft skin brush against his own roughness and then she kissed him. It was a simple kiss that lingered for a moment or two on his lips, just a simple kiss that humbled him in its innocence and then broke his heart with its intent.

Goodbye.

He pulled his head back and she was crying.

No.

'Don't say it,' he shook his head. He moved away a little and sat back on his knees.

He was going to shout, fucking scream like he had no tomorrows left.

'Oh God Tom, don't look at me like that!' she cursed him.

'Don't cry,' he whispered.

She grabbed at her chest and with her two hands, met his eyes and shook her head sadly. Tears ran down her face and for the first time that evening he understood the weight of it for her.

He felt his own emotion close to the surface and he nodded at her slowly.

Alice nodded too, then jumped to her feet. She looked around her quickly and grabbed her bag from the floor. He was watching her but couldn't get his head together.

'Goodbye, Tom,' she wiped her eyes and started walking to the living room door. Her shoulders slumped and head low she reached out for the handle.

There goes your life…

'Alice!' he shouted.

None of it meant more than her.

She stopped.

'Do you want me to let you walk?'

He watched her head flick slightly, seconds passed and her bag slid from her hand onto the floor.

Just one word…

'No,' she replied.

He jumped off the sofa and practically leapt five paces and skidded to a stop behind her and wrapped his arms around her tiny back. He had accidently pushed her towards the door with some force because of the short sprint and massive burst of adrenaline. She put her hands out to steady herself then let her head fall back against his shoulder.

He should have asked if she was sure. He didn't. She wasn't sure – she just knew, like he did that there was no way it couldn't happen.

He breathed in the heavenly scent of her hair and prayed he wasn't dreaming.

THAT OLD FEELING

Monday 2nd August

Alice looked franticly around her feet for her bag. She needed to find it. She needed to get the hell out of there. Everything had gone wrong. He was doing what she knew he would and the problem was she was starting to feel what she knew she shouldn't.

'Goodbye, Tom,' she wiped her eyes.

The tears had started and she knew they weren't going to stop.

She looked at him. The thought, for one last time, came into her mind and her breath caught in her chest. He was sat kneeling on the sofa, an empty space in front of him where she had been. That space had felt like everything. For a few moments, with him towering above her it had been perfect again.

His expression was vacant now and he stared into the middle distance and said nothing. His eyes full of hurt.

Tom...

Alice turned and walked towards the door. If she hadn't come here tonight her heart wouldn't feel this heavy. Her body wouldn't feel so unfulfilled, and her mind so confused she didn't know which way was up.

A thousand memories of him swam towards her.

Mr Chambers.

The first time she saw him. He was flustered, angry and late on his first day at her school.

'Sit on a chair young lady…'

The first time they were alone was after a lesson in his classroom, there he had nearly touched her lips.

'Sorry, Alice you were upset and…'

The first time they had kissed.

'Call me Tom, for fuck sake, Alice…'

The first time they had made love had been the most intense experience of her entire existence. Her teacher moving over her, inside of her, so overwhelming…

Then the end came bringing with it tears and a wicked hatred. Not knowing if she would ever get over the pain they had caused.

'You… You can be everything without me, baby…'

Two nights ago the face of the man that was once her whole world had been sat in a car behind her own. His eyes telling her without a shadow of doubt that he wasn't finished.

'I'm going to try and win you…'

Now everything was here and open. The only place to run was into his embrace or a million miles and a thousand lifetimes away from that face.

'I see the woman that should have been my wife…'

Fear, love, family, loyalty, happiness, hope, future, pain, guilt and comfort all merged into one emotional entity – that's what was at stake here. That's what she stood to gain and to lose.

For him. For one night of frenzied passion that would kill her when it was over?

'Alice!' his mesmerising voice caught her off guard and she stopped dead.

Her heart pounded so hard she could feel its quick beat all the way to her ears.

'Do you want me to let you walk?' his strong accent cut straight to her core. An upward surge of lust tickled her scalp and her hand let go of her bag.

This was Tom.

This was where it had to get to.

This was the most important answer of her life. It meant a choice between the memories of delicate night-time promises she had made as a teenage girl and the holy and binding lifelong promises she vowed as a loving wife…

'No,' she replied.

Was that her voice?

He ran into her and she was pushed into the door as he wrapped his strong arms around her middle. His embrace weakened her knees and her head fell back against his shoulder. He held his face close to her ear and said, 'stay.'

Alice nodded slowly.

He pulled her around and grabbed her face. His eyes were almost crystal clear, his thick eyelashes were moist and his jaw twitched impatiently.

'I'm going to kiss you.'

She nodded again.

'God, I need to touch you,' his hands trembled.

She tried to look away but he held her face still. His left hand dropped to her waist, then moved to the front of her jeans. She felt him press is fingers against her pubic bone. Alice tried to speak, tried to say no, that it was too fast for it to happen tonight but he put his thumb to her lips to stop her, so she shook her head instead.

'Stop,' he ordered.

'Tom,' she searched his face. She was so afraid. Could she handle all of him again, so suddenly and so out of the blue?

'It's too quick, Tom. I want to kiss you. Heaven knows I do but anything else… I just can't,' she said quickly.

Would a kiss be enough to take away with her? Could this one stolen evening with him be the closure she needed?

Moments passed slowly. His eyes looked confused, like he was having some kind of internal battle. Finally, he smiled at her and he moved his lips towards her own.

Suddenly her mobile phoned beeped as it received a message. Her husband's face crossed her mind and for a moment it broke the magic spell that held them. He paused and they both looked toward her bag on the floor.

'I better see what that is…' she sighed, 'just in case it's my…'

'Okay, sure baby, of course,' he dropped his hands from her face and fished in his pocket for his own mobile, 'I'll send a quick message to Neil,' Tom started typing quickly.

She watched his handsome face fall a little, the anger visible as he punched the keypad. She didn't move for her bag, instead she reached out and touched his wrist lightly. He took his eyes off the screen and glanced at her. Then he moved.

He threw his phone onto the sofa behind him, he didn't seem to mind if it landed safely or smashed to bits. He grabbed her face again and pushed her out of the living room doorway and towards the stairs. Her back met the wall with a light thud.

'You didn't send it,' she looked up at him shyly.

'I got distracted…' his eyes drilled into her gaze.

Tom's head bent towards her and his smooth lips touched her own. She closed her eyes. His mouth moved drawing her into the kiss. Everything she remembered about kissing him was here still… but ten times more compulsive than before.

His hands delved into her hair and he pushed her harder against the wall. His body pressing against her like an immovable piece of wood. His lips moved with clear purpose and she kissed him back.

Her whole body was poised on the edge of something fantastic. Attraction burned wildly inside of her. She clung to his back and through his shirt she felt his hot skin.

She was losing herself.

Tom's tongue sought to find hers and she gave it willingly. Alice was lifted up on a wave of his perfect attention. He never faltered or hesitated. He only ever gave what he was confident he could deliver.

She traced her hands around his sides, feeling the defined contours of his body. She wanted to see him naked again. She wanted to know if what she remembered was just a figment of her hormone induced imagination or if he was the real deal.

She heard him sigh. The noise transferred through the kiss into her mouth. It bounced off her teeth and slid soundlessly down her throat like a pin ball. Her prize was a small piece of Tom inside of her.

He twisted her a little, moving her back away from the wall and towards the staircase. She fell onto the carpeted steps clumsily and he followed. His hands started to work their way down her body, quickly lifting the edges of her t-shirt. His warm fingers splayed over her hips and he pulled her under him.

Tom moved his face away quickly and leaned back a little. Looking down at her, Alice didn't think she'd ever seen a man look at her like that before. It was pure sexual need mixed with a lifetime of unanswered what-ifs.

He quickly started to pull at his belt. Alice placed her hand over his own to slow him.

'Tom, just wait,' she was breathing fast.

'What?' his eyes met hers.

'Let's not rush.'

'You don't want to do this?'

'Damn it, I'm not saying that,' she felt confused.

'Alice, I don't want to stop this.'

'It's just…'

Tom looked around him, 'we'll go upstairs, come on…'

'I'm scared.'

'I know you are. I understand you're the one taking risks here,' he replied messing with his hair in frustration.

'That's not what I'm scared of,' she looked away.

'Then what is it?'

'I'm scared of you making love to me.'

Alice covered her face with her hands and Tom pulled them away, 'I know baby it's a big deal. It's not just…'

'No, Tom, you don't get it. I'm worried about… sex,' Alice looked away.

'Physically, you mean?'

'Yes and no. If you and I have sex that means I'll know our connection again. How deep it ran and how good you can make me feel.'

She couldn't tell him that since being with him she would struggle to reach orgasm through sex. When they had been together all he had to do was tell her she could and she would climax without it ever being an issue. If they made love now and it was how it used to be she would be addicted to him and unable to function without his love, and without his body she feared she would shut down sexually with Stuart. But if she couldn't orgasm with Tom this time then it would change the past and he might not understand why she needed the memory of the way they were, intact and unaltered.

'How is that bad? I've never felt what I feel with you, with anyone else. Sometimes it just clicks. Once in a blue moon you find someone and it feels like home,' he smiled and added, 'a really amazing dream home.'

'I've only had sex with you and Stuart,' she said, 'not that it's relevant.'

'What?' he sounded like someone had slapped him.

'I've only slept with two people.'

'Why?'

'For over a year after you left I didn't even want a man near me. I met Stuart soon after that and we got on well. When we did eventually have sex – it was good…'

Tom cut in, 'I don't want to know that.'

Alice continued, 'I cried myself to sleep the first night we did because I thought I had erased you. By sleeping with him all trace of your memory had been wiped from my body.'

'That's why you're scared?'

'It's silly,' she smiled.

'You're afraid that I will erase him now? The way he erased me?' Tom looked angry.

He never erased you.

He continued, 'you don't want to risk my making you feel the way he does?' Tom grabbed her arms and pulled her up against his chest. He lifted her with one arm around her waist.

'It's not what I meant…' she whispered against his warm cheek.

'I'm not sure I understand any of it, Alice? But I'm taking you upstairs. If I have to tear down walls with my bare hands and beg you till the sun comes up, I'll do it. I need to make love to you until you forget you ever had anyone else. Just the thought of you with anyone else…'

She didn't correct his assumption. She wanted to be honest but she couldn't give him that kind of power, not yet. She held him tightly as he began climbing the stairs with her in his arms and she knew without a shadow of a doubt that he would be able to make her forget.

He already had.

TOM'S CONFESSIONAL

Monday 2nd August

This is what Tom couldn't tell Alice – certainly not after the things she had just confessed to him.

He had travelled back to Ireland four days after they split in 1996. He had caught a ferry on Saturday at dawn. He drove his little blue Peugeot onto the parking deck. It was full to bursting with his personal items, clothes, books and computer.

Neil had waved him off and Tom had left his friend with the keys to his house, a meeting booked with an estate agent to arrange the sale of the property and an empty storage lock-up to clear his stuff into, plus enough cash to cover his costs.

He was going to miss him.

Tom walked to the viewing deck and looked back at a country that would forever keep his hearts-desire. Holyhead faded into a misty haze and the Irish Sea engulfed him.

He breathed out and watched his breath dance into the cold morning air in front of him. He was running. His life was changing and he couldn't do a damn thing about it.

Tom looked down at the angry waves hitting the steely side of the boat. They seemed annoyed that it had stopped their pre-destined course. He toyed with the idea of jumping in for a moment or two. Those strange irrational thoughts that sneak up and tap you on the shoulder occasionally and make you question your own sanity – but luckily he wasn't *that* crazy.

Then the rain had started. He wondered if he had made it come, to add weight to his sorrow, to further humiliate the pitiful shell of a man he felt like he was becoming.

He didn't move or run for cover, he just let the relentless blanket of precipitation pound at his face. He turned towards the forceful barrage and the heavens opened onto his skin taking his breath away. Tom stayed outside until his hair, clothes and shoes were saturated and he was shivering uncontrollably.

A man ran over to him some time later. He must have worked for the ferry company. He ordered Tom to go inside and get a hot drink.

Tom nodded and followed the man.

Once inside he was handed a blanket by an older woman with shocking red hair she was standing by the door watching the whole spectacle. Clearly the guy had drawn the short straw to brave the weather and rescue Tom from the rain. He thanked her and used it to remove some of the water that literally poured from his clothes. They looked at him like he was mad and/or a little dangerous. He was pointed towards the café and told to warm up.

Tom didn't really care. He was wet. He was cold, but he couldn't feel it.

There were a few people in the cafeteria, mainly business men at this time of day. Tom ordered a coffee and sat in the corner of the room.

He drank the coffee while it was still hot and had to admit he had needed it. While he drank he silently prayed.

He asked God to look after Alice because he couldn't anymore. He asked him to bless her with a happy life, with health and laughter. He told God that whatever it would cost to let her have those things he could gladly take out of his own life. He would take any of the hurt or hardship that was meant for her as well as that meant for himself. He needed to hand someone stronger than himself the job he had ran from.

An hour later he was still staring into the abyss when a young blonde woman came over to clear his cup away. He remembered she was wearing a green uniform and a little green hat. She asked if he was okay and if he would like anything else? She smiled at him and he thought he would cry.

To this day he couldn't remember what he had said to her, or how he had ended up screwing her against his car on the parking deck. He didn't know her name and ashamedly he didn't care.

He drove his car onto Irish soil a few hours later.

That same night he went out with some friends as a welcome home thing. He was functioning on autopilot and pulling off a pretty good act of normality. They all went to a bar near his home town and started drinking. One pint followed the next and his friends had started singing, then so had he. He was actually singing – but he should have been crying.

That night he went back to a woman's house. She was blonde, petite and younger than him. He thought her name was Maxine.

But to him she was only, Alice.

For five months he did this. Mindlessly fucking nameless blonde women and pretending they were her. It was like torture. He would drink. He would convince himself that was what he wanted. He would make love to them and afterwards feel like he had betrayed Alice over and over again.

If it wasn't for Neil talking to him on the phone over the next few months, talking him down if you like, he may never have stopped.

He met Estelle a year later. She was a teacher at the same school as him and they just kind of fell for each other slowly. Day in, day out they talked about pupils, coursework and parents' evenings.

Then they laughed. Then after six months the laughter didn't make him feel guilty.

Soon he thought he was in love.

They had some good years together and two children that changed who he was entirely.

Since his marriage ended he had stayed clean of empty sex and doing the wrong thing. He had seen several women but nothing like before. He was a better man and his children had helped heal him.

But now as he carried Alice against his chest he realised she was probably right, making love to her again was scary. It was putting himself in a position of weakness. Even though he wouldn't be walking away this time, he couldn't guarantee she would choose him – if there even was a choice to be made?

Maybe this was it?

He got to the top of the stairs and put her down, he looked into her eyes and he knew he would take the risk regardless. He had to. If all those years away from her were for nothing, then someone up there was having a massive laugh on the both of them.

If you go full circle and still feel this kind of connection, it had to be right – didn't it?

'Are you alright?' she asked him.

'Yes, just thinking.'

'What about?'

'Whether or not I'm winning you yet?' he grinned.

Give me something, Alice please...

She smiled shyly, 'it's not a competition, and I can't just drop my life for you.'

'I know that.'

'I wouldn't be doing this unless I wanted to. This wouldn't be with anyone else but you. But I can't answer a question like that, Tom.'

'I know.'

She went up on her tiptoes and kissed him lightly on the lips.

'Fuck it,' he whispered against her mouth. He pulled her into one of Neil's large spare bedrooms and closed the door.

His clothes were scattered around the floor. Some spewed out of a bag in the corner. His bed was unmade and yesterday's boxers were sitting next to the bedside cabinet. He cringed and grabbed them off the floor throwing them not so discreetly on top of his bag.

'Well at least I wasn't a foregone conclusion,' she joked looking around at his things, 'I know you well enough to know you would have tidied up first.'

'I'm embarrassed – forgive me?' he winked at her.

'We'll see,' she smiled.

Her wide playful smile filled him with lust. He wanted to throw her on the bed and show her how crazy she made him, but instead he just watched her for a moment.

She looked around the room. Her little body was perfectly still. He loved just looking at her. Her perfect pixie-like features always seemed so perceptive, always so aware.

Her eyes met his.

His heart rate picked up and he started towards her. But a little raise of her hand had him stopping about three feet away.

'What's wrong?'

Please don't say you can't do this again.

'Take your clothes off.'

He paused.

'Do I have to ask twice?' she said sweetly.

'No,' he said shaking his head.

Tom pulled his belt open, then the buttons on his jeans. Next he started work on his shirt buttons. He struggled with the last two so he just tugged at it and they popped off falling onto the floor.

Alice laughed.

He looked up at her and smiled.

Tom kicked his boots off, then socks. He pulled his jeans down and stepped out of them.

Alice never took her eyes off him.

'Everything?' he motioned to his boxers.

'Everything,' she confirmed quietly.

He was feeling a little bit high with nervous excitement now. He really wanted to move, but he had to do what she asked. He had Alice in his room again and he wasn't about to screw this up.

He looked down at himself. He hadn't had an erection like this in a long time. Feeling the tiniest bit self-conscious he stepped out of his pants. His arms dropped to his sides and he looked over at her.

She grinned at him – but her eyes held back something more primal.

'My God you're quite the specimen, Mr Chambers...'

He gritted his teeth to make himself stay on the spot. She had called him Mr Chambers. It was the hottest thing he had heard since the last time she had said it. But this time it didn't hold the guilt or the sad reminder of his position.

'I advise you not to call me that,' his voice sounded harsh but he hadn't meant it to. He was just so tightly wound.

She smiled at him again, 'do you prefer sir?'

Fuck, don't play like this...

He waited for a moment.

'Yes,' he said honestly.

Alice bit her lip, reached up and removed the pins from her hair. The beautiful golden strands fell around her face, 'me too,' she whispered.

He closed his eyes and counted to ten in his head. It had been too long. She had belonged to another man for far too long. He hated himself so much deeper for never coming back to her in the days after he left, for all the times he had gone to the airport and convinced himself it was the wrong thing to do. If he had, then maybe she would have never known any man but him.

'Tom?'

'Yes?' he opened his eyes and she was standing in front of him.

She placed a small hand onto his chest, then the other. Her head fell against him and he could hear her breathing. When she did look up at him her face was anxious. If he was ever sure of anything though, he was sure she did want this. But it felt like she was waiting, stalling. It was like asking him to strip was so she didn't have to and as much as she wanted to take charge and be herself with him, her own guilt still held her back from fully letting go.

He had to drive this. If he didn't she would tear herself to pieces later. He knew her. She would condemn her actions and regret everything she felt. If he could take some of the blame away from her he would.

WHAT IS MINE

Tom closed his eyes and didn't open them.

Alice breathed out.

Her eyes darted to the side, then back to his body.

She stared at him. There was nothing about this man that didn't turn her on. He was as near to perfect as she had ever seen.

She wanted to study his amazingly wide chest and the smooth tan skin of his strong arms. The rippled muscles of his belly had her palms sweating, and his dominant thighs and strapping legs that stood slightly apart should have been enough to quench her growing thirst, but her eyes were pulled away.

Her gaze should have lingered on his formidable shoulders, all powerful and protecting. They would make a girl want to hang off him like she was a feminine 1940's black and white movie star, but as soon as he had stepped out of his pants, his impressive erection jutting out from his body so proud and unashamed, she had been totally lost in him.

She stepped closer.

She wanted to touch him in a million ways. Taste him and hold him. She wanted to show him she wasn't a girl anymore and she could handle all the things she knew he had once held back. All the times she felt him check his actions before he reacted, remembering he was her teacher as well as her lover. He had cared for her with the most tenderness of heart. He had loved her passionately and deeply. But he had never given himself fully in the physical sense.

Though if she was being honest what he had given her then had been more than enough. He had known that and he had never pushed it.

She wanted to do this with him again. She just had to switch off all thoughts of… well basically everything outside of this room. For the next hour, if she could, she had to leave it all at the door.

'Tom?' she reached up and placed her open palm onto his chest. Its heat surprised her and she lifted her other one.

'Yes?' he opened his eyes and looked down at her.

She let her forehead fall against him.

'Sorry, Alice,' he said touching her neck.

She shivered, 'what do you mean?'

'I'm sorry,' he shrugged.

'Oh don't get all self-doubting and moral on me now. That's the last thing I need,' she smiled.

'That's not what I meant,' he said, his eyes narrowing.

'What then?'

Tom grabbed her hair suddenly and pulled her head back, captured her face and bent towards her. He kissed her with strong determined lips. Starting on her mouth then trailing down her neck. She heard herself sigh as he traced his tongue over her sensitised skin.

Her body was high now. She reached up and clung to his shoulders, kissing her own path down his chest. She could feel his heart beat under her lips.

He yanked her cardigan from her arms and dropped it on the floor. She trembled when he lifted her t-shirt over her head and grabbed her breasts underneath.

'Alice, you're so beautiful,' his voice caught in his throat.

'You too,' she whispered against his skin.

Tom pushed himself towards her. His erection pressed into her belly. He backed her over to the bed, lifted her legs and tipped her onto it. She tried to sit but Tom pushed her down with a single firm hand.

'Not yet...' she breathed, 'wait.'

'I can't do it like that, baby. I can't wait.'

'Tom, let's just take it slow,' she touched his arm gently.

'I can't,' he gritted his teeth and climbed onto the bed.

She watched him as he pulled at her jeans. His features both determined and on edge.

Was she ready for this? Was she ready to cheat? Every part of her wanted Tom... except for the small part in her damn head that had said 'I do.'

Tom's hands were on her again. Her jeans were gone and so were her knickers. He traced his fingers down her torso. Her body shook and she closed her eyes.

He moved his hand between her legs and she felt him lightly trace circles over the wildly responsive flesh. His delicate but precise touch had her lifting off the bed to meet him, pushing towards his hand.

'Tom,' she grabbed his wrist.

He pulled back from her, picked up her left leg and repositioned himself between them.

She began to tremble uncontrollably. He looked at her with passionate all-consuming eyes and moved towards her.

Suddenly the picture hit her – what she was about to do. She was going to have actual sex with another man. Here and now, for real and not in her dreams. Tom was going to make love to her.

'No,' she pushed him off lightly as he moved closer to her, 'I can't... this is too real. This is wrong.'

He frowned at her and shook his head, 'Alice, please don't do this to me – don't make it about anyone else, we've come too far.'

'I'm sorry I can't let you put it inside me. I'm the worst kind of cheating whore if I let you do that,' she felt tears fall on to her cheeks. They weren't tears of guilt though they were tears of frustration and need. She needed him to do it.

Tom's eyes glazed over too and he wiped his hand across them. 'Baby...' his voice was stern, 'please move your hands.'

She looked down and realised she had placed her hands covering herself so he couldn't enter her – she felt like an idiot – but she didn't move them.

'Tom, please...' she begged, 'we have to do the right thing.'

'I'm trying to do what's right for us.'

'I didn't mean that. I just meant we have to think about others...'

'No, you didn't.'

He lifted one of her hands away and held it over her head the way he always used to. More of her hot tears slipped down her neck and onto the pillow.

He grabbed the other hand and she struggled against him a little. With his thighs he pushed her legs towards her body. He breathed deeply, his face was set and the muscle in his jaw twitched.

Tom bent down and kissed her. She turned her head away sharply and struggled beneath him again.

'Why are you still doing this?' she squirmed, 'Just let me go. You can't do this if I don't want to.'

Why was *she* acting like this? All she wanted was him inside of her – desperately she wanted it. If he turned away now and gave up, she would fall to her knees and beg him to finish. But something was making her resist. She didn't understand herself at all? She just kept silently praying he wasn't going to do the right thing. She bucked against him.

'Fucking stop it,' he half shouted, 'stop fighting me.'

'It's not right,' she cried turning her face towards him.

'That's it, that's enough baby,' he tried to keep his voice calm.

'I can't,' she looked him square in the eye, 'I can't just do this willingly. Help me...' she whispered.

'It's just you and me,' he whispered back. She felt him push slightly forward. His whole body was tight. Beads of moisture grouped on his chest and upper arms and his voice was laboured, 'you're seventeen and I'm your English teacher,' he pushed forwards a little more and she felt that part of her body open to him, 'this is my old house and that song is playing...'

'Don't say that...' she looked at him, 'can we really pretend we're those people again?'

Tom grabbed her waist, stilling her. He closed his eyes, 'I love you,' he whispered, then he flexed his hips driving himself deep inside of her with one blunt thrust.

'Oh no, Tom!' she cried out, scrunching her eyes shut.

'I'm so sorry, baby,' he pulled back and pushed forwards again. The feeling was unlike anything Alice could describe. She had felt it before, but nothing prepared her for the instant explosion in her head, cheeks and throat.

Her inner muscles tightened around him and he moved faster. She was suddenly and speedily building towards what she thought had become impossible. There was something about him – about the way he made love to her.

Tom let go of his composure and grabbed at her body. He pushed into her over and over. Each time raising high above her, she began to stroke his hips and urge him forward.

She could hear her own cries outside of her head someplace. But all she could feel was him inside of her. This wasn't romantic sex. It wasn't tender or considerate. It was letting go. It was drowning. It was what she needed. Her own concerns had flown out the window as soon as she realised what it meant when he was with her.

'Alice,' he could barely get the words out, 'next time I'll make it amazing for you I promise.'

'Shut up, this is… it is amazing,' she kissed his arm and he thrust harder.

'I love you,' he said again, 'I know it's not like that for you, but I love you, Alice Rutherford.'

He called her the name she had waved goodbye to seven years ago.

'Tom, I think…' she couldn't say the word. She didn't want to jinx it.

'Okay, wait for me. He positioned himself higher and every movement ratcheted her up and up. His whole body tensed and his already corded muscles hardened further. She felt her tummy clench, then her head dig into the pillow. Then she felt it – her moment of absolution. She was falling or drifting and he was cursing. She felt his climax, and her own orgasm belonged only to him.

I love you.

In the heady aftermath of what was the best five minutes of her life and as her body came down and the small ripples of pleasure still teased her limbs, she heard only his voice. His beautiful Irish accent kissed her ears. She had missed him so much and now her heart remembered what her body always had.

'Baby, I'm not moving until you promise me you're not going to freak out?'

'I won't,' she kissed him.

He smiled.

'You won't run?'

'I won't.'

'Lastly, you won't say that this was a mistake? I'll keep you in this room forever if you say we're done.'

She smiled at him again, 'I can't...'

'Because I didn't take no for an answer? Do you think I forced you?' he cursed himself.

'You didn't force me. I was going to say it *wasn't* a mistake and I hope I don't ever believe it was.'

Wait till morning.

Tom smiled and let his head fall to the pillow beside her.

'Thank God. It was a close one, I was about to give up,' he laughed.

She giggled, 'I needed you to do that.'

'I love you,' he said for the third time, 'if I keep saying it you might take pity on me?'

'I could never pity you.'

'Could you love me?' he grinned.

'Tom.'

'I know.'

'I've got to go I don't even know what time it is?' Alice looked for a clock.

She saw a flicker of sadness on Tom's expression as he looked at his watch.

'Eight forty-five,' he winked.

Alice laughed, 'don't pull that one.'

'What? It is.'

'I have to, Tom,' she kissed his neck. Breathing in his woody scent she hoped it wasn't the last time she would smell it.

'You can't go yet. I'll tell you the truth. Its ten thirty... early really?'

Tom went up on his arms again and pulled her underneath his body.

She sighed.

'If you leave you'll make me feel really cheap and used,' he smiled and kissed her nose.

'Can we do this, Tom?'

'Absolutely…' he looked down his body and smiled again, 'yep, I'm ready.'

'Again that's not what I meant. And how at your age are you ready again?'

Tom's mouth fell open, 'I'm hurt.'

She giggled and stroked her palms down his chest and wished she was stronger. When it came to him she was pathetic. When you mix genuine honesty, a touch of playful humour and the best sex of your life together it was hard to be anything but weak. Add into the pot a visual feast of dirty prince charming you may as well throw the towel in.

'The question is, are you ready?' he asked.

Alice nodded.

She was high right now. But she knew the low would come later.

He pushed into her again with no less urgency of just minutes before. No less want or vigour. He was only ever all or nothing.

'I love you,' he breathed.

Her eyes welled up not with fear or sadness now. Not even with love for this man. It was how she felt when he was taking her. She was a mass of nerves and memories cumulating with every stroke. Nothing could ever raise her to the point of no return and keep its foot on the gas the way becoming one with him did.

You stupid girl…

LEAVING

Tuesday 3rd August

It was quarter to two in the morning. Tom knew she had to go but it didn't make it any easier.

He watched her gather the clothes from the floor quickly and dress in silence. From the warm burrow of his bed he wished that his door would lock and never open, trapping them together for eternity with nothing to do but talk and screw.

They had fallen asleep for a while and Alice had woken moments ago in a panic. She tried to get out of bed immediately but he had kept her in his arms for a full forty seconds until she wriggled free from his hold.

'Alice?'

'Tom, have you seen the time? I've got to go – I'm sorry,' she said pinning her hair up franticly.

'Alice?' he said again.

She stopped pinning and turned to him.

'You know what I'm going to ask?' he swallowed.

'I take the pill. You don't have to worry.'

'What? Why would I care about that?' he shook his head.

She was unbelievable sometimes. Did she really think that he would mind if she was to become pregnant with his child? Like that wouldn't make him the happiest man alive? Giving him the claim he so desperately craved, as well as a baby that was theirs. Made from two people's souls that should exist together above all else in this world.

'Oh, I thought seeing as how we hadn't discussed it and you weren't in any hurry to... you know, that you would be worrying by now. You always did before?' she picked up her bag.

'I'm not worried now, baby.' Tom started to get up.

'Don't see me out, stay in the warm. It's too emotional anyway,' she smiled tightly concealing her feelings the best she could, 'what were you going to ask then?'

'I have five more days. Will I see you again before I leave?' he tried to stop his voice from choking on the words.

Alice moved to the bed, leaned over and kissed him. Her hands ruffled through his hair. Her large eyes looked sad, 'of course, I hope so,' she whispered, 'but right now I'm in a whole heap of trouble.'

'Not with me,' he grinned.

'No, not with you. With you, I've made a whole heap of trouble.'

She walked to the door and the feeling of uncertainty in his stomach stepped up a gear. His body wanted to stop her and his head was full of ways he could make her stay.

'Rutherford?'

'Yes, sir?'

He closed his eyes, 'don't forget.'

'I won't.'

'What won't you forget?' he asked in his teacher voice.

'That you love me,' she paused, 'and that I think I still might love you too.'

She hurried through the door and didn't look back at him.

She might love you.

He was stunned.

He wanted to jump out of bed and pull her back. But she needed to go. She was a mother and her child would need her soon. Morning would come and things would look different, but hopefully not that different.

His brain was tired. Tom turned over and willed sleep to come back to him quickly.

She loves you…

———◆———

'So, how was last night?' Neil asked as Tom stumbled into the kitchen a little after nine.

'Good,' Tom growled, 'any coffee on?'

Mornings provided more of a challenge as he had got older. The only way to blast away the cobwebs used to be an early run before school. These days caffeine came first.

'It's fresh,' Neil placed a phone on the breakfast bar. Tom's phone.

'You left that downstairs last night and you forgot to call me.'

'Sorry, I was just so tired. What time did you get back?'

Tom fidgeted in his seat and sipped his drink.

'About half past eleven.'

'Good night was it?' Tom asked cheerily, as he began typing a message.

'I'm more concerned with hearing about yours,' Neil smiled and raised his eyebrows.

Tom didn't respond he wanted to keep Alice out of this.

'We talked – it was good – she left.'

'You left a beer on the coffee table and it was uncharacteristically half full.'

'Did I?'

Neil started to butter some toast, 'you did, and I don't want to be rude, but when I walked up the stairs to bed last night I'm pretty sure I heard 'sex' noises,' he started laughing then.

Tom smiled and grabbed some of his toast, 'I must have been dreaming.'

'Nice dream. Did it happen to leave at about two this morning?'

'It may have, Lieutenant Columbo.'

'I told you,' Neil looked at him smugly.

'Well it wasn't the way you said it would be. She wasn't just out for a quick thrill,' Tom's jaw clenched.

'What was it then?' Neil asked suspiciously.

'More than I expected,' Tom replied, avoiding any details.

'Why aren't you sharing?'

'You know why.'

'Because you love her,' he mimicked Tom's voice and clutched his heart in an overly dramatic fashion.

Tom nodded and finished his drink, 'indeed.'

'So what do you hope to have gained?' Neil asked.

'A second chance,' Tom replied.

'Do you think you got it?'

'The beginnings of one I think.'

'Where's this going to end, Tom? You bedded her, isn't that enough?' Neil said finishing his toast.

'Of course not, if anything it's made it worse. She's gone now and I'm burning with jealousy wondering if she is playing happy families with her fucking husband? That's how crazy it makes me. I won't be done until she is back where she should never have left.'

'Tom, you need to wake up and realise this isn't 1996. You aren't the king of her world anymore and she isn't the teenage girl you left there. I can't stand by and watch you fall apart again.'

'No one's falling apart,' Tom sighed and looked at his friend.

'I hope to God you're right, man.'

Tom nodded, 'me too.'

He looked at the newspaper on the worktop. His eyes were drawn to the date. He was leaving on Saturday and even though she had said they would see each other again he wasn't sure if he believed her.

He wished more than anything she would wake up this morning without regret. With a heart full of a love they still shared despite all the complications. Most of all he didn't want her to ever forget how it felt when they were together, because if she remembered that, it would be hard for her to deny their fated paths and bound hearts.

And he prayed for her to choose him.

CHEATING HEART

Alice opened her eyes slowly. She looked at the alarm clock, it was gone nine. She turned her head to the right expecting to see Stuart next to her sleeping soundly. But the bed was empty aside from herself. She went up on her elbows and looked at the camp-bed and that too was empty.

In the distance, from somewhere within her parent's home she could hear the faint sounds of her daughter's laughter and she let her head drop back onto her pillow with considerable force.

Shit.

When she had returned in the early hours of the morning the whole house had been asleep. She washed frantically in the bathroom and crept into bed beside her husband. Turned away from him and pretended to sleep. She pretended to sleep through 3am and then 4am and most of 5am at which she had dozed off at some point.

Her mind had been spinning. Her body had felt twitchy and restless.

She turned over again and stared at her husband's back for a long time. It felt like she had just slipped a knife into his unsuspecting flesh.

She stroked his familiar hair and tried to stop herself from wishing if he was to turn over to meet her touch she would be greeted with Tom's face and not his.

Guilt gripped her mind for long hours. She found herself mouthing her confession to him in the darkness but allowing no sound to spring forth from her lips. Just the silent whispering of it had aided in easing some of her darker thoughts.

Then she would close her eyes and Tom would be there.

He was making love to her over and over. The feel of him inside her made her skin tremble and the sides of her mouth pull up in the start of a smile. She found her hands touching her breasts and thighs when her thoughts were full of his voice and his strong embrace.

The years that had passed between them had meant nothing. As soon as she was lying beneath his glorious body, watching his hips move and becoming lost in the exquisite sensation they evoked. All thoughts of the word 'mistake' had scattered from memory like the flippy-flappy dance of the pastel coloured confetti that had caught her attention on her wedding day, and had always remained one of her more vivid recollections.

Alice had played the events of the evening over in her mind more than once since leaving Neil's house. The things they had said to one another. How obvious it had been from the moment that they had laid eyes on each other again, that it would end up here, like this.

And, time and time again she thought about the sex.

Tom had said he had forced himself onto her – and in a sense he had. She had said no, and he had taken her anyway. The image of that should have made her angry and hurt, scared even. But in reality she had never experienced a more physically gratifying moment in her life. The choice removed from her and her submission expected.

He knew her better than she knew herself. Tom always did everything right, in the right way, at the right time and with the right words. That made him a pretty impressive man, if not a little intimidating.

How can I fight that?

Alice heard footsteps coming up the stairs.

She breathed deeply and got ready to recite her lie. Something else she had thought about repeatedly in the small hours of the morning. She closed her eyes and once again pretended to sleep.

The door opened.

'Wakey wakey,' he whispered. She felt the bed de-press as he sat next to her.

Alice peered out and yawned, made a few morning noises and the little rub of her eyes made the whole despicable farce feel more convincing.

'Morning sweetheart,' she reached up and stroked his chin playfully, 'what time is it?'

'Just after nine. Hayley and I let you sleep as you got in so late – I was getting worried?' he asked what she had been doing without actually asking it.

'Gossip, wine and girls,' she smiled, 'I tried to text you but the signal was rubbish from her place.'

'I messaged you several times.'

She had ignored every one of them.

'I didn't get any of them honey, till I was on my way back and then it just seemed pointless to reply when I was nearly home.'

Stuart nodded.

'Your parents have taken Hayley to the park. Fancy me joining you?' he winked.

Alice panicked. She loved her husband but she didn't want to sleep with him. She had only managed to wash when she got back. A shower at three in the morning would have been too obvious and she may as well have screamed 'I just fucked a man that wasn't you!' at the top of her voice. Sex with Stuart would be an insult, a slap in the face, with the smell and lust of another man still clinging to her repulsive skin.

'I'm all yucky and sweaty. I don't really feel at my most attractive. Let me hop in the shower?'

Stuart looked at her and narrowed his eyes, 'you're always attractive to me, Alice.'

'Thank you, but really I feel gross.'

'Okay… I'll stick the kettle on for you? We may get a cuppa and a quick read of the papers before they get back.'

'Thank you, Stu – love you,' her eyes glazed over and she looked away and rubbed her face again.

I'm a whore.

'It's just a cuppa,' he smiled.

He disappeared downstairs and Alice pulled her phone out from under her pillow. She had stashed it last night and only just remembered about it. She looked at it, she had a new message from Tom.

9.02am
Morning baby…breathe…relax…don't stress, please xxx

Like that was possible?

9.11am
Morning, sorry I was sleeping – or something close to it. I'm texting you now before I see my daughter and start living again in my real world.

Last night was amazing. I forgot I was once the girl that had you all the time – she was lucky. I'm so glad you never changed and even if this is all we have I never want to wish it different. xxxxx

She read the message again, sent it and then deleted the conversation. She wouldn't change it now but when this was over she wouldn't even have his words to comfort her. She would be broken and in pain, secretly licking her wounds and pretending to the rest of the world that she was still the same woman.

And this would end, how could it not? Maybe last night had been the end? Did knowing that make it easier to put the two men in different boxes? Tom was here and for whatever reason she'd had to re-live him. She loved him the same as she ever had, but he *was* a fantasy. Her husband and family had the bigger stake in her life, so she would just have to accept that and deal with the sadness that she was dealt.

She thought about her old journal. She never did get a replacement. She wanted to write down everything that had happened so far, but she knew she never could.

This is what infidelity felt like. It was like being as free as she could imagine, but at the same time in a prison built by your own hands. From which there was no early release or parole because unless you confess your crimes, the blood would always stain your hands and sleeping with one eye open would become normal.

She felt the weight of deceit heavy upon her shoulders as she glanced at her phone.

9.16am
I can't accept that last night was it. I know how it is for you, but I just can't think like that – I won't. I'm not going to put more pressure on you though, it's hard and I get that xx

9.21am

Tom, you know I want to see you again but really with all of this around me how can I do that? Last night we were Tom and Alice again, student and teacher, lovers. This morning I'm Alice Lyons, wife to Stuart. For the past two days I've let myself be someone else and I've got to stop now.

She pulled her legs up to her chest and grabbed the duvet around her a little more. Had she ever wanted anything as much as she wanted to carry on?

Alice's phoned beeped again.

9.25am

If you have ever loved me I'm asking you now for something I know I don't deserve but I'm asking all the same. Don't leave me without letting me have just one more day or even just an hour please? I can't leave what we did last night there and move on. I will fight for you baby whether you want me to or not. And, I'm not above begging x

If she didn't see him he wouldn't stop. He would always be there. If not physically then in her thoughts. That's what she told her conscience anyway. Of course it had nothing to do with the fact that she was already addicted to this man. That she had never, not for one day ever stopped thinking about him.

9.30am

Tomorrow. Then it's got to be it. We can't play at this forever x

In less than ten seconds he had replied. One sentence that both scared and excited her.

9.31am
Tomorrow I'll win you – I promise xx

She hoped that wasn't possible because it was something she hadn't allowed herself to consider yet.

"SCENES FROM AN ITALIAN RESTAURANT"

Tuesday 3rd August

The restaurant used to be her favourite, 'Sofia's'. It was the place Stuart had asked to marry her, the place her parents took her to celebrate her A-level results and where Hayley had her christening dinner. It was a small family run Italian restaurant that was at the heart of the town and people absolutely loved it. It even had a waiting list at weekends. It had been a focal point of her life for as long as she remembered and its owners Frank and Sofia felt like family. So whenever they visited Stuart would call a few weeks ahead and secure a table for them, it had become sort of a tradition of theirs.

He hadn't told her until late afternoon that he had booked for tonight he also hadn't told her that he had invited friends. Lewis, was more Stuart's friend than Alice's and his wife Bethany was way too confident for Alice to ever feel totally comfortable with.

It was the last thing she wanted to do tonight. She had too much on her mind to be able to successfully traverse conversation with two people that she really had no inclination to entertain.

'Why are they always late?' Alice tapped her fingers on the table.

Stuart laughed, 'I think its Beth. She takes forever to get ready, drives Lewis mad.'

'It drives me mad. I keep looking at what I want to order!' she was starving having eaten nothing since yesterday.

'It's still going to be the meatballs for me. And before you say it, I know I should try something different but I just love the meatballs here, baby.'

Alice's head shot up from her menu, 'What?'

'What?' he looked confused.

'Nothing… the meatballs are good,' she smiled.

He had called her it. In as many years as she could recall he hadn't called her that. That's what Tom called her. Why would he do that? Guilt ridden paranoia made her grab her gin and tonic and finish it quickly. She raised her hand for the waiter.

'Slow down Alice, you're driving tonight I want to have a few beers.'

'I'm always driving,' she snapped before thinking. After what she had done how on earth did she have the cheek to moan about that?

'Don't start. They'll be here any second, we can get a taxi,' he looked down at his menu again and she stared at the top of his head.

Don't start?

'No, I'll drive,' she couldn't risk being picked up by the same driver who had dropped her off on Saturday night.

She looked away from him towards the window. A little table for two was set with a bottle of wine chilling in a bucket, a 'reserved' sign sat on the edge and a single yellow gerbera smiled at her from a tall vase. It reminded her of those dancing sunflowers in pots that were all the rage from childhood. Some wore sunglasses and held a guitar, swaying from side to side as it played some cheesy summer tune.

What was she doing? How could she sit here with him? This time last night she had walked into a house with another man knowing she would end up sleeping with him, wanting to sleep with him.

You know it's true...

No.

Yes.

'They're here,' Stuart rose from the table and waved them over.

Lewis, also a sports physiotherapist was an absolute dead ringer for Dec (Ant and Dec) in Alice's opinion. Beth, well she was tall, voluptuous and always primped to perfection. Always tanned, with the silkiest raven coloured hair Alice had ever seen. She was loud and confident. She talked about sex and fashion and flirted with Stuart way too much. She made Alice feel even plainer then she thought she was, and boring for not being as open about their relationship as them.

Alice stood and hugged Beth. Then Lewis grabbed her and squeezed her tightly.

'Alice, you're so tiny,' he squeezed on, 'you're like a little doll, I could snap you in half,' he laughed.

'Hey, don't do that, put my wife down,' Stuart joked patting Lewis on the back.

'Wow you look amazing Beth. Your hair looks fab,' Alice complimented her. She felt like she had to. If someone cares that much about their appearance, you almost feel rude not saying how great they look – and she did look great.

'Thank you Hun!' she swished her new do and pouted at Alice, 'you always look lovely too Alice, so natural – you're lucky.'

Plain.

Alice smiled back. Tom called her beautiful all the time. When he said it she believed him. He looked at her and she felt like she was the most desirable thing in the world. The passion in which he needed her made her feel sexy, made her feel like she had something that a man like him could crave. But here she was just ordinary Alice.

Stuart hung off every word that Beth uttered for the next five minutes, until their waiter came over to take their order. She practically sang *'don't you wish your girlfriend was hot like me'* to him. Lewis looked on smiling, he didn't care. They were an open couple and happy to watch the other make a show of themselves.

'Beth's having the meatballs too,' Stuart smiled smugly at Alice then back at Beth.

'Nice choice,' Alice replied.

'So, Al what's new with you?' Lewis leaned in towards her and rested his arm on the back of her chair.

'New? Nothing much really. The artists are still doing well, we're getting more interest than we can handle *and* my workshops are starting to pay now, so I can't complain.'

'And how's that beautiful little double of yours?'

'Hayley, she's amazing as always, but she wants a new puppy,' Alice smiled at him.

'We all fancy something small and cute from time to time, you can't blame her,' he raised his eyebrows and she felt his fingers brush the back of her sweater.

So now she's a puppy… great!

Stuart glanced over and saw him touch her, he shook his head in a playful way, as if to say 'what're they like?' he didn't care either. And, in turn she wasn't supposed to care that Stuart wanted to screw Beth. Marriage was kind of mad like that. There were some thing's that just got overlooked.

Tom wouldn't have overlooked it. He wouldn't like a man flirting with her and he wouldn't lust after another woman in front of her. He would sit beside her; he might even pull her chair a little closer to his. He would rest his warm hand on her leg under the table and she would know that for the whole night he would be thinking about when they could escape and be alone together. Tom would probably brake a man's thumb if he saw it drift seductively down her back.

She looked towards the door quickly. Thinking about him here made her nervous.

'Waiting for someone?' Lewis asked.

'Um... no.'

'Alice, you've been odd all day,' Stuart looked over.

'Have I?'

'Leave her alone boys, honestly,' Beth laughed, 'you won't get laid tonight if you start picking on her?' she aimed her last comment in Stuart's direction.

'If she kicks me out I'll have to come and sleep on your sofa,' he winked at Beth, who at least had the decency to blush a little.

'I don't think my wife would banish you to our sofa, mate,' Lewis took a large sip of wine, 'and in return if Alice needed some company I would be a gentleman and offer my services.'

She wanted to grab her bag and leave, instead the other three cracked up with laughter. She tried to smile along, forcing some fake chuckle to pass her lips. They might as well throw their car keys into the basket of bread and oils that had just been put down in front of them. She truly believed if the couple they were dining with, openly offered, Stuart would happily enter them into some kind of orgy/wife swapping scenario.

The evening continued in the same fashion. Stuart and Lewis got drunker and more cringe-worthy. She was stroked and breathed on more than she thought she could handle whilst still pretending to enjoy herself and Beth encouraged the sexual innuendo like it was her favourite dessert.

Alice had abstained from any further drinking since being told she was driving so just sat back and watched. Engaging in the conversation, but totally disengaging her mind. She watched her husband lean towards the other woman, talk to her and watch her eat. But even though she knew that women found him attractive she had never really been distant enough to notice how much he thrived on it until tonight. She wasn't jealous, more annoyed really, and in the car on the way home, an hour or so later, she had to ask him.

'Do you want to fuck Beth?'

'Bloody hell Alice, do you want to be anymore foul mouthed?' he coughed and turned to her, 'no, I don't.'

'Why lie?' she asked him, 'we're adults and human, I wouldn't blame you she's very attractive.'

She didn't know if she was trying to make herself feel better about what she had done by getting him to admit a similar desire or give her actions some kind of justification?

'She is really pretty. But I'm married to you, very happily. I wouldn't do that to you.'

'But you would do it if I wasn't around? So, you do fancy her?'

'What? If I was single, why not?' he looked like he was on trial.

'They practically offer us to swing every time we see them. What if I was to sleep with Lewis and you with Beth, would that be different?'

'Do you want to?' Stuart stammered, 'what has Lewis said to you?'

'Forget it Stu, I'm just being silly… Beth makes me feel inadequate that's all,' she laughed as they turned into her parent's street.

'You shouldn't feel like that,' he rested his head against the back of the seat and closed his eyes, 'I'm knackered… and a bit pissed.'

Three days ago that would have been enough. Her husband telling her she didn't need to worry, that he loved her and she shouldn't feel unattractive. But now all she could do was compare the two men. She had visions of Tom rushing at her, silencing her with a kiss that told her she was going to find out exactly how much she shouldn't feel like that.

She pulled onto the drive and glanced over at her husband. She loved him so much but he didn't make her feel the way Tom did, he never could and it wasn't his fault.

He was her family, the father to her child and her life partner, hell even her best friend. But here, right now in this car she knew that wasn't enough to keep her away from Tom. She wasn't strong enough to deny him one more day. And Tom wasn't selfless enough to give her up.

As a woman, she never believed that she would be capable of this level of deceit. She always held herself in a higher regard, and as a mother, the thought repulsed her. But tomorrow she was going to meet him again. Mrs Lyons would take her clothes off, make love to him and wish, like that silly teenager she once was, that it could last forever.

CALLING AT

Tom would never get tired of watching Alice walk towards him. He sat on the train, his face casually turned towards the window. She walked onto the platform thirty seconds before the train was due to depart. Fresh-faced, beautiful and smiling, his heart picked up. She didn't look into any of the windows, she didn't look for him. She just jumped on and disappeared from his line of vision for a few moments.

He never wanted to be the other man, yet here he was.

The electric doors opened four rows in front of him and she was there. Her emerald green eyes found him quickly, she smiled and held up two polythene cups.

He wasn't a 'coffee on the go' kind of guy. He mocked men under his breath for carrying them around. He disliked the way they subliminally said 'look at me, I'm very important and busy.' It was almost like sipping a well-known branded coffee from a little cardboard cup was the substitute for having a small penis. He was a mug man – instant coffee with two sugars and a little milk to lessen the bitterness. But if Alice had got him a take-out he would drink it with relish and let people happily assume he had a tiny cock. He loved her enough to suck it up.

'Mr Chambers,' she said smiling, placing the drink onto the table and sliding into the seat next to him.

'Thanks,' he looked at her.

Was he allowed to touch her? Kiss her? Monday night seemed like an age ago and given all the circumstances and barriers he wasn't sure what the proper etiquette was for second day of cheating?

'Are you alright?' she asked.

Tom sighed and moved his body to face her.

No, not really.

'I'm good, you? How did yesterday go?' he replied.

'Alright, it was horrible lying to him, but it went alright.'

'Good,' Tom paused he had no idea what to do, it all felt so alien to him, 'Alice?'

'Yes?' she glanced at him whilst she took the lid from her cup and started blowing her drink.

She seemed relaxed today, almost resolute. He on the other hand was wired and jumpy, the days were ticking by, his plane ticket was burning a hole in his pocket and all he wanted to do was push her, but he couldn't. He wanted straight answers that he knew she couldn't and wouldn't give him. Ninety-five percent of his brain and one hundred percent of his heart was ready to get down on his knees and declare that death would be preferable if she didn't agree to be his.

He shook his head, 'where are we going anyway?' he asked instead.

Late last night she had suggested each driving to separate stations on the same train line and meeting on-board. She said it was safer and less likely to be seen by anyone they knew. Tom would have happily got on at her home town station with a sign that said 'I'm with Alice!' if he had his way.

'Two stops on, then get off at Stratford-upon-Avon. I can't wait you know,' she dropped her hand onto his upper thigh and lightly pressed into the denim with her fingers.

'Me too,' Tom grinned.

'I've thought of nothing else,' she unconsciously bit her lip and squeezed a little harder.

Tom closed his eyes and silently both pitied and envied any man that had never felt like this. To know the woman you love completely can't wait to be alone with you. To have her sitting next to you, her body warming your arm and her smiles filling your eyes was all he could ever want. But at war with that euphoric regard was the fear that now constantly gripped him, debilitating his thoughts and emotions – what if she walked on Saturday? What if this, for her, was all it was ever going to be?

Man up.

Tom's default response was sex. It always had been. His weakening heart and mind never seemed to dull or dampen the need for it. So he chose that to cling to amidst the very choppy waters that he found himself just about surviving in. With his head bobbing above sea level and a threatening mouthful of distasteful salty refreshment washing towards him fast, he reverted to type.

'Since we aren't student and teacher anymore and for the sake of this story we're consenting adults… what do you want to do when we get there?' he asked her, his hand resting on top of her little fingers and pulling them backwards to his groin.

Alice flashed a look at him, her eyelashes blinked a little faster and she looked just like the nervous girl he had corrupted so many years ago.

'Honestly?' she asked him shyly.

'Definitely honestly,' he confirmed.

'I don't want you to hold back,' she stroked her hand over him.

Tom felt hot. He glanced out of the window. The countryside whizzed by merging into a Monet inspired panoramic watercolour. His reflection in the toughened glass looked skewed, one half of his face sort of disappeared into the background of the train carriage.

'Okay,' he looked back at her.

She nodded at him and leaned in to kiss his cheek.

'This train better hurry the fuck up,' he laughed.

What had he held back?

He wasn't that sure? Okay he had been very self-controlled. He had pulled back when he thought he was being too dominant and he had never tied her up and spanked her – but he got the impression she meant something more than that.

'What're you thinking about?' she whispered.

'Tying you up and keeping you prisoner,' he joked.

'Hmm nice thought…' she smiled back at him

'Alice, you know this is serious for me don't you?'

Grow some balls.

'What do you mean?'

'I know you think we're playing here but I do want you back.'

Alice sighed, 'I'm aware you're not playing. I'm not playing either. Do you really think I'm that shallow to risk my marriage for a week of sex with someone that I have no feelings for?'

'No, I don't. But the problem is you don't know what you want from all this?' Tom pushed his hand through his hair.

'True. You came out of the smoke like some kind of dream. You already knew how you felt. I was happily minding my own business when you told me you still loved me. That takes some time to digest, regardless of how much I still care about you. But I'm married to a great man, who I do love. We have a life that many people would envy. But then there's you… and that changes things,' she took another drink from her cup, a cloud of steam obscuring her face.

'And you think you love me too?' Tom tried to stiffen his voice.

'I do. I've always been in love with you.'

'Are you in love with him?'

'I love him and I think I'm *in* love with him. But the love I feel for you is so different,' she looked at him with tears in her eyes.

'How is it different?' he asked.

'It's mine,' she paused, 'It's not something that is shared or multiplied. The way I love you is selfishly and honestly. When I'm with you I have the ability to forget everything else. It consumes me and owns me. It's a feeling that I've never felt since and will never feel again with anyone else… it's unique,' Alice glanced around the carriage to make sure they weren't being overheard.

He knew that love.

'It's dangerous isn't it baby?' he held her small hand tightly and pulled her against his side.

'Make no mistake Tom, its deadly,' she sighed deeply.

'I should never have come. I didn't want to screw up your perfect…' he stopped.

'With you still in this world away from me it could never have been perfect, Tom.'

'What did we start?' he turned to her and kissed her lips softly.

'Something it seems we could never finish,' she replied.

THE PARSON'S NOSE

Wednesday 4th August

The woman who she used to trust and thought she knew pretty well gave the girl that sat behind the small reception desk her name, 'Chambers. I booked over the phone,' when did this respectable mother and wife become a total shit?

The girl looked at Alice then at her computer screen and smiled, 'Yes, Mrs Chambers, I have your booking here. I just need a signature and a credit card.'

Alice flinched when she called her by his name and looked towards Tom who was smiling broadly.

'I'll get that, darling,' Tom leaned over and signed his name and handed his card to the girl.

Alice thanked him. She hadn't thought that there might be a credit card trail leading back to her infidelity. So Tom's quick thinking had avoided the awkward moment.

She had found this seventeenth century pub with bed and breakfast online last night. 'The Parsons Nose' was the quintessential middle England good pub guide establishment.

While Stuart had slept off the beers beside her she was surfing the internet, pulling together the repulsive plan of deceit. She wanted to vomit, to hit herself in the face with her laptop... but still she made the necessary arrangements to exacting standards. She was doing this and there was nothing she could say to stop herself.

It was a total head fuck to be at war with one's self. Talk about bloody Jekyll and Hyde.

'We don't have any bags?' Tom whispered as they ascended the stairs behind a young skinny boy dressed head to toe in black who had been sent to show them to their room.

'I know, but they don't know that. They could be in our car.'

'True. Are we staying over?' he asked hopefully.

'No, for today this is our drive by motel,' she smiled and took his hand.

'Dirty sex then?' he mouthed.

'Here we are,' the young man opened the door and handed Tom the key.

'Lovely, thank you,' Tom grinned at him and Alice stepped inside.

'Anything else you need just give us a shout or dial 9.'

'We will thank you.' Tom put on his most charming Irish accent, letting his words roll a little more than normal and patted the guy on his shoulder as he slowly shut the door in his face.

Alice walked around the room. It was sweet. There was a large mahogany bedstead with a jacquard quilt and cushions, two side tables and a writing desk. The en-suite was fairly large too and very Italian looking in comparison.

She watched Tom unscrew the lid from one of the complimentary bottles of water and take a drink.

'You didn't have to do all this you know? I could have sorted something,' Tom looked at her.

'I know, but I didn't want you to think I was taking you for granted. That I thought I was some princess who always needs you to look after everything.'

'You are,' he smiled.

'Are you always the perfect guy?' she laughed.

'No.'

Alice wanted to rip his clothes off. She really didn't know what she was waiting for? She loved hearing him speak though and it's what often kept her sane when her entire body was screaming out to have him. He made her feel loved and very much like she was the only woman that he ever noticed.

She had decided that morning on her drive to the railway station that she would just let whatever happened today happen. She wasn't going to hold back and cover herself in guilt. She had already done the worst thing. There was no point in lying anymore, pretending that she didn't love him or want him. She wasn't going to hope anymore that he would change his mind and leave her alone – she didn't want that – she wanted this.

You can only tell yourself so many times that you're married, committed and hope it will make a difference to your choices – she was those things, but all the prayers and denial in the world can't change the fundamental and difficult things that make us human.

'Alice?' he beckoned her over with his hand.

She walked to him. Her eyes drawn to his tall, muscular frame. A body that had filled her dreams for as long as she could remember. His clothes always hung from him in just the right way. His hair never over styled, but always so damn hot. His brooding face was the constant little blue pill to her libido. But his heart and his smile is what had her, all the rest was just perfectly tailored window dressing.

'How am I going to give you up?' she sighed.

Tom reached for her hands and pulled her towards him and she collided with his hard chest.

'I'm going to do everything I can to make that not a fucking option,' he whispered harshly into her hair.

He moved his mouth lower and pressed a firm kiss onto her neck just below her ear. The sensation had her moving her neck towards his lips, like a cat urging the person stroking them to continue. His lips moved lower, he brushed her hair away from her neck with his hand and kissed her collarbone. His stubble raked her skin as he moved and its prickling quality only heightened her experience further.

'Tell me again what you want me to do?' he asked.

'Don't treat me like I'm seventeen,' she breathed, 'I want all of the man that is standing in front of me. Not the watered down version or the teacher scared to death of being caught,' she met his gaze.

His eyes were a heady shade of ice blue and they searched her face for the truth in her statement and found it lacking no conviction.

'You want to push me to the edge, Alice?' he asked.

'I want you to take me there with you,' she replied solemnly.

'I've never known anyone like you,' he kissed her nose and pulled her in tighter to his body.

'All I can think about is how much I need you. How many years we have spent knowing that we still loved each other and living like it didn't matter,' she said against his chest.

She meant every word. She had married a man knowing she loved another. But where did that leave things now? She knew she couldn't have both.

'Okay baby let's do this,' he pushed her away suddenly and rubbed his two hands on his temples.

'Be gentle,' she giggled nervously looking at his serious expression. She remembered so well that puzzled but determined gaze he would give her just before he caved in and showed her just how naughty a teacher he really was.

'That's a joke right?' he stared at her and waited.

'Um...' she fidgeted on the spot.

'Gentle?'

She shook her head, 'I just meant –

Tom laughed, 'relax, baby I'm kidding,' his eyes squinted in thought 'do we have all day?'

'Yes.'

'Shower then?' he flashed his eyes at her cheekily.

'We never did that, did we?' she thought back to the wondrous affair of her youth.

'No,' he gripped her fingers with his own and pulled her towards the bathroom.

Tom leaned his body into the walk-in shower and turned on the faucet. She watched as he sliced his arm through the powerful spray making sure the temperature was just right.

'Do you remember the first day we met?' she asked watching him.

'Of course,' he peered over his shoulder.

'You never told me what you thought of me? When you first walked in to the classroom – did you think anything? Or was I just another faceless student?' Alice asked absentmindedly as she unzipped her boots.

He turned to her and started opening his shirt buttons, 'Firstly, young lady, no student is faceless. But if you want to know what I thought...'

She nodded smiling up at him.

'I thought, fuck. That's the truth, I actually sat there after you had left the room with the rest of the class and my hands were shaking. I thought who the hell is that enticing little fairy that I have to pretend I'm not having visions of screwing? It was bloody scary.'

Alice watched him pull the shirt from his waistband, 'I think I was thinking about some random teenage thing, just minding my own business really. The bell had gone already and you were late so everyone had started kicking off. I remember the door opening and you walking in a few minutes later. You looked so angry at everyone. You really scared me. Then you sat down at your desk and started talking and as I stared at you my skin became hot and my mouth got dry. I licked my lips when I watched you click the top of your pen...'

Tom moved towards her quickly, 'you don't have to say anymore. I got it. If you want me to lose the plot then carry on,' he growled.

'I'm just trying to tell you how I felt.'

'You're trying to get a reaction,' he said pulling his shirt off aggressively.

She ignored him, 'as I was saying, I thought if he turned to me now and told me to crawl over to his desk and well...' she blushed, 'I would have. I would have sat at your feet and followed your lead instantly. All that and the mad thing was I had never even thought much about *stuff* like that before.'

'It was amazing that I resisted for so long,' he said staring down at her. He was almost naked. But she was still fully dressed.

'I really thought I had no chance. I was a student, I shouldn't have even been contemplating it,' she kicked her boots aside, stood and moved her hand to his chest and traced his skin with her fingertips.

'Get your fucking clothes off,' he demanded. His voice was serious and his eyes told her she had said enough. Yet, she wanted him worked up. She wanted him ready to fulfil her desires, absent his control.

'No,' her lips trembled.

'What?'

'I've touched myself hundreds of times dreaming it was your hands on me. Even before we made love and for all the years after...'

'Alice. Stop. I know what you're doing. You don't have to goad me into the state that you want me in, I'm there. Now get undressed or I will make sure you don't come for hours. I'll build you up and keep you waiting as punishment for ever thinking I need priming to be what you want me to be. I am that – now let's see if you can handle it.'

She looked at him and then began to remove her clothes slowly.

He raised his eyes. Her whole body sang with delight as she studied his face watching her. His jaw was set with impatience. His chest rose and fell faster than normal but his brow was heavy with a concern she didn't understand.

'When you're just like this you're still mine,' he breathed as she stepped out of her knickers. But he didn't touch her.

Tom turned and moved into the shower. Alice stared as the small beads of water clung to his sculpted torso and gently wove a seductive path down his beautiful frame.

She was captivated.

His erection stood proud of his body, she shivered a little, not knowing if it was because she was naked or the thought of things to come.

Tom raked a hand through his wet hair, efficiently removing any excess moisture. He found her gaze and smiled at her obvious distraction.

'Get in here,' he ordered pulling her under the beautiful warm flow of water.

'Is it crazy that I never want another woman to see you like this? With me being married and everything?' she whispered and wrapped her fingers around his penis.

'Well all you have to do is choose me,' he half joked, 'if you don't you'll have to live with the image of me screwing around with other girls forever.'

Alice smiled sadly, 'I don't want that.'

'To be perfectly honest baby, if I were you, neither would I... I mean look at me.'

They both started laughing and in moments the laughter had turned into a hug. They both held so tightly they could feel eachothers heartbeat. This was too real for either of them to make light of, the jokes only served to soften the blow of potential ruin that might follow.

Tom snuggled into her neck and his strong hands fell onto her bottom and gently kneaded her flesh, 'right,' he said into her ear, 'it's time to get serious.'

'I know,' she pulled away from his arms and looked up to his face.

'Get down on your knees,' he ordered.

She blinked a few times, then placed her hands on the wet floor of the shower carefully and bent in front of him.

Tom reached out and pulled her face towards his body. She opened her mouth and he silently pushed himself past her lips. She moaned at the instant feeling of heat and the sudden stab of arousal in her pelvis. She heard him sigh as she moved her mouth slowly over him.

Tom grabbed her hair in his fists and pushed her head lower. She felt his hips thrust forward and she struggled to catch up with his strong movements. Water covered her face and dripped from his body, making it an extremely powerful mixture of sensations to control.

She looked up at Tom. He was lost in the moment. His blue eyes so transfixed by the spectacle that he could have been in another world. His muscular arms were taut as he continued to push forward, while holding her head still. She loved what he was doing. She loved that it could be considered base and degrading to be held like this and used, yet she felt neither.

She would do this for her husband from time to time, he would never push her or order her to her knees and she did enjoy it. But she never felt the need to try too hard at it. She never really let herself worry that she might not be doing it right or as he wanted.

With Tom it was different. She only wanted to do everything he wanted. He challenged her without ever saying a word. He set a pace and he expected you to follow without question. If your jaw ached you didn't complain or stop, you could only carry on. If he asks too much of you then you simply find a way through the panic, not because he's expecting you to but because you want to. There was nothing soft or loving about the way he felt at the back of her throat, it was primal, exhausting and it shocked her. Her knees hurt from resting on the hard tiles and her eyes stung because of the constant stream of warm water splashing into them. But nothing had ever left her climbing the walls with a need to totally submerge herself in sin the way he left her.

'You're insane,' he half shouted.

She grabbed his body and pulled him closer.

He stopped moving then and looked down at her, the grip he had on her hair tightened and he wouldn't let her pull back. He held her mouth over him, as far as he could go and she could look nowhere but into his tortured eyes. Alice tried again to move, she was finding it hard to control her breathing, her reflex to swallow overwhelmed her and when she finally did he swore loudly and dug his fingertips into her scalp a little harder. Her hands went to his legs to find her balance, her body poised and all too aware of her own building need for release. She swallowed again and this time it was easier to do. He shook his head and closed his eyes. She needed air now though and she lightly stroked his thigh. He looked down at her and with her expression she asked him to give her a minute.

He narrowed his gaze, like he had just realised what was happening and ripped himself away from her abruptly, turned his back and slammed his two palms hard onto the tiled wall. Alice caught her breath quickly and wiped the water from her face.

'What's wrong?' she asked reaching out and touching the back of his calf.

Tom rested his head against the wall.

'Tom?' she stood. A little scared to find out, she covered his back with her small body and snaked her arms around his waist. He took her hands and wrapped them tighter around his middle. She reached down and he was still hard under her fingers. He stiffened as she ran her fingers up and down its length marvelling at its smoothness as the water eased her way. She stretched her neck up and kissed the top of his back and across his shoulders blades.

'I love you, Tom,' she whispered, 'I know how hard you find this?'

He made a noise then began to shake his head, 'Do you believe I can treat you like that and hope to have any kind of second chance?' his voice was hard.

'I want it,' she answered, 'do you know how much it turns me on?'

'No.'

She took his hand, pulled it behind him and placed it between her thighs. His fingers found her arousal and she trembled, 'I love that little dark in you – I always have.'

'I only want to please you; you know that?'

'I do, and I you.'

Tom turned around suddenly and with an expression that could only be described as possessed he leaned forward and pushed his fingers inside of her, thrusting upwards and making her cry out. She took a breath to gather herself.

Her eyes filled up a strange kind of fear, tears threatened to fall with the force of what she knew would follow. His hand moved steadily for what only could have been a matter of moments and she began shaking her head against the pure emotion coming at her like a stampede.

Her gaze dropped to his arm between her legs, the strong tendons in his wrist flexed and jumped as he spread his fingers inside of her. She felt her entire body tense when he twisted his hand slightly and pressed against the small bundle of nerves hidden deep inside of her.

The hot spray of the shower cascaded over her breasts and down her thighs but her mind was no longer connected to anything but him. Tom applied pressure to the ultra-sensitive spot with expert precision. She felt her limbs go numb and he caught her gently when her legs buckled. Just seconds after that she promptly exploded onto his fingers.

She'd never known anything like it. It felt like the top of her head had been struck like a match, the heat so concentrated at first gently separated and slowly rippled down her body, touching every inch of her flesh in its wake. The many strands of pleasure then regrouped deep inside of her and pulsated until she was shaking and unsure of what had just happened.

'Fuck...' she panted.

'Hey, that's my line,' he smiled.

'Sorry,' she shrugged.

Tom lifted her in his arms and carried her through to the bedroom. He placed her on the bed and moved back to the bathroom to grab towels.

He reappeared with one in his hand and another wrapped around his waist. He placed it over her shoulders and rubbed her arms slowly.

Alice stared at him.

'What?' he smiled.

'You'd get sick of me without the danger and excitement and we've never known each other away from it. I'd bore someone as passionate as you eventually if we were ever together properly.'

'Sometimes I wonder if you know me at all?' he said with mild anger in his tone, 'danger doesn't turn me on or make this whole thing better. It makes it harder, more painful and fucking impossible. If we never had sex again, but instead you told me you would be with me, I would happily live the rest of my life celibate, more contented and more in love than any man alive,' he dropped to his knees in front of her and pushed her towel up her legs a little more.

'You couldn't live without sex,' Alice smoothed his wet hair away from his face gently.

'I can't live without you,' he replied solemnly.

'Tom, I have to ask you a question.'

'Go on?' he looked puzzled.

'What if I don't know what to do? What if I want to be with you but can't leave my husband right away?' she watched his eyes narrow and instantly wished she could take back her words.

'What're you asking, Alice? If I'll be your bit on the side until you're brave enough to leave him?'

'No, not like that... indefinitely,' she bit her bottom lip, 'would you wait until I was ready?'

'I'd wait forever baby, but not while you're screwing another man. I'd wait to move in with you for the sake of your child and I'd wait to ask you for our own. I'd wait while you beat yourself up with guilt every night and I'd dry your tears when you think that you've made a mistake and Hayley needs her father. But I won't wait in my house, in another country for a call that may never come. Holding out for the next stolen moment I can feel your body against mine,' he was angry, 'I can barely stomach the thought of you leaving here today with these rings on your finger,' he grabbed her hand and let it fall again.

What answer had she expected from him? He was the most hot-blooded person she knew. How could she ask him to stand on the side lines and watch? If the shoe were on the other foot and he was the one going back to a beautiful wife every night she would be going crazy with the very same jealousy that burned within him.

'I'm sorry. I'm just so confused. I wouldn't ask you to do that. Forget I said it.'

'You haven't been with him this week have you? Since we slept together?' Tom asked angrily.

'No.'

'Alice?'

'No, I haven't. He tried and I made up an excuse. I didn't want to.'

'That sounds crazy, doesn't it? But in my head you're mine and you always have been, so he is trying to fuck my woman and not the other way round,' Tom laughed scathingly at himself.

'I know how you feel. I felt that way about you for years.'

'Rest assured baby, every woman I have been with has been you,' he tapped his head, 'up here.'

'Come here,' she pulled his arms towards her. She had to cut the tension the only way she knew would tempt him out of a massive Irish temper that seemed to be brewing. Something that she had seen before a few times and knew wasn't where she wanted him to get to today. She had upset him when all she really wanted to do was make him happy.

He moved her legs apart and manoeuvred his body between them. But his eyes were hurt.

'I'm sorry,' she muttered and pulled him close to her, 'I wasn't thinking straight.'

'It's okay, baby, I get it.'

THE QUEEN OF HEARTS

Tom had lost. She wasn't going to leave her husband; her question had told him that. She would be one of those strong, selfless women that would put her family first despite breaking her own heart in the process. In a way he had to admire her for being able to do that, because as his divorce had shown him, he could not.

What now? Give up and walk away? No, that wasn't his style, he would fight till the end and hold on to the tiniest hope that still flickered, however fleeting.

With a lust that dripped with sadness and anger he pushed her back onto the bed. He wouldn't let her see it though, but he could use it the only way he knew how to.

He looked at her laid out, naked. He pictured her in a grey skirt and white school shirt, breathing rapidly and awaiting his next touch. But that image seemed wrong now. She wasn't that girl anymore, she was so much more and worth so much more than he had ever given her.

Her green eyes held his gaze and a small smile passed her lips. Her little hand moved to his face and stroked his hair.

'Why have you stopped?' she whispered like it was a secret.

His eyes travelled over her body slowly, her full breasts, exquisite pink nipples, then her quivering little belly, thighs...

'I'm not your man, Alice. I shouldn't be allowed to see you like this.'

'You are.'

'You know what I mean.'

Why was he giving her opportunity to run?

'Don't tell me you aren't mine,' her little face frowned at him. Did she have any idea how much all of this was hurting him?

Tom looked down at himself, his penis was practically shouting at him to shut up and get on with it. He ran his hands along the insides of her smooth thighs, spreading her legs further.

'I'm going to have you until you're begging me to stop,' he said honestly, 'at least that's one way I know you want me.'

Alice shivered, but shook her head, 'Tom, that's not the...'

It's the last time you will be with her.

His temper suddenly shot through the roof at the prospect of her leaving. Did he have it all wrong from the start? Did she only value their physical connection? Was the love he felt for her truly reciprocated?

He cut her off, 'No, baby if all I can do is this...' he gestured towards his body with anger, 'then that's what I'll do for you.'

'That isn't all you can do...' she started.

'Just leave it, Alice. I know my place. You love me fucking you, but you don't love me enough to follow your heart?' he snapped harshly without thinking.

'That's not fair. Where's all this bloody coming from? It's not that easy,' she bit back.

'You married your fucking rebound Alice, and now you expect me to beg for crumbs from his plate?' he was shaking.

'How can you say that?' she stared at him as if he was a stranger.

Tom pushed down some of the bubbling anger and breathed. This wasn't her fault.

Make it right, Jackass…

'I'm sorry baby – I didn't mean that,' he reached down to kiss her lips but she turned her face away from him. 'Alice, I'm sorry. I just lost it.'

You have just lost it…

Her expression crumbled against the pillow and she began to push at his shoulders, 'Fuck you, Tom,' she sniffed, 'do you think I'm some sex addict that can't wait to jump you? I have a husband I married because I fell in love with him and believe it or not we have sex that's good. I don't need you for that. I also…'

'Shut up!' he boomed suddenly in his teacher voice.

Her mouth snapped closed.

He gripped her cheeks hard with one hand and shook his head, 'please stop,' he whispered, 'or I will kill him.'

'Why are you being like this? What the hell is wrong with you?' she shouted.

Tom opened his mouth to speak but shut it again quickly.

'What?' she said again.

'Alice, I…' he wiped his eyes, 'I can't stand you loving another man and not knowing what is going on between you both. Then you start telling me about how fucking great your marriage is? Really!? Are you trying to rip me apart here? I can't…'

'I pick you,' she tore her face away from his hand fiercely, 'you fucking crazy bastard!'

'What?' he asked not quite understanding.

She lifted her head off the bed and shouted, 'I hate you! Sometimes I can't stand you. But I've always chosen you, I've been doing it my whole damn life. I don't know how I'll sort it all out, it's such a mess – but I can't leave you again,' she hit at his chest with her fists, 'you stupid stubborn fuck. I should tell you to go jump. You did all this to me… you walked away from us. Now I'm the evil one messing *you* around?'

Tom grabbed her hands that were still punching him and held them at her sides. He was breathing fast, his heart exploding in his chest. He positioned himself over her and pushed forward with a stroke that he hoped told her everything he was feeling. Her wide eyes locked with his and her face both hated him and worshipped him, but her body responded as it always had – like it was home.

ECSTASY

She couldn't do it any longer. She couldn't watch him hurting, falling apart, all the while never truly knowing how she felt. The anger was his way of showing his emotion and it scared her. He would have ended up pushing her away because it was easier for him to deal with, but she didn't want to be moved aside this time. Dumped, because he couldn't handle it coming to a gentle close. What she had told him was the truth, but how she would follow through with her decision was beyond her?

She wanted to spend the rest of her days with Tom, but at the cost of so many people's sadness and heartache?

God, what had she said?

Tom moved over her and not so delicately pinned her to the bed and proceeded to push himself inside of her.

She moaned as he thrust deep and grabbed her waist lifting it off the bed and pulling her body towards him. This instant rush of his flesh hammering against her thighs sent her mind spinning. He dug his fingers into the skin on her sides, fighting with each stroke to gain more ground and join their bodies further.

His face was determined. He moved like he was born to do this.

Then Tom winked at her. It was a simple gesture that meant so much. It meant I love you and I'm sorry. It also meant we're okay, me and you. Whatever happens, I'm here.

She smiled back.

He bent his head and captured her lips in a solemn kiss.

'I won't ever make you regret me baby,' he pulled away a little and whispered.

'Yes you will Tom, probably many times, but I don't care. That's who you are. We will always be butting heads and making love – it's what we do.'

'Yeah, maybe you're right, thank heavens for the making love bit then.'

He pushed deeper, his thrusts that were seldom gentle or weak felt stronger than ever. She had sensed and tasted some of it when she was a teenager. But now she had asked him not to hold back he was giving her what she wanted.

Her cries grew louder. If she didn't love the feeling of this type of sex so much it could have bordered on crazy. But the lines of pleasure and pain often blend, meeting somewhere in the middle. A murky grey area where a simple orgasm becomes boundless. Where men and women set aside their preconceptions and are allowed to live without proper thought and conscience for a few short moments.

He understood this. Where many men would hear her cries and ease their speed or purpose, concerned they were doing something wrong, Tom heard them and listened to the part that most men couldn't, and with it making sure that the next sound was louder than the last. He had a way of looking into your eyes and reading what you wanted without ever having to ask.

He just kind of got that she had a backwards type of logic. Sometimes she said no and meant yes. Sometimes what appears savage is in fact the one thing she burnt for. Tom was capable of gentle love making too, he had shown her that before. It's just right now, since they had met again, the urgent, frantic, crazy love seemed all they could do.

He controlled her when they made love. Not in the obvious 'dominant male' way – he was that – but he actually controlled her with sex. Tom, to her was something she would never be able to fully harness. She would never be able to overpower him in anyway, emotionally or physically. She would always crave him and when he wasn't by her side she'd ache for his touch. He could gain his way by pushing her against the nearest wall and simply staring at her, regardless of whatever fight or heated exchange had gone before.

Alice knew being with him would change the way she lived. Could she be the girl she was now and still have enough time to satisfy both their desires?

Tom placed his hands under her bum and lifted her effortlessly in his arms. He twisted and sat on the bed. Alice now on top she moved quickly, she felt herself building without any hope of slow-ing and any moment she would come apart in front of him.

He watched her face as he guided her movements with his hands, pushing her away then powerfully pulling her back.

She wasn't embarrassed where normally she would be – it was daytime, she was naked, her body no longer that of a teenager. Tom, on the other hand was still somehow in peak condition? Something that put her in mind of *Dorian Grey*. She was fully exposed to his ice blue stare but instead of shying away as she thought she would, the whole experience excited her.

'This time I'm never leaving,' he said as Alice moved her own hands to her breasts, 'I like that,' he whispered.

She smiled back.

'I'll take care of you. I promise,' he vowed.

'I know.'

END OF THE LINE

Wednesday 4th August

Later, after they had re-showered and dressed and Tom was waiting for Alice to fix her hair before they left, he had a flash of guilt, real guilt. For about five minutes while sitting on the edge of the bed they had just made love in Tom felt like the bastard he was.

Alice's husband was probably a good guy and a good father. Tom had stolen another man's wife and hadn't even given the guy a chance at a fair fight. Her daughter was going to live away from her dad because her mother loved a stranger and he knew all too well how that felt.

Tom shook his head and pushed his hands through his hair. He couldn't think like this it wasn't helpful to anyone. He had to be strong now, for all the things that were to come for Alice he had to maintain a solid, unwavering front of calm confidence.

You won.

That didn't sit well right now.

You won.

Shut up.

You won.

He had. But now he had to make his peace with God, her family and his own.

Tom smiled though. He couldn't help it… she said she was his and however you looked at it, the outcome for him, integrity aside, was fantastic.

'You ready?' Alice appeared at his side and he looked up at her.

'You're sure?' he asked.

'Yeah, I am.'

On the train ride home they said very little to one another. For Alice, a head full of tough decisions and even tougher conversations lay ahead.

For Tom, he quietly made mental notes of silly things he must do before they started their life together.

He started working through his finances and thinking about logistics of when they would have all three kids under one roof during school breaks and weekends. He thought about his little car – that would have to go in favour of a larger model.

He looked out of the window and fantasised about taking Alice away on holiday, visiting all the places they had dreamed about when they were both younger. He didn't know where she had travelled in the years they were apart. Before that thought would have pissed him off but now he longed to talk at length with her about their lives and what the other had missed.

Now she belonged to him he could swallow his jealousy and embrace everything she was.

He took her hand and she stirred from her absent gaze for a moment, looping her fingers around his, but not looking at him. She needed time and she'd get it.

His mind flicked back.

Then of course there was the issue of living in different countries. Would she move to Ireland? Since being back there he had really put down roots and didn't relish the idea of starting again over here. He had just got the job he had always wanted and looked forward to the new challenges that would bring.

It all seemed too early for questions like that, he didn't want to push her, and whatever she decided he could work around.

'It's nearly my stop,' she sighed and tucked herself a little closer to his side.

Tom wrapped his arm around her and kissed the top of her head, 'Do you know when you're going to do it?'

He felt her head shake, 'No. I don't know how? I'll get sorted in my head everything I want to say and then do it...'

'Will you be alright? He's never been violent has he?'

'Hell no. He'll be broken though,' she sighed again.

'So what now for us?' he just needed to know what she needed him to be doing.

'Well I've got a few days before you leave – I guess I will try to do it before then. If I can sneak out at all I will. Otherwise just texting and phone calls until the dust settles,' she looked at him and smiled a tight smile, 'I'll need your strength when this is done.'

'You never need ask.'

She nodded just as the train pulled into the station she had boarded from hours ago.

Tom looked out, this station was so dated, it had a definite eighties vibe about it. Red and blue gloss paint glistened from the benches scattered along the platform. The small cafeteria offered homemade Battenberg and Victoria sponge from a chalk board outside and on its window a big Mr Whippy sticker was peeling and faded from the sun.

An old man in a brown suit puffed on a cigarette while studying the timetable on the screen above him and the station clock ticked over another minute.

A railway station with its own sense of mystic and romanticism never failed to draw Tom's interest, until today, today all it brought him was another goodbye.

Tom raised his body from the seat and she shuffled past. He walked behind her to the train door and followed her down the two small steps onto the platform. They were met with a gusty wind that made him smile.

'Alice.'

She turned and hugged him tightly, 'I love you. You better get back on.'

'I love you too,' he held her hand and kissed her fingers.

The guard blew his whistle and Alice jumped, 'Go,' she urged quickly.

Tom hooked one arm onto the inside of the train door and leaned out again pulling her close. The guard waved his hand at them, but Tom ignored him.

'Tom, you've got to go,' she said into his chest.

'Sir!' the guard shouted.

'I know,' Tom shouted back.

'Sir, the train is about to depart!'

'I know,' Tom shouted again. He kissed her once and jumped on board just as the doors closed and trapped his upper body. Tom grinned at her and slipped the rest of him inside. He shrugged as the train pulled away and watched her wave for a moment, then turn for the car park.

Tom slumped back down in his seat. It was up to her now, he had done all he could.

Who would have thought only days ago he was sat on a plane longing to see the love of his life – not to talk to or to hold – but just a glimpse would have been enough he had thought. Then she had walked into that living room and changed his fucking world again.

His phoned beeped. He reached into his jeans pocket and pulled it out.

4.50pm
Tom, we are for keeps, aren't we? x

What was she thinking?

4.51pm
Baby, do what you have to do then come to me. Forever looks like us, together. I know you're confused but in your mind just picture me waiting – cause that's what I'll be doing. I love you xx

4.54pm
I love you too x

4.57pm
You need me at any point, just shout - I'm minute's away xx

Tom closed his eyes and pictured his own children. They would be happy that he had found someone to be with, like their mother had. But Estelle would be a different matter she would be angry and understandably hurt when she found out who he was bringing back. To her, Alice was the reason they spilt and it would take an awful lot of smoothing over if they were ever to be comfortable with each other.

He imagined all the children together playing in his backyard, laughing and smiling. They would love Alice, they really would. In the picture in his head she was round with his child growing inside of her. She looked back at him with a love in her eyes that never changed.

As he had always prayed for heaven to exist, his own would look like this.

SOFT PLAY

Alice bent to untie Hayley's other trainer while she stamped her foot impatiently. Her cousins had already escaped onto the massive red and yellow coloured squashy apparatus. Rainbow coloured slides and rope ladders called to the already half-crazy children.

'Calm down Hayley, you can go in a sec.'

'But they've gone already, hurry mummy.'

'Alright go,' Alice replied as Hayley tore past her towards the ball pit.

Stephanie set down a tray of tea and cake and laughed, 'the only thing missing is Pat Sharp.'

Alice smiled, 'and the power prize.'

'A Mr Frosty... each!' Steph continued mimicking the host's voice.

Alice joined in, 'A Spirograph... each!' she laughed it was good to feel something other than worry for a few short moments.

'Just imagine how much fun it would have been to go to one of these places as a kid. No wonder they get so hyped,' Stephanie poured the tea.

'Thanks.'

Alice had done nothing yet. She got back home from her afternoon with Tom to be met by tales of fishing trips that the kids wanted to go on with Stuart and Tony in the next half term and the present Hayley had bought for Zach being shoved into her face to look at and then wrap, because 'daddy doesn't know how to do it properly.'

This was her life and she loved all of it, however mundane it felt sometimes. How on earth do you go about pulling apart what they had spent so many years building?

How could she be around Tom and feel like that's all she'd ever need and then come home to her family and feel exactly the same about them?

The only change she had noticed was sexually towards Stuart. He was a very attractive guy, tall and athletic. She had always found him sexy and never looked at sex with him as a chore. But since she had been with Tom that had all changed, her body was Tom's again and under his spell. However much she had tried to look at Stuart in the same way she had only days ago, she couldn't. She looked at him with love and affection and friendship and respect, but not with any desire to be with him in that way.

What did that mean? That she must leave him anyway because her body was hard-wired to Tom's? Or could she just put her head in the sand and stay with what was safe? Dealing with the same broken heart she had always had. Hoping that her sexual feelings would return for her husband and all could be as it was.

When she left Tom on the train yesterday she had no doubt that she would be telling Stuart today that things had changed and she was leaving. When she got into the car park to retrieve her car and Tom's train pulled out of the station her real life came crashing back onto her shoulders and its weight was considerable, its cargo equally as precious to her.

Alice now understood the decision that Tom had been faced with as her teacher and an adult. How sometimes you do things just because it's the right thing. As a young person you only see what you need and want, but as an older person with responsibilities there was so much more to consider. For the first time she didn't hate the part of Tom's character that had walked away.

'So then, what actually happened on Saturday night? You've been so busy catching up with everyone else I've barely got to talk to you over the last few days.'

Alice felt her face flush, 'I told you already it was fun, everyone really seemed up for having a good night. Your year group should definitely have one.'

'I meant after, when you text me about being late, then not getting in till I'd gone to bed. What was the deal?' she widened her stare and grinned.

'We just decided to go on to a pub for a nightcap that's all,' Alice lied. Should she just come clean and hope that her sister would understand?

'Which pub?' Steph asked casually cutting her cupcake in half.

'Um the one near the school.'

'Didn't think they opened past eleven?' she met Alice's eyes and narrowed her gaze.

'Well they were, so…'

A child started crying on the large trampolines and the noise drew both women's attention away from the conversation for a second until they caught sight of their own children, saw they were fine and that the problem this time, was somebody else's.

'Stuart was asking me about the friend you visited the other night.'

'Oh, what did he say?' Alice fidgeted in her chair.

'Just asking if I knew where she lived and how close you were and stuff – just making conversation I guess,' Stephanie took a sip of her tea.

'Why didn't he ask me I wonder?'

'Don't know?' she shrugged her shoulders and continued drinking.

'Tom's here.'

Stephanie coughed, dropped her tea cup onto its saucer a little too loudly, ducked her head low and moved towards Alice quickly, 'what the fuck?'

'Tom is here,' Alice swallowed hard.

Stephanie darted a look towards the door of the soft play centre, then to the line of people waiting to be served at the counter.

'Not here, but here in town. Idiot!'

'Oh my God you've seen him.'

'Yes,' Alice nodded, picked up a little packet of sugar and started adding it to her drink – she didn't even take the stuff.

Stephanie put her hand over her mouth, then slowly let it fall to the table and whispered, 'You were with him the other night weren't you?'

Alice bit her bottom lip and took a deep breath, 'I was.'

'Oh shit… he came to the reunion,' her sister stared at her with wide eyes.

'Just wait, I'll tell you.'

'You didn't… you slept with him didn't you?'

'Steph, please it wasn't like that…' Alice hushed her.

'It wasn't like sex? What was it then?'

'Well it was like sex but he…'

'So it was sex?'

'Yes.'

'So you had sex with Mr Chambers behind your husband's back. Oh my God Alice and I thought I was the rebel child.'

'Fuck,' Alice dropped her head into her hands.

'Whoa the F bomb?'

'Don't make this a joke, it isn't funny. He came to the reunion, not inside but he was there afterwards. He was waiting.'

'Waiting for you?' Steph cut in.

'Yes. I was with Stu so I let him drop me off and then I got a taxi to where I thought he would be staying and confronted him,' Alice paused and looked again towards where Hayley was playing.

'She's fine – go on.'

'I actually went to his friend's house and demanded to see him?! What was I thinking? I was a bit drunk I guess and I needed to…'

'You knew what you were doing didn't you?' Steph narrowed her eyes.

'He was… he was just the same. We talked for a few minutes and I left. But he gave me his mobile number and I text him.'

'You made the moves on him?' Steph looked shocked.

'No, I didn't. I left. When I got back to yours I was all over the place, but I text him to say it was great seeing him but it wouldn't be happening again because…' Alice paused took a deep breath and went on, 'he had grabbed me and he had said that he still felt something for me… it wouldn't be fair to lead him on by having further contact you see. So I tried to draw a line under it.'

'So you *did* put the moves on him?' Her sister half smiled.

'No, I meant it.'

'Uh huh, the same way I'd mean it if it had been Ryan Gosling? I'd *really* mean it.'

'I wanted to see him but I knew I couldn't, okay?' Alice replied.

'How did he talk you round?'

'His honesty just like always. The way he doesn't care how intense he's being or how it looks to others… hell, I don't know?'

'Don't stop I need the full picture,' she urged.

'So I agreed to meet him on Monday night, just to talk, straighten a few things out that were left unsaid from back then,' Alice paused, 'he was just the same Steph, so different from most men, so amazing.'

'Really? Still bloody *amazing* after all this time?'

'He is. He did a throw down and…'

'Oh you can never underestimate the power of the throw down,' Steph rolled her eyes.

Alice nodded in agreement. When a man pretty much throws you down and takes charge and tells you how it's going to be is pretty hard to resist in most cases and certainly in this one.

'I wasn't going to do it even when everything was telling me to, but it just kind of happened in the end. He took me upstairs and I managed to forget I was married,' she cringed.

'Was it what you remembered?'

'So much more,' just thinking about it was making her need him.

'Alright, the man can fuck. He can charm the pants off you with his smooth talking and mess with that stupid head you've got,' she mimed shooting herself in the head, 'how do you know he's not just playing you?'

'God, Steph if you knew him you would know that just isn't in his DNA. He's not that kind of guy. He wants me to leave Stuart.'

'He's an absolute lunatic – I thought that at the time too by the way – crazy, crazy! After one night he thinks you're going to give up your marriage for him? God, he's arrogant!'

'It was yesterday as well.'

'Alice,' she scorned.

'I know.'

'So he's begging you to run away with him? Saying he loves you? The insane bastard probably does still love you!'

'I love him,' Alice stared into her sister's eyes and willed her to see that she was telling the truth and that this was serious to her.

'Please tell me you're not thinking about this? I know Stuart can be an arse from time to time but he's a good guy,' she took hold of Alice's hand, 'I can understand why you slept with Tom, closure, great sex, freedom, whatever and I don't blame you. God knows we've all thought about cheating but...' she paused, 'I hate to tell you this... you're brainwashed by a penis!'

Alice smiled a little, 'I'm not. I would hope by now I know the difference between love and lust. When I'm with him he's everything to me – I need him.'

'And when he's not with you?'

Trust her to pick up on that.

'I'm me, here, a mum and a wife with a great life. I'm happy but I'm not full.'

'Oh he "*completes you?*"'

'Don't take the piss.'

'I'm not. But I think you're in love with the idea of him.'

The idea of him?

That hit her somewhere. Was she seduced by what he stands for? In a clear contest between the two men would Tom win without their back story? Would he win if the sex had been less than she remembered?

She wasn't brainwashed... was she?

'It's not the idea of him,' she stood her ground.

'Are you going to leave your daughter's father?' Steph asked coldly.

'You bitch,' Alice bit back.

'I'm calling a spade a spade – so you get a real clear picture here.'

'I get it Stephanie; I get that I'm playing with more than my life here okay? I'm not a reckless person. But, he thinks I'm going to leave Stuart – I told him I would.'

Stephanie shook her head, 'why did you tell him that?'

'Because I believed I was going to. I think I still am.'

'If you truly love the man that practically crushed you, owned your life for years then by all means be with the knob. You know I believe in living and not just existing Alice, but please be sure of what you are about to do. I'll stand by you always but this won't be easy.'

'Thank you, I know that,' she whispered.

'I still can't believe he's back in your life?'

'Neither can I, but Steph he is unlike anyone else, you have to believe, that I believe he's worth the risk,' she didn't want her sister to hate him.

'I do believe you.'

'I can't let him go again. I can't say goodbye,' Alice looked over at the children, 'but I'm not ready to end my marriage right this minute. I know he won't wait though.'

'Why not? If he loves you as much as he says he does than he can wait till you're ready surely?' Stephanie took a bite of her cake.

'He doesn't see it like that. He thinks if I stay and take my time to work out a tidy break then I will never leave. He thinks that I'll be playing happy families and sleeping with Stuart – to some extent I would be. If I don't do it soon he will feel like I'm betraying him. I know that sounds odd.'

'The balls on him!' she spluttered.

'He's not like you're thinking, he just see's us as very black and white.'

'He's a jealous man, Alice. You have to be careful, what if you get together with him properly and he turns into a total nightmare?'

Tom was jealous but she didn't believe in the way her sister imagined. He was giving, confident and selfless but he didn't compromise or share. Switch their places and she wouldn't either.

'You're going to have to stall him. You can't do it this week at mum's house and everything.'

'I know that. But he goes back to Ireland on Saturday.'

'Tough shit he is just going to have to deal with it,' she warned.

'I'll call him later and explain, as long as it's soon I think he will understand.'

'How do you think this will affect Hayley?' her sister asked.

She had opened the gates that Alice had not yet dared to touch. How her daughter, the love of her life, would cope with her parents separating?

People say that children get used to it. That couples break up all the time and although there is an adjustment period most kids get by. Now that was probably true, but Alice wasn't happy for her only daughter to just get by. If there was one thing that would stop her in her tracks and make her see the bigger picture, then it would be her daughter's tears.

Alice looked down at her cup and felt her heart wrench towards her throat, 'Not now – I can't now.'

'Okay,' her sister said resting her arm on Alice's lower back, 'I know this must be shit.'

Alice heard her phone beep in her bag perched on the chair next to her. She reached for it.

'Bet that's him,' Stephanie said scowling.

'It is,' she whispered.

3.27pm
Hey, what're you doing today? Is everything okay? I'm thinking about you almost every second, as sad as that sounds, it's actually true. I'm not 100% sure when I became a girl but it looks like I am – what joy! I will try to keep the mushy love texting to a minimum, but it's not guaranteed x

She smiled sadly. He was the missing part of her, he hadn't taken something that belonged to her when he had left he had only taken himself. The emptiness that she had felt for so long was gone every time she heard his voice.

She didn't reply though, she couldn't until she had figured out what the hell she was playing at. Her fingers hovered over the small keys, he would be mad, but he knew she needed time to do this.

She placed the phone back into her bag and picked up her cake. Stephanie smiled, 'make him sweat.'

CLEAR WEB HISTORY

Tom sent the message then cringed, he really had to either censor himself before texting some of the shit that he did or get rid of the bloody thing altogether. She knew he loved her did he really have to keep saying it every five minutes? She liked his dark side and she definitely liked a man to be a man so why couldn't he shut up?

Right, the next message he sent would be testosterone fuelled and smutty to make up for the hearts and flowers he was currently churning out.

It was mid-afternoon and Tom was bored. He walked from room to room thinking about little other than their future together. He had spent two hours that morning cutting Neil's expansive lawn and fixing a few fence panels that were loose. At lunch he had prepared a tuna salad for them both and Neil had ventured from his office for all of twenty minutes to eat.

They were seeing friends tonight so all he had to do was stay busy for a few more hours, before beers and chat would while away another evening not knowing what she was doing.

Tom stopped outside Neil's office, the door was slightly ajar and he pushed it open soundlessly the rest of the way and poked his head around.

'Hey dude, can I borrow your car I'm going to go out to the…'
Tom stopped mid-sentence. Something on Neil's desktop had caught
his eye. Neil's hand shot out and turned off the monitor quickly.

His face was red and flustered, 'what were you saying?' he
stammered.

'Who the hell was that?' Tom's mouth fell open.

On Neil's computer screen he had seen a beautiful looking,
half naked, Asian woman blowing kisses at his friend via Skype.
Tom was shocked – he was expecting to see a page full of web
addresses and computer hacker stuff, not a half-naked girl making
out with a webcam.

'What?'

'Who's the woman getting her rack out for you?'

Tact wasn't one of Tom's strong points. It wasn't any of his
business really, but the amount of times he had been given a hard
time or grilled about woman by his best friend made him hungry
for revenge. Neil was such a private so and so too, which made it
all the more intriguing.

'No one – yeah borrow the car just don't kerb the alloys,' he
turned back to the screen and shuffled some papers around.

Tom smiled. He had him on the back foot.

'Are you sex chatting with random Thai women online?' Tom
tried to keep the laughter from his voice, 'Neil, you have about
seven "girlfriends" you're banging, why bother?'

Neil didn't look at him, 'I'm not sex chatting,' he said quietly.

'Oh did she pop up for online help?'

'Shut up,' he turned around, 'her name is Jatu and she's a friend
I met in Phuket last year.'

'A bit more than a friend, maybe?' Tom smiled trying to coax
it out of him.

'A bit,' he agreed.

'Don't turn her off on my account – not that it looked like you could,' Tom put his hands up and started backing out of the room in comedy fashion.

'We're getting married.'

That stopped him in his tracks.

'Sorry?' Tom couldn't quite believe his ears. Neil the last person he ever thought would take the slow walk of doom as he called it, had actually said the 'M' word.

'Married – I've asked her and she's said, yes.'

Green Card was Tom's first thought and he hated himself for it. Of all the judgements that Neil could have made of him over the years, that just wasn't fair.

'Congratulations?' he asked carefully.

'I think so,' Neil replied motioning to the armchair in the corner of the room.

'Tell me about it?' Tom sat.

'We met last year as I said. I'd taken that month off to clear my head of work if you remember? She was working in a bar at night and studying in the day to become a nurse. I stumbled in there one evening about half way through the holiday. I was floored by her appearance and she was really sweet too. We talked all night in the little beachside bar, until I was kicked out by the owner just before dawn. Her English wasn't bad and even when she didn't understand me it was fun laughing at each other trying to make sense. I went back the following night and the same happened. For five days I kept going back and then I asked her out,' Neil opened the drawer next to his right hand and pulled out a picture of them both and handed it to Tom, 'that was taken on my last night in Thailand.'

The photo was taken on a beach with the crystal blue sea behind them. They both wore shorts and t-shirts and Neil looked about ten years younger than he normally did.

Jatu was a stunning girl and they both stared at each other smiling broadly. Happy, came into Toms mind, they looked really happy.

'Wow you know how to keep a secret,' Tom looked up from the picture.

'It wasn't on purpose, mate. I just wanted to see how things would go when I was back home. I would have told you.'

'Well, obviously things are going well?' Tom smiled and handed it back.

'We chat all the time, I miss her and she misses me. She's happy to come over here to live, so I'm going to marry her,' Neil shrugged.

Tom wasn't about to ask him if he was serious or if he thought that was a good idea or not. He knew Neil and he knew he wouldn't have made this decision lightly. He would have gone through all the implications ten times over and if, having arrived at this point – he was definitely sure.

'When do I get to meet her?'

'Her course finishes in three months. She's flying over straight after her exams.'

'I'm not making a judgment here, so don't get moody, but you know the lads are going to say that you've ordered a Thai bride off the internet don't you?' Tom again held back his laughter.

'Why do you think I haven't fucking told anyone? I know I'll be the butt of jokes for years over this,' he laughed too.

'At least I'm not the only one chasing younger women now.'

'She's twenty-seven – younger than Alice! If you want me to fix you up I know she has loads of really pretty friends that you could have your pick of? They are really sweet natured and boy can they cook. Bring one over and Bobs your uncle.'

Tom smiled, his friend was so old fashioned when it came to women, all he really wanted was a pretty wife that could cook and clean, keep him happy in the bedroom and not challenge him too much. If that's all he needed in a life partner then good luck to him, he really hoped she would work out to be everything he desired.

'Thanks man but I told you yesterday Alice and I we're really good, we're together,' Tom pulled the phone out of his pocket and checked for messages. No reply yet.

'I still can't believe you managed it. In less than a week you've convinced her to leave her husband?'

'Am I really going home with her do you think?'

'I think you are. But be careful her husband looked like a big fella.'

Tom swatted away the comment with his hand.

'How weird the next time you're over here it will be as a couple… no actually a family with your kids too, at my wedding – freaky!'

'I still can't get my head round you in a morning suit. You're actually going to pay out for a wedding? Mr Tight is going to open his wallet?' Tom pushed his shoulder lightly as he stood.

'Anything she wants, Tom,' he replied.

'I'm rubbing off on you, I'm impressed.'

'Go on now, get out. I have work to do,' Neil pointed towards the door.

'Is that what you call it?' Tom added.

Neil grinned, 'the same kind of work you were doing when you were teaching Alice, mate.'

'I text her ten minutes ago and she's not replied yet. Do you think she's alright?' Tom asked changing the subject.

'OUT!' Neil shouted, 'and stop being such a girl!'

MISSED CALL

She had to call him. He had sent her four messages that afternoon, each one becoming more frantic than the last. She grabbed her phone, run up the stairs into the bathroom and turned on the shower. She re-read his last message sent ten minutes ago before she deleted it.

> 7.20pm
> Alice please reply to me right now if you're okay? If he has fucking touched you – I'll kill him. If he has your phone now and is reading this – I will kick the fucking living daylights out of you if you have raised a hand to her. I am coming to get you in thirty minutes unless I hear from you, baby. And again, if this is her husband, I'd probably call the police for when I get there, as you're going to need them.

She had rushed her dinner in a bid to escape the table before his thirty-minute deadline and call him off. She had ignored his texts all day because she just needed some time to decide what she would say to him and if she had called him right away she would be seduced once again into doing it all his way.

She was going to ask for two weeks, to get back home, finish her marriage in private and make the arrangements for Hayley and herself to leave. If he couldn't wait for her then she would walk away from him. He had to bend somewhere and understand what a big deal this really was for her family.

'Alice?' his voice was angry.

'It's me – I'm fine.'

'What the fuck has happened?' he growled down the phone.

Alice took a deep breath.

'I have to be quick, I'm in the bathroom. Sorry I didn't text back I have had so much to think about and I needed to do it with a clear head,' she started.

'You're staying with him?' his voice changed suddenly and she wanted to run to him and hold him tight.

'No. I need more time Tom I have to go home and do this, I can't do this in front of my parents – it's just not fair on him. I need about two weeks to get everything in order,' she pleaded.

Silence.

'Tom?' she whispered.

'I'm here. Okay I'll wait baby,' Alice closed her eyes in relief, 'I know it's hard. I know what I said yesterday about not waiting, but that was before we had promised each other, before you made your decision.'

'Thank you.'

'Please don't thank me… you never have to thank me. But don't ignore me again, I've been like a caged lion this afternoon – I even punched a hole in the bedroom door, Neil hasn't seen it yet thank heavens,' she could hear the smile through his words.

'I'm sorry I didn't think you'd be going that crazy?'

'Alice, I was imagining all sorts. Him beating you, calling you all the names under the sun...' his voice turned dark, 'I was ready to kill somebody.'

'He wouldn't do that I already told you.'

'You have no idea what men are capable of when cornered or wronged. I hope you never have to find out.'

She sighed, 'you'd never hurt me.'

'I'm glad that wasn't a question,' he said, 'do I get to see you before Saturday?'

'I could try and get out tomorrow night for a while maybe? Meet you on the old road we used to meet? About 8pm? I'll text if I can't make it for any reason, okay?' she would do her very best.

'Okay. That's good I'll be there.'

'You sound so much more Irish on the phone, I'd forgotten that,' she whispered.

He laughed, 'I'll wait to hear from you then – I love you,' his rich tones kissed her ear and she trembled like he was in the very room with her.

'Me too,' she replied.

'Before you go I've got to say one thing. I'm sorry I didn't trust you when we were together, when I was your teacher. I'm so sorry that it's taken this long to right that mistake. I will spend the rest of my life making up for the years that I robbed us of, I promise you that. You will never have to go to sleep or wake up wondering if you are loved. You might not want to be on a pedestal, but you are and it's where I want you.'

She closed her eyes.

'Tom...' she breathed.

'What's the chance of me driving over there now and you letting me take you away?' he asked, making her laugh lightly. 'I'm serious Alice, I need you.'

'No sex-talk,' she scolded him.

'I'm thinking about your mouth on me…' he smiled.

'Cold shower?' she suggested.

'I'm supposed to be going out tonight with some of the gang – I think I need one.'

'Not in that state I hope? I don't want any women around you when you're turned on – I know what you're like,' she joked but was actually quite serious.

'Just say something to keep me going till tomorrow then?' he joked.

Alice bit her lip, he still made her feel like a nervous girl, 'the feeling I get just before you push inside of me is one of the most confusing things. It's far beyond desire and lust. I know how it's going to feel, I know that it's going to blow my mind. It's scary that I can feel so high on the memory of the last time and anticipating the next time. It's one of my most favourite emotions.'

'I love it when you cry.'

'I don't cry.'

'Yes you do baby, sometimes you cry when we're making love, don't deny it,' he was teasing her.

Alice blushed and was glad he couldn't see her, 'It's intense,' she whispered.

'I know.'

'I've got to go,' she said.

'Okay,' Tom sighed.

Alice looked around the small room then met her own gaze in the bathroom mirror.

'Don't forget you're mine,' she reminded him.

'God, I love you,' he said and hung up.

Alice stripped the clothes from her body quickly and jumped under the warm spray. She wasn't going to have a shower, but now needed to cover the conversation they had just had.

She felt so scared, more scared than she had ever felt. She was going to leave her husband within a week of being back here because she had rediscovered the love of her life. In many ways she was wrong and very much the bad guy in all of this, but she was also refusing to live a lie. She wasn't going to waste anymore of Stuart's life by stringing him along.

But she did love him and she really loved the family that the three of them made – was she just being really selfish? Was it fair to Hayley if she stayed? Setting the example of, 'it's better if you never follow your dreams because the price of dreaming is far too great.'

She washed her body with the fluffy shower mitt thing and closed her eyes as the water rinsed away the glorious smelling suds.

If she didn't leave him she would live the rest of her life with regret, wouldn't she? She would always look at her husband as the person that stopped her having the only thing she ever truly desired.

She towelled off and opened the bathroom door.

'Shit, Stuart you scared me!' he was sitting on the top step of the stairs. His eyes followed as she stepped out of the room and started the few paces to their bedroom. He got up and walked behind her into the room, closing the door behind them.

'It's a little early to be going to bed, honey?' Alice said aloud grabbing some pyjamas from their suitcase.

'I wasn't thinking of going to bed yet,' he reached out and pulled her waist towards him and she stumbled backwards, 'we haven't had any us time all week... this is why I hate coming here. You're always busy and your family's always around,' he laughed against her back, but his warm breath on her skin felt like the biggest betrayal.

'I know Stuart,' she replied screwing up her eyes to push down any strange reaction, 'but Hayley's downstairs and we really need to get her to bed soon,' without turning to face him she continued, 'we're only here a few more days, I'm sure you can live without it for a little longer.'

'What's the matter?' he spun her round to face him sharply.

She swallowed hard but looked him in the eye, 'what do you mean? Nothing's the bloody matter,' she snapped.

'You've been avoiding me all week. Don't think I haven't noticed it. So what's going on?'

She watched his mouth move. She had seen him angry a few times in their marriage but it wasn't really his style, he would rather just give each other space if there was an issue, knowing it would sort itself out in the end. But right now he looked confused and sad – he was asking her why she had forgotten about him? Standing in front of him with it on the tip of her tongue, she couldn't do it, not like this with her back against the wall.

'Stuart, don't be silly nothing's going on,' she moved her hand to his hair, but he pulled away.

'Saturday you go to that party at the school, the minute we leave you start acting weird. You were strange in the car and the next morning and then stay out till all hours the night after that. You haven't kissed me all week, touched or anything. I've made moves and it's like you haven't even noticed them. So I'll ask again what the fuck has happened?' he didn't shout the words but they were definitely stronger than she had ever heard from him in the past.

How could she have been so dumb as to think he wouldn't have noticed anything? She spent all day everyday with this man of course he's going to know if his wife is acting out of character, just as she would if it were him.

'Stuart, please don't be like this here, I don't want to argue with you in front of my parents. I don't believe I'm acting any differently. If I was strange on Saturday, it was because I had just seen all my old school friends and it reminded me of how old we had all got and how quickly time passes. I was feeling nostalgic that's all.'

What?! Oh please…

'Were you thinking about him? Being back in the school where he abused you?'

The age old comment that never failed to rile her.

'He didn't fucking abuse me!' she nearly shouted.

'What did you just say?' he looked shocked.

'You heard me,' she said pulling on her vest top and raking a comb though her hair.

'Was he there?'

She stopped, her skin went cold and she had to decide right now whether she was going to tell him.

'No,' she sighed, 'he wasn't.'

'But you wanted him to be, didn't you?' he stared at her hard, ready to read any lie she attempted to tell him.

She stared back at him unmoving.

'I guess so…'

What?

'Why Alice, why?' he shook his head and then grabbed her arms, 'what is the matter with you, have you lost your mind?'

'Stop it,' she pulled away from him, 'I don't know why? I just wanted to see him that's all.'

Stuart slumped onto the edge of the bed, 'I knew going to this reunion would be trouble. Is this why you've been distant? Because of that bastard?'

'I still don't think I have. But if you feel it then, yes, he's been on my mind a bit.'

Why couldn't she do it? Why couldn't she just use this moment to be honest with him? Looking at the man she had spent over ten years with so upset and knowing she had caused it, didn't feel good. She thought about Hayley, and how not having this man with her everyday would make her feel?

'He was your first love you told me once?' he asked.

'He was.'

'That's hard to compete with, even as just a memory,' he looked at her and he had tears in his eyes.

'Stuart, please. I don't know what to tell you?'

The truth?

'Have you tried to contact him over the years?'

'Not once.'

'Do you still love him?' he grabbed her hand.

Alice took a deep breath at last a question she could answer honestly, 'I think I always will, but I do love you.'

Stuart nodded like he already knew the answer. Maybe he had always known part of her still loved Tom?

'We need to go home. We need to get away from this house, this town. Go home where it's just you, me and Hayley. Where no part of him belongs and his ghost can't follow us anymore. I'd say we should leave in the morning but your dads planned a barbeque for tomorrow night. So we'll leave first thing on Saturday?'

'I guess we probably should,' she sniffed lightly and wiped her eyes.

'I don't blame you, Alice,' he pulled her to sit next to him on the bed, 'I know you don't think there was anything sinister about your fling with him, but I do. You can defend him till you're blue in the face, but he did take advantage of you. He was your teacher and every time…' his face turned distasteful, 'you and he had sex that was abuse of position and morally wrong. Have you ever thought of it like this, he was the age I am now, how would you feel about me if you found out I was sleeping with a girl who had just turned seventeen? Even worse than that say it was someone that I was teaching?'

She thought about it for a moment and in truth she would be disgusted by him doing something like that. So how was it so different for Tom? It shouldn't be, but it was.

'I know what you're saying, I really do. I would doubt every bit of your character if you did that.'

'See? And put it this way, say Hayley's doing her A-levels and a teacher tries it on with her and he's handsome and charming and she sleeps with him – worse, gives him her virginity?'

'He didn't try it on with me… I've told you before I confronted him,' she corrected his story indignantly, 'and Hayley will make her own decisions. Would I be happy if she had a relationship with a teacher? No way – and yes I know that sounds hypocritical.'

'No, it sounds like a mother. As a mother you're all too aware of what that situation reeks of. You say you confronted him, what if he played you into making the first move? I don't want my wife thinking about another man. Alice, least of all the kind of man I would happily see on a *Crime watch* reconstruction.'

She couldn't argue with him. He would never see it through the eyes of a teenage her and how could he? She would stand by her actions and Tom's against any criticism. They were the only two people there at the time and they both knew what it had meant to them and means to them still.

She turned to her husband, he was a lovely man and it would be so easy to just carry on the way they were. Could she push Tom out of her head and replace him with the guy that had made her very happy? A dad that Hayley really deserved to have a hug from every morning and every evening to kiss her goodnight. Would the kisses Tom gave her mother be enough to compensate for that?

For the umpteenth time in the last week the word, 'whore' played across her vision of the future. She really was putting her own feelings and desires over the happiness of her daughter.

It was exhausting thinking this way. She wished she had never come down this week. That fate hadn't decided now would be the time to draw the two of them together... and it was fate, it was always going to have to be like this. You don't find a love like theirs that doesn't have a price.

'Alice, can you forget him?' he asked then, 'please just forget him, he doesn't matter anymore.'

He'll always matter.

'I don't know Stuart? I can try...' she replied.

'I'm being really patient here you know,' he whispered.

'I know that. I love you for that.'

'Do you think I can keep doing this year in, year out? I know when he's on your mind. I know when we're in bed you think about him sometimes. I've never said anything because I love you and I know you love me. But it hurts Alice, it really hurts.'

He stood and walked over to the window. The top of his head caught the evening sunlight and it bounced off his dark blonde hair. He pushed his hands into his pockets.

She hated that he felt unwanted. Her husband felt like he was second best and in a way he was. He didn't deserve to be.

'I'm so sorry,' she closed her eyes.

'Let go of the past Alice, or you'll ruin our future.'

OLD GHOSTS

Tom opened his eyes. It was pitch black. His head ached. He sighed and picked up his phone from the bedside table.
3.11am.

Shit, he hated waking like this and it had been the third time this week. It was an odd time of night, the sort of time that nobody should be awake. A time that was the night's property and it was private.

He let his head drop backwards to meet the soft pillow, closing his eyes once more. His mind found an old memory of a night just before they had split up.

He had woken very much like this in the early hours and had turned over to find Alice sleeping next to him. It had been one of only a handful of times she had actually been able to sleep over with him. He remembered the momentary shock as he had forgotten she had stayed.

She was sleeping soundly like a beautiful angel, her golden hair fell down her small back and she looked... she looked like a young woman that shouldn't be there with him.

In that split second he clearly remembered who he was, most of the time it seemed clouded and unclear. Their love was the invisible filter that sat atop all of his responsibilities and made him unable to fully process his actions. It had, however been eerily removed in the presence of the witching hour.

He was looking down at the girl that held his heart – she would always hold his heart. But the demons that held for him, he saw with perfect clarity in the darkest hours of the night. It should have been enough to send him running in fear from the warm nest that they'd created.

At this hour all problems seemed scarier and the burden of lies so much heavier. The beady eyes of old knowing souls stared at him from within the four walls of his bedroom, mocking his choices and condemning his very right to love the person he did.

Uneasy lies the head that wears the crown.

He knew if he closed his eyes and pulled her to him, sleep would come and the morning would bring her laughter, and with it, the veil would once again descend upon the happy couple and tonight's realisation would become just another bitter tasting dream.

He didn't close his eyes, he didn't hold her and sleep didn't take him.

He stayed awake for the rest of the night and in the morning when she woke as bright as the sun itself, kissing his face and sending his head spinning, the shroud did settle over their heads. He did feel calmer, braver and more protected. But this time the delicate veil neglected to offer him quite the same coverage as before. For every now and again and very slowly at first he would catch a glimpse of something mildly repulsive in his own reflection and something approaching regret would grab his gut when he touched her.

It had been the beginning of the end. The first steps to open eyes and rational thoughts. The transition from lover back to teacher and vice versa was not so easy anymore. The truth that soon he would have to make a choice for them both was snapping at his heels daily and as much as he tried to shake it off it just wasn't going away.

And the choice he had finally made was wrong – but for the right reasons. It was the same pathetic decision people made all over the world a thousand times a minute. But the minute that had belonged to his choice had haunted him every moment of his life since.

Tom opened his eyes again. He didn't want to think about that night, he wanted to drift back to sleep with the images of something happy, maybe sexy and definitely about her. He wanted her face to fill his dreams until her body filled his bed and at last he would have the right above all else to call her his girl. No one could dispute it. He wouldn't have to fight to have her or lie to keep her ever again.

He lay awake for a while longer; the heavy silence became less foreboding as his eyes adjusted to the darkness. It wasn't all that sinister now, as it had seemed at first. The past was half buried and the next couple of weeks held the promise of a new start, forgiveness and the re-building of a rare and true connection.

To Tom, Alice was like the one toy that your parents could never afford to buy for you as a child. The same toy that maybe one or two of your friends had – the rich kids – and you craved so badly. Even if, as adults you were given that toy you know you would want it and treasure it, with the biggest part of you feeling eight years old and bursting with excitement.

He sat up and swung his legs onto the floor, found his bag in the dark and grabbed some boxers. He wasn't going back to sleep tonight; he was too wired. He needed a coffee, some food and maybe paracetamol. He pulled on a t-shirt and headed downstairs quietly.

Today was going to be a good day, if he was seeing her it was bound to be. But before that, he was going to have a little look at this Xbox thing and see what all the fuss was about and how it kept Neil amused for so many hours.

MORNING

Friday 6th August

'Hayley, baby, wake up,' Alice lay her hand on top of her daughter's chest and as always was both comforted and scared by how much the small motion of her breaths meant everything to her. They say you shouldn't live through your kids, but let's face it as soon as they enter your life that's all we live for, it's all that really matters. Her family mattered of course they were her safety blanket, the people that knew her the best when she was as precious as Haylcy was now.

Stuart? Well he was the one that saved her from the big black hole she was swimming in and taught her how to like herself again and how to love without guilt.

But Tom, he was the part of her life that reminded her she was a true, living person. That she was Alice Rutherford, a girl she really liked before life got in the way. He showed her that a love outside of motherly love and loyalty could still be as crazy as she remembered.

'No, mummy I'm tired,' Hayley pushed her hand away and turned over. She was a teenager already.

'Sweetie it's past eight, we need to get you up.'

'No, please I'm having a lie-in,' she grinned without opening her eyes. She had such a sense of humour, it was both beautiful to watch and slightly annoying at times when coupled with her stubborn streak.

'I love you,' Alice kissed her cheek lightly.

'I know that silly pants,' she giggled and opened her eyes. She looked so much like her own mother had when she was a girl. Alice remembered looking at the browning, retro white edged square photos of her parents as children. She used to love spending time sorting through them and asking her mum how old she was in this one and where was the other taken and so on. By the time Hayley was two-years-old everyone commented how alike they were.

'I need a hug from my baby,' Alice pulled her into her arms and squeezed tightly and she tried really hard not to cry.

'Get off me mummy! Why do you need a silly hug?' she wriggled, but Alice didn't let her go.

'Sometimes mummy needs a hug, that's all.'

'Oh mum,' she muttered in exasperation but submitted and wrapped her arms around her neck.

'Thank you,' Alice giggled softly.

'What are you two up to?' Stuart appeared in the doorway freshly showered.

'Mum says she needs a cuddle,' Hayley promptly informed her father.

'Does she now?' the question in his voice wasn't sarcastic or suspicious, but a bit lonely almost asking if he could be the one to provide it.

Alice sighed and held out her hand to him, he walked over and put his arms round both of them. It was his embrace that had kept her warm for the longest time and it was his love she felt radiate out to his little family now.

'I love you,' he whispered into her hair so only she could hear, 'and I love you,' he said raising his voice and kissing Hayley's head.

'I told mummy I needed a lie-in daddy.'

'Is that right,' he raised his eyebrows and smiled at them both.

HOOKED

Okay this wasn't his usual gig, and yes it was technically geek territory, but he had to admit it this was pretty addictive stuff. He had turned on the machine at about four that morning and the game that was already loaded he decided to try.

Call of Duty proved to be just that. The first person play appealed to Tom's boyish action hero complex and the graphic missions were helping him to work out some of his stress. He hadn't left the room to re-fill his coffee in three and a half hours and if he was given a pound for every curse that left his mouth he probably could take six months off work.

'Well slap my arse and call me Judy!' Neil spluttered as he walked in to the lounge at about eight that morning.

'Leave it,' Tom replied without turning away from his game.

'Tom Chambers playing *Modern Warfare 2*, who would have thought? What was that you're always going on about? Computer games are crap? Only for nerds? I could go on.'

'Things have moved on since *Pac-Man*. What can I tell you?' he answered hitting pause on the game and turning to face his friend.

'Welcome to the 21ˢᵗ century my man, move over and I'll show you how to multi-play.'

'No. I haven't finished yet, in a minute okay? I'm Jack Bauer right now – I'm up against it,' he laughed, 'make us a cuppa.'

'Yes boss.'

'And a bacon sandwich?' he added quickly.

Neil started jotting his order down on an imaginary notepad.

Tom turned and raised his eyebrows.

'Like I keep saying, I worry about you.'

'Alright, alright I need to man up a bit before Jatu arrives. I need some tips,' Neil smiled.

'You've been living on your own too long. Getting used to country vegetable soup for lunch and fancy telling me the other day that your favourite programme is *location, location, location*. And whilst we're on the subject of your masculinity, what the fuck is with the four cushions on my bed that aren't actually pillows? You know that you have to chuck them on the floor before you get into bed, right? You've got this big arse house that you paint cream, you add no pictures to the walls, yet you have a thing for random girly shit.'

'They're scatter cushions of course you take them off first. Clearly you have no taste for soft furnishings.'

'Soft furnishings isn't a term that you should even understand.'

'You're a cave man Tom and I'm glad you've found a woman that finds that appealing. I have a feeling Jatu will enjoy my metrosexual side,' Neil replied grinning at Tom.

'You lost me at 'metrosexual' I don't read *GQ*.'

'You do surprise me,' Neil rolled his eyes sarcastically.

He departed the living room and returned twenty minutes later with coffee and warm bacon rolls. Tom could get used to living here, he took the piss but Neil was a great host. He would make a brilliant husband as long as he could get used to having someone around him all the time. He was a sociable person but he also loved being alone, he was a great thinker and he was all about process and problem solving. So if she could be patient with him while he adjusts to his new set up there was no reason why they wouldn't have as good a chance as anyone else going into marriage?

'What's your plan for today big man?' he asked chewing nosily and watching Tom's technique on the controller, 'you need to loosen up your fingers they're too tense and it puts too much pressure on the buttons and gives you less control of the game. It's got to be relaxed.'

'How do you relax when you've got a small army of mercenaries at your back and you're trying to secure a safe house and re-load your side arm at the same time? He wouldn't be fucking relaxed would he?' he said pointing to the man from his game.

His friend laughed, 'you'll get the hang of it. It's like sex, we were all shit starting out then with practice you hone your craft.'

'I can't remember ever being shit,' Tom smiled and cast him a cheeky sideways glance.

'That's what they all say,' they both laughed.

'I'm going to hang here this morning. Go out later and pick up a few presents for the kids – I have the list they emailed me. Then I should be seeing Alice tonight, catch up, see where she's at with things and stuff.'

'Stuff?'

'Lots of stuff hopefully,' he continued.

'I feel for her husband, Tom. The poor guy didn't stand a chance.'

Tom paused the game again, 'don't think I don't feel for him too. He's by all accounts a good man and I don't want to hurt anybody. I didn't come here with that agenda. I was never going to actually approach her, she found us remember?' Neil nodded, 'Then how, after seeing her and speaking to her again could I do anything other than be honest with myself? I didn't plan any of this, but when she was stood in front of me she was the very same girl that I lost a long time ago. She looked into my eyes and the emotion was unchanged regardless of everything. She looked at me and I saw every last thing she wanted. It was written as clear as day, as if our connection had never been severed at all.'

'I guess. I know you're not a bastard I just hope no one else will see it that way?'

'The kids will be fine,' he said reading what Neil was implying. Tom paused.

'And Estelle will come round eventually – she'll have too. I fucking accepted Frank and all his bullshit didn't I?' he frowned thinking about his ex-wife's boyfriend. He was a total idiot in Tom's opinion. The kind of man that knew everything, had been everywhere and happily dispensed his worldly wisdom to everyone daft enough to listen. He was a successful sales professional, as he liked to remind Tom. Always spouting on that a teacher's salary was capped but in sales the sky was the limit, totally forgetting Estelle was a teacher too – the douchebag.

He was a scout leader and a long distance runner. He played cricket and golf and was tee total. Okay, he was good with Tom's children and he had three of his own, but he was still a shit.

'Maybe given time she will?' Neil concurred, 'Frank is an android though.'

'At last someone gets it.'

'He's like Ned Flanders,' Neil joked plugging the other handset into the games console.

'Poor Estelle what an earth is she thinking?' Tom nodded.

'She's probably thinking how nice it is to be driving round in a brand new Mercedes courtesy of the man himself – nice birthday gift! What was it you used to get her, flowers and a card?'

'Steady, she's not like that,' Tom would defend her honour despite being unable to fathom it himself.

Neil put his hands up, 'Joking, I love Essie.'

'Right let's stop talking about Frank the plank its making my head hurt. Let's see if your expert fingers can teach me a thing or two,' he picked up his controller and started tapping the buttons aggressively.

'Don't turn me on Tom, we're the only two people here and as we have already established I *am* metrosexual...' Neil flashed his eyes at him.

'I knew that would mean something I didn't want to understand...'

JUST CAUSE

'So what's going on?' Stephanie pulled Alice outside into their parents back garden and led her away from the children who were playing marbles on the patio.

'Nothing new, I told him I needed a bit more time and he was fine with it,' Alice replied pushing her sunglasses down from her head to cover her eyes.

It was mid-afternoon and the sun was full on, summer had a second wind and her father was intent on capitalising on it. He had been checking the weather all week and had been giving them daily updates. This morning he stepped outside, looked up to the sky and announced, 'Yep, just as I thought this is going to be the best day we've had so far.' He changed his chinos for shorts. Got into his car and headed to the butcher's dragging Stuart along for the ride.

'Fine with it, was he?' she glanced back at the house 'that's a turn up. Thought anymore about what you're going to do?'

'I've thought of nothing else. Stuart confronted me last night, said I was acting strange and asked if I had seen him.'

'Shit no! What did you say?' Steph asked holding her hand over her mouth.

'I lied. I hate doing this I really do.'

'People get fat from having their cake and eating it sis.'

Alice nodded, 'I want him… it's just our family?' she shrugged.

'I'm still convinced it's just because you have the chance to get something back that you think is yours. If you don't claim him then you're scared that someone else will.'

'It's not a game.'

They walked together to the end of the walled garden and stopped again pretending to look at their mum's overflowing and pretty impressive flower beds.

'Steph, tell me something honestly?'

'Sure.'

'The whole time you've known about what happened between Tom and I you've never once said you thought he was in the wrong… like I mean creepy wrong. Stuart's convinced that Tom's a child abuser or something and I hate it. But did you ever think that too?' Alice wasn't sure why she had to ask this now. Maybe it was talking to her husband last night and him referencing Hayley as an example? She just needed the opinion of someone who was there at the time, who knew Tom then.

Stephanie sighed quietly, 'I wish I could say I thought Mr Chambers was a nonce, Alice, really. But the truth is I don't think there was ever anything creepy about you and him. It was never that weird to me, then or now. He was just a dude who happened to be a teacher. He fancied a girl who was too young for him, fell in love and then panicked. Now he's just a dude with a big arse ego. You've got to admire him in a way.'

'Thank you,' she said and squeezed her sister's forearm.

'It's only the truth. Look he was hot then and if he's still hot now then I see the attraction – but all that aside I would still think very carefully about changing all of this…' she drew a circle in the air, 'all for a pretty face and lucky smile.'

'Steph, I love you.'

'Urghh!' her sister replied pulling a face and they both started laughing.

'Dad's going to get the barbeque going soon so the kids can eat early. I need to get away later at about eight. I said I would see him before he leaves tomorrow.'

'For fuck sake how the hell are you going to pull that off mid-evening? Just cancel, it's too risky,' she hissed back.

'I can't cancel I need to see him,' Alice stopped to re-clip her hair up and stared at her sister like what she was planning was the most normal thing ever. Her sister stared back at her with her large brown puppy dog eyes in disbelief.

Steph thought for a moment.

'All we could do is use a drink run as an excuse, I'll say at about half seven that we're running low on something and you pick up on it straight away and follow my lead, say you'll go get it because you haven't been drinking or something?'

'Have I ever told you that you're the best sister in the world?' Alice hugged her quickly.

'Get off me,' she shrugged her off and looked around to see if anyone was looking at them, 'some of us have a reputation to uphold you know?'

The rest of the afternoon passed in the most pleasant of ways. The children played at water fights with the dads before their dinner, causing a big fuss when it came to sitting down in wet clothes so everyone piled upstairs for a quick change, while her father moaned that the sausages were overdone.

Stuart didn't question why she herself had changed out of her jean shorts and into a summer dress at about half past six, assuming that she wanted to dress up a bit for a family evening. She looked up at him and smiled when he tucked her under his arm and told her she was beautiful and she still felt genuinely happy.

When the kids had settled down, her mother had ushered them to their beds for stories and by 7pm Alice was ready for a drink. Her nervous energy was building but she had to refrain if her escape plan was ever going to work.

She was checking her watch constantly and making eye contact with Steph, who glared back at her to calm herself. Her mum came back down and announced the children were all asleep and everyone visibly relaxed a little more. Stuart grabbed a beer and smiling handed one to her dad.

Hayley was asleep, she was safe and now suddenly despite everything she felt for these people all Alice could think of doing was running to where Tom would be waiting. He would be there now, early, on that road they used to meet – he was always early to meet her but late wherever else he went.

'Tony, did Stu tell you how much these burgers were?' her dad, since retiring and taking more of an interest in the shopping budget liked to play the 'guess how much' game.

Tony swallowed the bite he was chewing before answering, 'He didn't Max, but they taste pretty damn good.'

'Twelve burgers £13.50. That's at the local butchers. I could have gone to the supermarket but you don't know what they put in them these days… rabbit's stomachs and horse hair probably,' her dad replied and Tony nodded in agreement with another mouthful being relished.

Her father was the kind of man that kept other men in line, but in such a way that you didn't ever realise you were being moved until your surroundings had altered. His son-in-law's were no exception. They respected his position as head of the family and sub-consciously sought his approval in all matters.

He had stayed in pretty good shape since leaving office life and now swam almost every day at the local pool. He always threatened to build their own in the back garden to save on gym membership.

Her mum on the other hand had got a little rounder as she had got older, not large just cuddly, contented and very, very nanny-like. She was always the type of woman that should be a mother or have children around her.

'Suzie, are they good?' he asked his wife as she started blowing her burger after a small test bite.

'Give us a chance, Max!' she laughed kindly.

'And why isn't the girl eating?' he turned to Alice, 'lady, if you don't put some weight on soon I'm going to have words with your husband,' he shot Stuart a look, 'no one wants a scrawny wife – whatever he says,' he joked.

'I've told her! It's not my fault,' Stuart held his hands up.

'Excuse me,' Alice interrupted, 'I am here. I'll have something in a minute,' she replied.

She couldn't eat.

'Pregnant are you?' Tony butted in with his annoying voice that made Alice want to punch him, 'you're not drinking either huh?'

'Shut up,' Steph pretended to swat his head, 'she was just saying how she fancied some Pimm's but I couldn't find any in the kitchen.'

Alice's eyes connected with her sisters, 'yeah I really do – you know when you just get a taste for something?' she nodded.

'We'll get some,' Tony agreed quickly, 'I've got the car here.'

'I'll go Tony, but thanks. It's me that wants it and you've had a drink anyway,' Alice panicked.

'No, Tony can go babe. He owes me for the bet we had on the tennis match,' Stuart laughed, 'loser!'

'He's right, it's cool Al,' Tony put his drink down and patted his jeans to be greeted by the jangling sound of his keys.

'If Alice wants to go…' Steph pulled Tony back, 'let her.'

'Yes, I could do with getting some bits for Hayley for the trip back tomorrow,' she knew she sounded desperate and she tried to shake it off.

Stuart looked at her closely. She felt like she was under an infidelity microscope. She reached behind her and pulled her summer cardigan from the back of one of the garden chairs and slipped it on.

'Look babe we can get some stuff tomorrow on the way, don't worry,' Stuart said again rubbing her arm.

She looked at her watch quickly. It was ten minutes to eight. She glanced up and they were staring at her. She must have looked odd? Grabbing her cardigan and checking her watch... how obvious could she get?

'What is the matter with you?' Stuart glared at her but tried to keep the anger from his voice.

'Nothing.'

'Tony's going,' he nodded at Tony who was already half way out of the garden gate anyway.

'Okay,' she whispered, 'I just didn't want to put anyone out.'

'Don't be silly darling,' her mum piped up, 'he doesn't mind at all.'

'Fine.'

She wanted to fall to her knees and cry. Just knowing Tom was a few miles away and waiting for her and that she couldn't get to him was too much. He was leaving tomorrow and she wanted, no, she needed to hold him once more. It would make her decision so much clearer.

A few painful minutes ticked by, but when her dad moved back to the barbeque she used the distraction to casually walk to the kitchen. Stuart was chatting with her sister about a new artist that he had been impressed with and her mum was humming along to a tune on the radio.

She slipped inside and after retrieving her phone from her bag that was hanging from a dining chair she hurried to the living room and out of view of everyone.

She started typing a quick message to Tom.

7.56pm
I can't get out, Stuart has

'Who are you texting?' Stuart was behind her. She jumped and pressed send by accident without finishing the message.

'I… I was just going to text Tony to get some strawberries,' she swallowed hard.

'Your mum has some in the fridge. I had them on my muesli this morning and so did you.'

'Oh course, it's a good job I didn't send it then,' she smiled as sweetly as she could and flicked her phone off.

'Alice, is something going on? You're not yourself, is it that row we had last night?' he asked in his pissed off tone.

'Look Stu, it's been an odd week, let's just get through tonight then when we get home we can talk about it… all of it.'

'What the fuck is that supposed to mean?' Stuart snapped, pulling her shoulders round to face him.

'It's not supposed to mean anything,' she snapped back, 'and stop grabbing me like that it's really annoying.'

'Don't fucking tell me how to touch you,' the words came at her like a slap in the face.

'What?' she stared at him open mouthed. He never spoke to her like this. He was always respectful and had never once stepped over that line.

He was desperate and he wasn't stupid. Just because she hadn't admitted anything she was ignorant if she believed he couldn't read it all over her face or that it wasn't patently stamped over all of her silly actions this week.

'You're going to talk now,' he said, not letting go of her arms.

'I've nothing to say here and if you want my dad to come in and find us arguing like this then you can deal with the aftermath,' it was a threat of sorts and Stuart wouldn't want to upset the family whatever he thought he knew.

'Sort yourself out Alice,' he let go of her arms and shook his head, 'your phone?' he held his hand out.

'What?'

'I'm going outside and I'm going to put your phone away as you don't need it now,' he said smugly.

'You're being ridiculous…'

She felt herself falling.

'Phone.'

She slammed it into his open palm and watched as he turned without speaking and walked towards the kitchen, opened her bag as he passed by and dropped it inside before he stepped back into the garden.

He didn't even look at it.

She slumped onto the sofa and as much as she wanted to cry she didn't. Her hands were shaking and mouth was dry but she didn't let the tears fall. If she was going to do this at all she knew it was never going to be easy. But seeing Stuart like that had shocked her. He was a fiercely competitive man and any challenge to what he held dear he was never going to handle well or take laying down. She was watching him hurt for a reason he was yet to discover and the most upsetting part was she still loved him very much.

She had never felt more confused and she had never hated herself the way she did now.

Maybe Steph was right? Did she only want Tom because he was here and telling her she was his?

That couldn't be the answer.

One thing was certain though, her husband deserved better than her. His actions were a direct result of her guilt and she had the cheek to look at him like he was the one in the wrong?

UNINVITED

Tom smiled to himself as he got out of Neil's car and noticed how dusty the alloys were after the half mile drive down what was now a totally disused, gated road. Fourteen years ago it had been a short cut between the main town and a small hamlet four miles away. Since then a by-pass had been built and had proved the road redundant. The verges were over grown with pretty coloured meadow flowers, poppies and bluebells. The road itself was covered in a dry mud, probably churned up by the odd tractor that still ambled down it from time to time.

He was alone and for the next half an hour until she got there that was a comforting thought.

Tom breathed in the lush air.

The summer evening, there really was nothing quite like it. It held a poignant grace like no other time of the year. It was, for Tom, when he was at his most peaceful. He might have had a god awful day at work. The children might have been over excited and restless to be set free. The teachers might have smelt of stale coffee and dry cleaning fluid, but as soon as he got home on those precious evenings he left it all at the door. He would run up the stairs of his little cottage, take a cool shower and sling on a t-shirt and shorts or whatever was to hand and head out back.

His house overlooked fields. Not fields that were farmed, just open space, free space and with that came the feeling of happy isolation. To the left about a half a mile away was a tiny wood. He knew that the village kids called it a fairy wood or fairy den. It was a perfectly circular haven of enchanting trees and shrubs, untouched and holding a great deal of mysticism for children of Irish decent. He was damn sure their parents would play on the fact it was a fairy den and recount tales of evenings they themselves had seen the fairies as children – just as his own mother and father had done with him.

He loved sitting out on his deck with a beer in his hand just listening to nothing and like now, nothing always sounded pretty good.

Sometimes he would take work out with him and plough through essays until the light dimmed and even his reading glasses no longer helped. Until the air turned cooler and he could count the goose bumps on his arms. Giving in, he would retreat to bed with a misunderstood sadness that another day had passed him by, another day was over.

He hated when he felt like that and maybe until now he didn't get why it was sadness he experienced? He used to think he was getting old or all the feminine love classics he'd had to read and recite in his lifetime had started rubbing off on his normal 'manly' life. But maybe it was more than that? Maybe it was subconsciously another day he had lost without sharing it with her?

He wanted her out on his deck with him. A bottle of chilled wine open on the table between them and her delicate voice talking to him about the things she had done that day. He wanted to be able to reach over and grab her hand, kiss her fingers and know she was really there.

He leaned back against the bonnet of the car and the warm metal felt good against his neck and arms. Neil would kill him if he saw this. Tom closed his eyes and the soft breeze tickled his profile and the warm sun kissed his eyelids a hazy shade of orange. He could doze off like this.

Imagining her wrapped in his arms under a blanket when it turned colder, knowing that when he finally did have to give in and return to the house it wouldn't hold the same melancholy it had before. It would be arousal that would accompany him up the stairs. The thought of making love to the prettiest woman in the world may even make for a lot more early nights when they got back home.

His mind drifted to the week after they had first made love, they had met here on this road and she had done things with him in his car... a man of experience and a teacher was being taught how to love without limits by a girl barely old enough to know what she was doing. Binding him to her in a way he could never dissolve the ties. Showing him that this was living, and all that mattered was the two of them.

He felt himself harden. She was in trouble when she finally arrived. They would be separated tomorrow and that meant this evening was going to be filled with the slow, steady love he was day-dreaming of. He knew he needed to see her and the feeling had been steadily getting stronger all day.

His phone beeped in his pocket and his heart sank. Tom sat up.

7.56pm
I can't get out, Stuart has

Tom frowned and re-read the text. He waited for three minutes to see if the remainder of the message came through – but nothing.

He rubbed his head and started typing.

8.01pm
What do you mean, baby? Are you okay? X

He sent it and waited again. He paced up and down the length of the car over and over. No reply came. He opened the car door and started the engine. He sat with one leg outside and sent a second message.

8.11pm
Alice, I'm worried you didn't say what was wrong? Has something happened with your husband? I'm going to lose it over here in a minute. Text back please…

He looked at the message she had sent again. She had said 'I can't get out' then mentioned her husband. Did she mean she couldn't leave because he wouldn't let her? Tom felt his jaw tense.

Was she unable to finish the message because he had caught her and taken the phone away? Was he going to hurt her? You wouldn't say 'I can't get out,' if you couldn't make a date, you would say 'can't get away' or something like that. What was she trying to tell him Stuart had done? Why couldn't she finish the fucking message?

8.17pm
I'm coming over. I can't sit here if you're in trouble, baby – forgive me x

He pulled his other leg in and shut the door. He was about to make a move that could change everything, but he couldn't stay here if there was the slightest chance she needed him.

Fuck this.

He put his phone on his lap so he could hear any incoming messages and in a cloud of dust he booted the car back down the road he had come.

Rural beauty was quickly replaced by expensive looking housing estates.

As he drove even more images assaulted his brain. Alice with a bloodied face, she was crying and huddled in the corner of a room trying to get away from her husband.

He drove faster.

When pushed, Tom's temper was bad at best. He feared the odd times he had lost it. Truly Irish in nature and without someone to pull him back he was very hard to stop when provoked. He didn't doubt that he would kill him and the thought alone had his hands shaking despite the vice-like grip he had on the wheel.

He tried to control himself, but his walls were coming down fast as he turned the corner onto the street where her parents lived. In the distance he saw the big Audi parked in the drive and knew they were still there.

He skidded to a loud jack knife stop at the kerb, crunching the pristine wheels into the concrete and wincing to himself. The back end drifted dangerously close to the expensive 4x4 but stopped inches from the metallic paintwork.

Tom pushed his hands though his hair to try and calm himself. He checked his phone once more and slung it onto the passenger seat in anger before he jumped out.

The first thing he noticed was the smell of barbeque. The next was a trim looking man in his sixties flying out of the side gate holding a pair of large tongs heading towards him. Tom didn't have a lot of time to think or care and to be honest his only concern was where Alice might be.

'Was that you?' the man shouted at him aggressively gesturing towards the abandoned car perched half on and half off of his driveway, the door open and the air pungently fragranced by the smell of burnt tyre rubber, 'Is that your car?'

'Yeah,' Tom replied walking straight past him and towards the gate.

'What do you think you're doing, pal? Who are you?' he shouted again pulling back on Tom's arm.

Tom looked at him for a second. It was Alice's dad, they had the same eyes. He didn't want to cause trouble with him, but he was wired and the older man's face dropped slightly when he stared back at Tom's death look.

'I'm looking for your daughter?' Tom said his voice was steely and his accent almost inaudible.

'Which one and what do you want with her?' he stood in Tom's way again and within seconds two younger men rushed through the same gate. One of them was Alice's husband.

Tom instantly ignored her father and turned to Stuart, 'where's Alice?' he whispered with venom, his eyes never leaving the man's face. He was ready to go at him, but he waited.

'Who the hell is this guy?' Max turned to Stuart for an explanation.

'What's going on here?' the stocky man next to Stuart shouted a little louder than he could clearly back up and he started looking backwards and forwards between the two men.

Stuart glared back at him. His hard face told him that he knew exactly who Tom was and like Tom he was equally prepared to fight.

'You cunt,' Stuart finally broke the silence.

Tom smiled a small smile that was the tiniest bit impressed. Then he started towards her husband quickly. His eyes had misted over by the time he saw Stuart move too. The scuffle that ensued between Stuart and the stocky guy trying to hold him back lasted only seconds and Tom was glad that he had managed to get free and that her husband was again coming towards him.

Tom had no self-preservation. The other guy was taller, younger and Tom was clearly outnumbered – but none of it mattered.

A few feet away from each other he heard her high pitched shout.

'Tom, don't please!'

Alice.

That did matter.

He turned to where he had heard the voice. She was running out of the gate followed quickly by her sister, tears ran down her face, 'Don't!' she shouted again. Her small body was silhouetted by the evening rays and a flowery sundress clung to her hips. She held her mobile in her hand. She looked safe and unhurt.

He breathed out, 'baby,' he started to move towards her.

'No, Stuart!' she screamed suddenly.

Just as her husband's fist collided with the side of Tom's face sending him off balance and tumbling onto his hands and knees.

Time momentarily stood still.

Tom couldn't hear anything. Hot pain shot through his head and his teeth felt like they had just done the Mexican wave. He opened and closed his eyes slowly. He felt like he was swallowing acid and he quickly spat out blood that had pooled in his mouth.

'Shit,' he heard someone say and he thought it was the man with the odd voice. He couldn't move his head to the side to look though.

'Leave him alone!' that was Alice.

'Hold him back for goodness sake,' her sister?

'Alice, stay where you are. I want you nowhere near these two,' her dad sent a strong warning to his daughter.

'I need to see if he's okay, dad,' she pleaded.

'Who the bloody hell is he?' her dad.

'Stuart, don't go near him,' Alice shouted again.

Her husband wanted to carry on, despite his low blow.

Okay.

Tom pushed himself up onto his hunches and held his head for a moment. His vision was clearing and the pain in his face was quickly being replaced by adrenaline. Thirty seconds more was all he needed.

'Let him come, Alice – I fucking owe him one,' Tom didn't recognise his own voice. He felt like someone had fired a gun right next to his ear, that or he had been underwater for some time. He stumbled onto his feet and looked around.

He looked towards the two men holding Stuart back. They had been able to manoeuvre him some distance away, 'let him go.'

'You heard him, let me go! He's been screwing your daughter!' her husband was as angry as Tom and with good reason.

'What?' Max asked confused.

Alice turned to her sister, 'the kids?'

'Mum's gone in, but I'll go check and I'll ring the police,' Steph hugged her sister and ran back inside leaving her alone on the driveway.

Alice looked at him then. When he had left her all those years ago he had seen that same look of utter desperation, shock and fear. She knew too within his own look that he was serious, that he would happily fight until he couldn't anymore. Stuart was confident right now, but she knew that Tom didn't have an off switch. She looked scared beyond anything he had ever seen. She looked like she knew what he had to do now.

She hurried towards him shaking her head the tears staining her pretty face and pulling at his heart.

'Don't go near him, Alice!' Stuart struggled against his human bonds.

'Stop fucking telling her what to do!' Tom shouted back and started towards him again. Alice ran up to him, her tiny body collided with his own. He could have picked her up and set her aside like a doll and carried on but he stopped dead in front of her as soon as her hands touched his chest. He looked down at her. He had never wanted to shout as much as right now, when he saw how clearly and how deeply she was hurting.

'I'm sorry Tom, I'm sorry. I didn't see the messages until just now. Please don't do this. Please don't hurt him. He's hurt enough. This is my fault,' she wiped her eyes, 'we did this to him. Please don't make it worse, just let it go,' she looked at the side of his head, 'are you alright?'

'I'm fine, baby. But I can't walk away from this,' he tried to soften his voice for her.

'You have to. Just get in your car and drive away, please.'

'I'm not leaving you here,' his temper falling slightly.

'You have to,' she said again, 'Steph's calling the police you'll get in trouble and so will he. You'll be arrested.'

'Come with me?' he said reaching out and touching her hair.

'I have to sort this,' she looked behind her and flinched at the scene that was playing out in this nice curtain-twitching suburban neighbourhood.

'Get your fucking hands off her!' Stuart shouted his face turning redder.

An upstairs window opened and Stephanie stuck her head out, 'just a warning for everyone the police are on their way.'

'Could someone make sure that they are sending the sex crimes division,' Stuart locked eyes with Tom and sneered.

Alice swung round with rage and ran back to where her husband was standing and Tom followed her quickly.

'If you ever say that again…' she screamed at his face, 'how many times have I got to tell you!'

'You're so blind Alice – look at him,' he shouted back at her.

'I remember you… you were one of my Alice's teachers weren't you?' her dad said stepping away from his son-in-law slightly and turning his body towards Tom, '…did you… have you, did you abuse my daughter?'

'What?' Tom looked shocked.

'The penny drops,' Stuart smiled smugly.

'No,' Tom felt his face beginning to burn.

'I think they call it statutory rape,' Stuart added.

'She was seventeen – it wasn't fucking statutory anything!' Tom clenched his back teeth together.

'Seventeen?' her dad looked horrified.

'…and sleeping with her teacher,' there were tears in Stuart's eyes now.

'What the hell is going on here?' her dad said quickly making connections in his head.

'Dad, it wasn't like the way Stuart is telling it, I can explain,' Alice gripped her hair in frustration and turned to stop her father. Her dad didn't meet her eyes he just rested a hand on her forearm to comfort her and instead he turned to Tom.

'I didn't rape her,' Tom looked at her father and shook his head.

'He didn't, I swear to you,' she pulled on her dad's hand.

'You better get off my property right now, you little son of a bitch. If, when my daughter tells me what happened between you two I think you're to blame – I'm coming for you. If you have ever hurt her in any way I'll kill you,' her father levelled a stare on Tom that he had to admit was disconcerting.

'That's fair enough,' Tom nodded, 'I haven't raped your daughter. I would never hurt her or abuse her. She'll tell you if she wants to, but hear her out when she does. She hasn't done anything wrong and she thinks she has. She's a wonderful person and sometimes the decisions we make don't always reflect the best part of ourselves... help her to see that.'

'Is that how you talked her into bed for the second time?' Stuart struggled again cutting Tom off. Her dad put a calming hand to his chest and told him to stop talking. He wanted this over, out of the view of the neighbours and most of all he wanted the truth.

'Have some respect for your wife. She didn't get talked anywhere,' Tom argued back.

'Just listen to how he gets himself into stupid little girl's knickers. Charming isn't he, Alice? So heroic – it's sick if you ask me,' her husband wasn't giving up.

'Shut up, Stuart,' she hissed.

'I can't believe the woman that I thought was intelligent and honest actually buys this arsehole's crap. He's a smug twat that has had his own way all his life, got away with abusing a student, not to mention how many more he might have fucked with...'

'Stop it, please,' Alice begged.

'Hope you enjoyed sleeping with another man's wife? Good was it? Can't you get your own woman?' Stuart was doing his best to call Tom into the fight. He breathed deeply and prayed his hands would stay at his sides.

'Just leave it now, Stuart,' her dad warned.

'Come on, Tom! You bastard!'

Tom had heard enough, he turned her away from the other men and grabbed her face in his hands and forcing eye contact with her, 'Fuck this guy, Alice... divorce him and marry me?'

'What?' she stared at Tom open mouthed and for a moment it felt like someone had hit a time-out.

Seconds later and someone whispered 'shit,' under their breath. Like before he thought it was the other guy and suddenly the spell was broken.

'What have you done to our daughter, Alice?' Stuart looked on shaking his head slowly, searching for anything he could hurt her with.

Tom watched her face crumble in his hands and he couldn't do a single thing to stop the sting of her husband's cruel words.

Like lightening he pushed past her father and grabbed Stuart by the throat. Stuart seized Tom's hands just as fast and tried to prise them from his neck. The stocky guy ducked out of the way and grabbed his phone and started dialling quickly.

Stuart couldn't get a good enough grip on Tom's arm's to free himself and Tom used his body weight to press against the other man's chest at the same time. He felt a savage kick against his leg, followed by another but he didn't stop, the sharp pain only made him madder. He looked up and their wild eyes met in close quarters for the first time.

'Now you've said enough. Do you want to ruin a father's impression of a daughter? Make me out to be some kind of monster and use your own child as a weapon? I don't think so – just keep it to yourself, you fucking righteous bastard,' Tom said clenching his teeth together and pushing down harder on the man's windpipe.

'Fuck you,' he choked.

Alice started pulling wildly at his arm, 'Tom, let him go or I'll never see you again I swear it.'

'Alice!' her dad shouted and pulled her away from Tom.

'Let him go, Mr Chambers! Damn, you heard my sister. If you love her at all…' a voice shouted from the window above.

'Please, Tom,' she screamed again.

He looked to the side and into her eyes.

She meant it.

Stuart started bucking against Tom's hands and his face was pink.

'Fuck!' Tom shouted at the top of his voice and pushed himself off her husband who slumped down gasping for air. He looked between her father who was rolling up his sleeves himself and then back to Alice. There was relief and anger on her face and he was well aware of what he had done.

'Go,' she mouthed.

Tom pushed down every bit of emotion he could. He swallowed all thoughts of retribution for the first time in his life. He nodded once sharply in her direction and walked quickly towards the car.

There was a strange silence as he did. No one behind him spoke. He didn't think they even moved. He could hear her husband coughing and a window close. He felt eyes at his back, but not one word was uttered.

Wow...

It was certainly a surreal moment when you realise you just fucked your life up.

THE PIECES

Alice stumbled to the kerb. She sat down clumsily and watched as Tom drove away from her parent's house.

He turned left without indicating and was gone. She could still hear the distinctive dip in the engine noise as he changed gears, but after a few seconds she couldn't even hear that anymore.

She closed her eyes. Surely what had just happened was a really awful dream. In a few seconds she would turn around and be met with the sight of cartwheeling clowns and her dad dressed as a ringmaster, or something as bizarre?

Not this time.

Why had he come? She knew why. He loved her, and to him only her safety mattered. He was always going to be the kind of man that would risk all to save her and in the process happily say to hell with everything else, including her life. But it wasn't his fault this time, it was hers. She was the married one, she had led him on and he had only reacted the way he believed he should, as the man that loved her.

'Alice?'

'Dad.'

'Are you okay? Let's get you inside,' he said picking her up under her arms.

'I'm sorry dad,' she was crying, 'I'm so sorry.'

'Don't worry about any of that now,' he shushed her and led her back to the house. Stuart and Tony were no longer outside and her sister had disappeared from the window. She leaned into her father and he hugged her against his side tightly.

'I'm just going to ask you this once,' he whispered, 'did that man ever do anything that wasn't what you wanted?'

'No daddy, I swear. I loved him. I can't help myself.'

Her dad thought for a moment, 'well I'm not happy, I can't lie. But I also understand nobody ever gets given a book of instructions in these matters.'

'Don't hurt him okay?' she begged.

Her dad nodded, 'What about your husband? That Chambers fella gave him a scare I can tell you, not that he didn't half deserve it, the way he was talking about you and my granddaughter like that.'

'He's hurting. I've hurt him so badly.'

'You have. You've done some shitty things by the sounds of it. But the heart wants what the heart wants.'

'What do I do?' she asked.

'Only you can answer that, love.'

'He's going to be so mad when we get in there,' she wanted to scream.

'He won't say another hurtful thing to you – not in my house – or he can leave right now, until he's calmed down. The minute I hear any raised voices I'll knock him out,' he laughed trying to make light of an extremely heavy situation.

They reached the back gate and they were met suddenly by Stuart coming the other way. He had a gym bag slung over his back and sunglasses pushed on top of his head.

'Stuart,' she said in surprise and her father tightened his grip on her arm for support.

'Hayley's still asleep. But I've been in to kiss her. I'm leaving, I'm going back home on my own. I'm not staying here a minute longer, I just can't look at you right now,' and he didn't look at her, instead he pulled the glasses over his eyes that were angry and surrounded by thick red circles.

'We need to talk,' she grabbed his arm as he tried to walk past her.

'We don't need to talk, Alice. The facts are this, I love you and you've cheated on me. You were too gutless to tell me even when I confronted you about it,' his voice broke.

Her dad moved away from them and into the garden.

'...and worse than that,' he continued, 'it seems that it's not just fucking around. I think this guy is obsessed with you and you with him. It's too much for me to comprehend at the moment.'

'Don't go like this. I need to explain to you why it's the way it is. I love you... you're my husband, my best friend...'

'Maybe that's the problem?'

'What do you mean?'

'No excitement for you with me anymore is there?' he snapped.

'This is not about excitement Stuart, I wish it were.'

'Whatever Alice... just answer me honestly though, was it just this week or have you been screwing him for years?'

'Just these last few days, of course I haven't been doing this any longer than that. I couldn't lie to you. I was going to tell you when we got home.'

'Do you really think there hasn't been many times when I wanted to cheat or had the chance to cheat? But I have more respect for you than that,' he snapped.

'When?' she whispered.

'Don't you dare have the cheek to ask me that after everything you've done,' he pointed at her harshly, 'two things before I go,' he paused and drew breath, 'one, that guy is crazy, he's dangerous and I don't want him to have anything to do with my daughter. Two, don't come home till you know what you're doing. I don't want to talk until I know that you and he are done. If you stay with him then all respect I ever had for you will be gone.'

'Please stay and talk this out with me, I need you to stay,' she was crying again. She could feel his body on the edge of falling to pieces, she knew him so well and she thought if she touched him right now that he would either kill her where she stood or he would beg her not to leave him.

'I'm not going to make this easy for you. You made your bed and you got fucking laid in it. You think about it all when I'm gone, and make your own fucking choices without depending on me to do it for you. Shit, Alice, if I didn't love you so much I would spit on you right now,' a tear fell onto his cheek and escaped from under his dark glasses.

She heard her dad cough twice, a not so subtle warning that he was still listening from beyond the gate.

'Sorry, Max,' Stuart shouted sombrely.

'That's alright, boy,' her dad called back.

Her husband was leaving. She had successfully ruined everyone's life.

'What about Hayley?'

'I told you she's asleep, she's fine, don't wake her till morning. Just say I had to go home for work or something and I'll see her soon,' he walked past her and made a noise like he was trying to supress his anger or pain.

'Stuart,' she begged.

'I'll leave the booster seat here.'

'Okay,' she sighed, 'okay.'

She never imagined that leaving, be it her or him would feel like this. She had been ready to end their marriage but had never fully considered how it would happen and what it would look like.

He turned back to her then, 'I knew you know, I knew when I first met you that a day like this might come. I was never what you wanted, a pretty good substitute maybe, but I never ticked all the boxes on the list he left you with, did I?'

He was right, she could deny it but he knew what he had said was close to the mark.

'You ticked an awful lot of boxes of your own, Stuart.'

'Bye, Alice,' he turned and beeped the car door open, 'Call and let me know what's going on.'

'Of course,' she wiped her eyes, 'I love you.'

He waved her away with his hand to leave him be. But she stepped closer.

'It was never about us,' she half shouted as he put is bag in the boot.

'Maybe it should have been,' he opened the back door and removed Hayley's seat and handed it to her.

'I know,' she nodded.

'Do you have money?' he was still being her husband. Considerate, caring and the man she married.

'Yes, we'll be fine. I'm so sorry Stuart, I'm…' she said again.

'I'll see ya,' he got inside and started the engine and started backing off the driveway.

'Bye.'

Her stomach retched and she suddenly felt freezing cold, she was crying again but she probably hadn't ever stopped. She was going to throw up. She ran towards the gate and pushed it open.

Past her dad who started calling after her and into the downstairs cloakroom. She made it just in time.

Her husband had gone. Tom had gone. She didn't know what the hell her life was anymore and in the morning Hayley would get to witness her mother lie to her over and over again in a bid to protect her from the pain that had been caused by her own supposedly nurturing and loving hands.

CUTTING TIES

Saturday 7ᵗʰ August

'Bleeding from the ear isn't normal, Tom, I told you, you have to go to the hospital,' Neil walked into Tom's bedroom a little past midnight with his laptop and flopped heavily onto the bed, 'I've been googling it.'

'It's just a bit of blood, it's nothing,' Tom carried on packing his clothes into his holdall.

'Is it watery blood or clear fluid coming out?' Neil looked worried.

'It's stopped now anyway and no, it was just blood, blood.'

'It could be a cerebral compression and that's life-threatening. Or it could be a skull fracture?' he consulted his computer again, 'any dizziness or nausea?'

'No. The guy isn't fucking Thor I don't think one lucky punch is going to cause a skull fracture,' Tom didn't want to get angry with his friend and he was doing his very best to keep it together and not make the situation ten times worse by pressing his self-destruct button.

Neil looked at the whiskey bottle on the bedside table, 'and that isn't going to do you any favours if you do get rushed in – they may not be able to operate.'

Tom shot him a look that said, enough.

'Just saying,' he mumbled under his breath.

'I know you mean well and you care about me and I love you for that, but really I just need to be on my own right now,' he smiled a tight smile and picked up his tumbler.

'Okay just tell me what she said after you tried to choke her husband? Was it a definite no?' Neil asked carefully.

'Neil just listen to your question again and ask yourself if you really need to confirm if it was a definite no or not? She told me to go.'

'But he was being a cock, and he hit you first. What were you supposed to do?'

'What you would have done, been the better man. He hit first, but I was fucking his wife! Shit, I should have shown her that I was worthy of her, that I had grown up. That I wasn't just a thug carefully disguised as a head teacher,' he shook his head, 'what was I thinking?' he said to himself.

'You can't change who you are.'

'I think that's the point.'

'What time are we leaving in the morning? Are you going to call her before you go?' he asked.

'Let's just get to the airport early. No, I'm not calling – she has enough to think about putting her life back together and if she's working things through with him then that's the last thing she'll want me to do. Like you said I fucked her life up once. Unfortunately, this is twice and I'm not about to make it a hat-trick,' he swigged his drink aggressively and slammed the glass back down.

Neil flinched, 'top up?' he smiled sheepishly.

Tom smiled back and shook his head, 'no man, you never know I might need that surgery.'

Neil laughed and pulled his body off the bed lazily, 'I'm going to turn in, if you need to shout at someone later... don't bother waking me up, just take it out on the Xbox.'

'Good plan,' Tom smiled sadly.

'And when I say take it out, I mean play on it, not smash it to bits.'

'Understood,' he saluted him, but could really have done with a hug. But how do you ask a guy mate for a hug without it sounding pussy?

'Night.'

Tom watched the best man he knew leave the room and the moment he closed the door behind him Tom sank onto the bed. He grabbed the bottle and poured another drink.

He wasn't surprised that it had ended like this. But that didn't mean he wasn't shocked by his calmness, that he wasn't crying or punching holes in things. He guessed because it had felt like a dream being with her again, that now the waking up part didn't feel real either.

He was sorry though. Sorry that he had brought it to her door like that. He had acted on impulse as he always did and this time he had got it wrong, sadly at her expense.

She wasn't going to call him.

He wasn't going to see her again.

Don't let that thought in...

Tom flung his head back on the pillow and instantly regretted it as the pain ricocheted around his skull, a bit like brain freeze after an ice lolly, but much worse.

He was convinced now that this week had been, for her, just something she had to do.

Bullshit.

Given the chance and being slightly bullied she had repeated history with him and now it was over. As with all unsavoury deception there was a price and they had both paid it.

She was a married woman and a mother. She would save what she could from the dust that settled and regret the rest.

Please baby, don't regret us...

That's what she had to do.

He would go home. Home to his little slice of the world and start over.

Bullshit.

He had done it before. Could he do it now? He was too old for screwing around and drink no longer held the appeal it used to. He had to remember he had children also, that they were more precious than his life. He would go home and pretend nothing had happened here. Pretend nothing had broken his heart... nothing had broken his soul and he would make damn sure nothing ever would again.

And that's what he had to do.

Fuck that, as if he could pretend that he didn't love her still and that his heart wasn't ripping into tiny pieces. His body might be calm now, he wasn't throwing punches and running round like a frantic dickhead. But his brain was pumping his veins full of old memories and the frail hopes he had dreamed of for their future. Those thoughts, this brain, would be a constant and unwelcome cell mate for the life sentence of pain and loss he had just been handed down.

He didn't get up again as he had planned to. He didn't want to sleep. He wanted to pack his stuff and brood over his actions. But he had closed his eyes and at some point drifted into a fitful slumber.

He dreamt of her face beneath his own, bending his head and kissing the end of her nose gently. The dream was them as their younger selves. Back then it had felt like they were up against so many barriers. But in truth the only barrier had been himself. As older people they were free from stigma to do as they pleased, but it seemed now they faced more hurdles than ever before. He dreamed of the time when he could have kept her forever simply by claiming her as his.

When he woke hours later it was pitch black, someone had turned his light off and thrown a blanket over him.

Neil.

He thought he had heard his alarm going off and that was what had pulled him from lazy stagnation, but now he was fully awake he heard nothing. He reached clumsily for his phone, he hadn't even set the alarm and he needed it for the morning. He pressed the round button and the room was illuminated by the bright glow, he squinted a little, quickly trying to adjust to the sudden light change.

1 missed call – Alice. He blinked again and re-read his screen. 1 missed call – Alice.

Fuck, that's what had stirred him. He sat bolt upright and rubbed his hand over his face. He was still fully dressed, absent his boots and he pulled the blanket back swiftly. He grabbed the glass and finished what was left in the bottom, but his mouth felt like a toilet.

He checked the call time, three minutes ago. He pressed call back and waited.

The phone rang twice and then she answered.

'Tom?' she was quiet.

'Are you okay? What's wrong?' he went straight into saviour mode again and cursed himself silently.

'I'm fine, nothing's wrong. Well obviously not nothing but you know what I mean.'

'Okay,' he didn't know what to say, 'I'm sorry I missed your call.'

'Sorry I rang so late – you were probably sleeping?'

'I wasn't,' he lied.

'Good.'

'What did you want?' fuck that sounded rude like he didn't want to talk to her, 'I mean what…'

'Its fine Tom, I know. I just had to talk to you and explain about everything. I'm so sorry I couldn't stop you from coming over. I'm sorry you got hurt the way you did,' she sounded like she was holding back a great deal of emotion and he wondered if her husband was there.

'I didn't get hurt, I'm fine,' he answered quickly. If she didn't count the possible head injury that is, he heard Neil say in his mind.

'Are you sure?'

'Positive.'

'Thank you for walking away and not making it so much worse.'

Why was she being so calm about this?

'Is he with you?' Tom's voice came out hard. He didn't want to be anybody's floor show if the guy was sitting next to her putting words in her mouth.

'No.'

'Are you lying?'

'No, he left ten minutes after you did. He's gone home to leave me to think about everything. I wouldn't call you if he told me to. I'm not a puppet and I wouldn't treat you like that,' she sighed and the line went silent.

'Sorry, baby,' he caught himself quickly, 'I mean sorry, Alice.'

He heard a sniff and a muffled sob.

'I know your leaving tomorrow and everything's different now, but I just needed to hear your voice and make sure that you were okay, that you hadn't done anything silly?'

'I wanted to call you too but thought you would tell me to die or something?'

'I'd never do that.'

'Maybe you should have? Then maybe your world wouldn't be upside down because of my failure to keep my mouth shut,' he pulled at his hair.

'Tom, we did this, not just you alone. Why do you always insist on taking the blame for every questionable choice I make?'

He flipped on his bedside lamp and pulled his shoes towards his feet, 'because I never want to see hurt in your eyes whether you're mine or not.'

He thought he sensed her sad smile.

'That's *so* you.'

'Where are you? Still at your dad's?' he asked tying his laces and balancing the phone between his shoulder and ear.

'I'm at Stephanie's house. She made us leave the kids with my parents despite me just wanting to grab Hayley, wake her up and hug her all night,' he could tell she was crying now, 'they said it would be the wrong thing to do, that she would sense my sadness. My mum said that I should take some time to think clearly about what had happened before I spoke to her. Steph has been trying to get me drunk all night, but like that's going to make all this go way? Her husband Tony, has been constantly asking me how I could have done it? And how it felt to have sex with a teacher – he's weird.'

Tom felt his jaw twitch with frustration, Tony that was his name was it? 'Tell him to mind his own fucking business.'

'I did,' she paused, 'can you believe my sister called you Mr Chambers like she was still a pupil of yours or something?' she chuckled sadly.

'No,' he joined in, 'it was so ill-timed.'

'Yep, that's my sister. But she's always championed us. Even when she didn't think what we were doing was the right thing.'

'Have I ever told you how sensible your sister is?' he joked.

'Oh God Tom, how did we get here? I keep thinking that I might wake up tomorrow at home, with you in my dreams, instead of this reality. You know? Just as a fantasy again. My life as it was before.'

He closed his eyes, 'I'm so sorry.'

'I didn't mean it like it was a wish. I just meant this all feels so strange now. I have had the white picket fence for so long. But tonight it's just me and my daughter and a future that's not certain anymore.'

'I regret that you had to deal with the way I forced you to tell him. It was never my intention, I just wanted to protect you. I messed up big time. But I can never regret being with you again.'

'I can't regret that either, Tom,' she breathed.

He walked into the en-suite and squeezed toothpaste onto his brush and turned on the tap.

'What are you doing?' she asked.

Tom laughed, 'cleaning my teeth.'

'Oh right... Tom, its ten to three in the morning,' she stated like he had gone mad.

'I know.'

'What're you thinking?' she asked.

'I'm not really thinking.'

'Oh.'

'I love you,' he whispered.'

'Tom...' she sniffed.

'Will you to let me pick you up?' he stopped brushing and waited.

'What?' she whispered.

'Let me pick you up… right now,' he said again. He knew he was pushing what was a very fragile situation, 'One more time before I go? I need to be able to take with me a goodbye that's not like the one we shared a lifetime ago, and if we leave it with the one from earlier it will feel just as desperate as before… do you understand?'

There was a long pause.

'I do.'

'Baby, I'm not stupid. I know you'll have to make things right with your husband and after what happened tonight I also know I've screwed up beyond redemption. I live in the real world and I know what works and what doesn't. But I do need to see you – if you will see me?'

Silence again.

'Hell, what have I got to lose?'

'Give me the address and I'll be there in five minutes,' he ran down the stairs and grabbed Neil's car keys and opened the front door. He looked again at the alloys with big scuffs and chips all over them. He hadn't seen it yet – all good things come to those who wait – he swallowed quickly and dismissed the uncomfortable thought.

'It's 32 Anderson Drive, near the tennis centre. But make it ten minutes I have to clean my teeth too and get dressed. I'm in bed, in my pyjamas.'

'Leave them on,' he started the car.

'Are you already in the car?'

'Yep – get brushing,' he said and hung up. He put the car in gear and started the drive to her sister's house. Adrenaline of a different kind powering his actions now. He needed to get to her.

He was down, but he wasn't out… and he wasn't done yet.

"YOU AIN'T JUST WHISTLIN' DIXIE"

Saturday 7th August

She jumped out of bed and pulled on a cardigan over her thin camisole top, she didn't bother with a bra. Her Ugg boots over her pyjama bottoms made her look like a Cossack dancer. She brushed her teeth and then her hair. She quickly applied mascara to try and go some way to hide her hours of crying. She looked like shit. But it was dark and a car would offer very little light, so she may well get away with it.

She crept down the stairs and looked out of the kitchen window. She saw his car parked at the kerb. His interior light was on and he glanced towards the house. She put her hand up to him, picked up her phone and borrowed a set of keys from the hall table. She quietly shut the door behind her and tip-toed down the gravel drive.

She studied his face in the dark, through the car window... and that was enough. She was young Alice again. He was nearby, she was looking at him and suddenly everything got fuzzy around the edges. No peripheral vision, just one singular thing pulling her body without ever asking her brain if it wanted to go along for the ride.

When he had said to her that he had ruined his chances by half-killing Stuart she hadn't corrected him. It probably should have been the case. But walking towards him now she couldn't think about anything more terrifying than leaving him again, even if she had to.

He reached over and opened the door for her.

'You really screwed Neil's wheels,' she smiled at the rhyme in spite of herself as she got into the car.

'It's been an expensive trip. New alloys and bedroom door.'

She turned to him and gasped, 'Oh my goodness that looks painful.'

He smiled sarcastically, 'yeah, I think it's going to leave a little bruise.'

'Sorry,' she said for what felt like the tenth time. She met his gaze, smiled a little and he smiled back.

'I'm sorry for letting him get to me. It's just what he said about your daughter and everything else. I'm too old to be doing stupid things like that though – I shouldn't have hurt him. You didn't need that.'

'I didn't, but it's done now. It would've been horrible either way. If I had left him, he would have found out about us sooner or later and the reaction would have been the same. More than the cheating it was who it was with that hurt him the most, I think.'

'I can understand that I suppose.'

'What's the plan, Chambers?' she asked with a smile. She was beyond upset and concern now, she may as well just live for a bit longer with him and add a little more onto the guilt pile for tomorrow's harsh light of day reality check. What genius said things always look better in the morning? She had a sinking feeling it wouldn't apply to her situation in the slightest.

'Let's get out of here,' he gripped the wheel and she watched his fingers move over the new leather and his left hand drop to the gear stick. She was always transfixed by him. Whatever he did, however bad she felt, it never failed to surprise or intrigue her. Watching him do the most normal things pleased her on a level she didn't understand. Stuart was right, she was obsessed with this man.

'It's been so long since I last watched you drive.'

'*Watched* me drive?' he raised his eyebrows.

'Shut up,' she smiled, 'you know what I mean.'

'Would you believe me if I told you I still have the same car?'

'No.'

'I do. She's still going,' he glanced in her direction.

'That's kind of strange – but I like that you still have it. It's how I always pictured you.'

'I always pictured you with long hair and a school uniform. I had been selling you so short, if only I had seen what your beauty had grown into sooner.'

'How have you stayed the same? Not aged?' she asked.

'I've aged. I think they call what you are suffering from 'eye of the beholder syndrome' it's very common in matters of true love,' he joked.

'Is that right?' she said shaking her head.

'The only cure is a course of rigorous sexual therapy, followed by long years of living in close quarters with the object of your desires. Only then will you see the man exactly as he is... so I've heard anyway?' he shrugged.

They drove for about ten minutes and when she realised where they were heading she smiled. This was where he wanted to say goodbye?

He didn't bother to indicate to turn left into the school driveway. At this hour they were one of the only cars on the road anyway. He pulled into one of the parking spaces but left the engine running for the heater, it was a chilly night and they both had forgotten coats.

'So?' she turned to him.

'So,' he replied, 'this was our place, Alice. This is where we met, this is where we fell in love and it's also the place…' he stopped and pointed towards the playing fields where her heart was broken, 'we nearly killed each other when I walked away from you.'

She looked out onto the pitch black field. He was parked here the night he had done it and she had watched him drive away feeling like the world had just pulled the rug out from under her feet.

'Do you really want a repeat of what happened, Tom? Because I don't think my heart can take it.'

He shook his head.

'What then?

'I want to erase what happened there.'

'You can't erase history,' she replied sadly.

'But we could re-write the scene, tweak it and maybe we would be able to remember things differently from now on?' he turned his head and caught her eye, 'I don't know about you but that day was one of the worst days of my life. I think about you crying and the things we said and I hate myself. This week has been so unexpected and so fucking unreal. I want to remember this, the way we are now when I get home and not what happened here the last time.'

'How do you plan on doing that? It's been that way for so long. Okay, we're different, but I still sit here and feel the same loss. I'll always feel it when I think about this school.'

'We make a new memory,' he half smiled, 'and we do it here, there…' he pointed to the playing field again.

'You want to go over there and say goodbye in a way that will make it all better?'

'I know it sounds crazy,' he waited for her reply.

'I'm wearing pyjamas. It's freezing, not to mention stupid o'clock in the morning,' she frowned at him.

'That's what's stopping you?' he asked, his eyes twinkling cheekily.

She felt a bit like a party pooper, but shrugged.

Tom shoved the car into reverse and pulled out of the space quickly. He turned the car in the direction of the playing fields and looked towards her flashing a wicked grin. He revved the engine and gunned the car forward, up the kerb, over the path and onto the grass.

'You can't do that, Tom… oh my god, what're you thinking!' she shouted and laughed at the same time.

He drove fast onto the middle of the field, churning up mud as he went. He swung the car around to face the way they had come and pulled the handbrake up to help them stop. She bounced back in her seat and stared at him with an open mouth. They were parked in exactly the right spot.

'Now you're warm, no one can see your pyjamas and we're where I wanted us,' he laughed a little, 'I haven't felt like that in quite a while. Maybe I should do bad things more often…'

'Oh my God,' she said again. She looked around them quickly, convinced security would be patrolling or the police would whizz around the corner any minute with their blues flashing.

Tom turned off the headlights and let everything fall dark and silent.

They were probably safe.

'You're crazy,' she looked at him.

'So you tell me.'

'Don't change,' she could feel tears threaten in her eyes but blinked them back.

'I couldn't anyway,' he answered truthfully.

'I'm never going to be able to forget you, Tom,' she said out of the blue, the words taking her by surprise, 'all these damn years and I'm still in love with my English teacher – you could write a book about it.'

'I will never forget a single moment that we spent together. I never hoped to even wish for a week like we've had. I didn't think I'd still feel the same about you, but I do and if it's possible I think I love you more.'

She turned to him and studied his profile, she wanted to touch his lips and feel his thick hair under her fingertips.

'Life has a way of standing in our path,' he looked out into the darkness.

She nodded sadly, 'Yes, it does. I think it's because the universe acknowledges that we're a wrong fit, but refuses to give up hope that we'll ignore her advice and do what feels right to us. That we just might be pre-destined to be together. It's like Adam and Eve and the forbidden fruit – the minute we taste it everything around us seems to go to shit. All accept the glorious taste of the succulent ripe apple, lingering just long enough to leave us wanting it forever,' she grinned at him.

'Nice analogy,' Tom said and reached for her hand.

'Thank you, sir,' she said quietly.

'Who's the apple?' Tom asked.

Alice smiled, 'you are.'

'No, you are,' he corrected her.

'Maybe we're both apples?' she laughed.

'Maybe you're the whole damn orchard,' he watched her closely as he spoke the words. Her eyes met his and she turned away quickly. Tom would never stop. She had panicked because within seconds she felt the age old pull in her gut, the light tap dance of butterflies over her skin and her heartbeat quicken.

'Why're you afraid?' he whispered, 'there's nothing we can do that is any worse than what we have already done,' he picked up her other hand and held them between both of his.

She didn't look at him, 'Tom, I'm not afraid I'm just...' his warm hands distracted her from what she was saying, '...complicated. I'm complicated.'

'I think in this place,' he looked around the confined space, 'we're only Tom and Alice. Nothing is complicated within the realm of us.'

'Just everything outside of us...'

He nodded, 'yes.'

She looked up at him and intertwined her fingers with his. She felt him squeeze her hand gently. He stared at her with the eyes of a sea god, so blue they still shone in the relative darkness. He moved closer to her face and she didn't turn away.

'Alice, I'll never give you up, you know? You might be a thousand miles away from me but in my heart you'll be right here,' he leaned in and kissed her lips so softly for just a few seconds. As he pulled away she followed him, her eyes were closed and everything about him filled her mind. His smell, his taste and the smallest touch of his skin, no amount of tender goodbye would be enough to sate her appetite for him.

'I never wanted you to,' she whispered as they parted.

She would never love or want anyone as much as she loved and wanted him. Honour and loyalty paled in the shadow of a truer love, as it probably always should. Nothing he could do would ever change the way she felt about him. For as long as he lived she would always be his to command.

'I'm leaving in a matter of hours. I don't want to go, but I have to. The thought of not seeing you again is scaring me like you...'

She stopped him with a second kiss. 'Don't think about that. Tom, we're here together and if we truly only have a few hours left together, we should make them count,' her eyes moved over his face quickly. His strong jaw flexed and his dimples appeared as she moved back from him.

'You want to do this now? Here?' he said feeling puzzled and promptly cringed at his comment.

She smiled at his look, 'there's not a second in your company that I don't.'

Alice reached up and slipped the cardigan from her shoulders.

'I should have done it here, that night, when every part of my body was screaming at me to lie you down in the rain and make love to you. My student? My lover? It shouldn't have mattered. Look at how little our age matters now. But instead my head had said leave…'

'A new memory then?' she blinked.

He grabbed her arms and pulled her on top of his lap. His large body beneath her made her feel powerful. He fixed her with an emotive gaze that radiated sexual possession and male heated pride. Making her yearn for him to touch her properly. She traced her hands over his chest and his own pulled her towards him forcefully.

Her breath caught in her throat.

He nodded in agreement, 'a new one.'

Tom reached up and slipped the straps of her top over her shoulders. The thin, feather-like silk fell away from her body pooling at her waist.

He smiled. Then he leaned forward and drew her nipple into his hot mouth. Slowly he pulled on the sensitised flesh and his tongue traced circles over the tip. Her head fell backwards and she felt herself respond to his exquisite ministrations with primal force. She felt reckless already and he hadn't even undressed. Her own reactions scared her, he scared her and losing this feeling terrified her.

His warm hands played up and down the flesh of her back, as his mouth continued to push her closer. He kissed the side of her breast and upwards towards her neck, she leaned her head back further offering herself to him.

'You smell so good,' she sighed as he kissed his way along her jaw.

'You smell like prey,' he growled biting her ear lope gently.

Another stab of arousal came at her.

'Tom, I think I want to tell you something... I don't know if I do though?' she breathed heavily and wriggled a little on his strong thighs and he responded by thrusting upwards against her playfully.

Why was she still talking? Why did she have this need to spill all her secrets to him, embarrass herself and spoil the moment?

'Oh?' Tom pulled impatiently at the elastic waistband of her pyjama bottoms and she lifted herself up to help him, he pulled them over her bottom and cupped her in his hands.

She unzipped his jeans, prising the stiff material apart, 'I can only orgasm with you,' she paused for a moment and wondered why she had said it as a throw away comment. He abruptly jerked her backwards to look at her face. His eyes narrowed, 'I can't orgasm through sex without it being with you...' she confirmed quickly.

Tom held his breath, if she had actually counted the seconds before he spoke she was sure it would have been a record or something.

'I... are you serious?'

'Unfortunately,' she replied, 'you're the only man that does what my body wants. For years I thought you'd put some kind of Irish spell on me so I only responded to your touch.'

A gust of wind coming at them across the open field rocked the car and made her tremble.

Tom shook his head slowly, '…no spell.'

'Anyway where were we?' she grabbed his hands and placed them back to her waist. Tom didn't continue though. He left his hands were she had put them and he just stared at her.

'What?' she bit her lip and waited.

"AND NOT THE WORDS OF ONE WHO KNEELS"

Saturday 7th August

Floored. All the fancy words in Tom's head and that was the one that best described the way he felt as she whispered a simple truth in the dark grey moments before dawn broke.

He watched her little face trying to gage his reaction. She waited a long time before she asked him what he was thinking and even then he didn't know how long it was before he answered her.

She *was* truly his.

Not only in his dreams or in a jealous figment of his imagination. She was his in reality. She had to be? She had just told him what he always wanted and prayed to be true… that they *were* meant to be, right from the very start.

How was it possible for a woman as passionate as Alice to feel this way with only him?

He wasn't stupid, it wasn't about what he did to her, it was about herself and how her mind let her feel when they were together. He wasn't a biologist but he was sure hormones and endorphins played a part too.

But the little fact remained the same.

Yours.

He wanted to squeeze her and kiss her and spend every Christmas with her forever. Travel the world by her side and treasure her honesty, beauty and laughter above all other things.

Shit, his marriage hadn't worked because of her and now her own lay in tatters because of him. Separated for over a decade and still they craved this. They had unlocked her body together on a school trip, one cold night in November, so many years ago. Together they still had the power to surprise and satisfy each other.

Had they been subconsciously searching and waiting for this day?

Did all roads lead here?

One thing he was sure of she wouldn't be taken from him now. If he had to sell his soul to the devil to make it happen she would never be with another man ever again. Fuck goodbye and fuck doing the right thing, from here on out it was only about them.

Calm down.

She had said to him the other day she was afraid that he would tire of her in the real world. He wondered if she would ever understand how wrong she had been. How could he ever feel anything but love when she turned her big emerald eyes on him and playfully smiled?

She pulled at his arm.

'Give me a minute, baby,' he touched her lips with his own.

I just need a minute…

The simple things he knew he would relish in their everyday relationship, like silly mundane arguments, wouldn't be tiresome to him, it would be foreplay.

'Tom, tell me what you're thinking?'

I will.

And as time passed, years rolled and the lust gently ebbed away from them, he would watch the lines around her eyes deepen and still think she was the most beautiful thing he had ever witnessed.

She in turn could tease him about his greying hair and plans for retirement that he refused to face. He could maybe even, at a push, imagine trips to the local garden centre for coffee on a Sunday morning as they grew *much* older – and he hated those places.

A normal life with her and all their children, however that worked out and however many they had of their own or didn't have for that matter, would be the purest kind of happiness he could think of.

'What is it, Tom?' she said again pushing at his shoulders, 'Talk to me.'

Okay baby…

How was he going to say what he wanted to?

'I asked you earlier this evening and I meant it,' he said. The words catching in his throat, '…in the heat of things, but I was serious. Probably out of order but when aren't I?' he gently stroked her cheek and her eyes moved quickly over his own, searching for answers, 'I swore I wouldn't ever do it again after it all went to hell last time…'

'What, Tom? You're making no sense?'

He grabbed her face in his two hands now, 'Marry me, Alice.'

'What?' she stumbled over the simple word and looked away from him in confusion and fear, 'I thought this was it? I thought you and me –'

He tightened his grip on her smooth skin and made her look at him.

'No baby, this time we have to stop playing.'

Tom lifted her up quickly with his two hands like she weighed nothing and pulled his wallet out of his pocket. She looked shocked and her shoulders shivered. He placed her back down on the seat next to him.

'Tom...' she started.

'Before you answer...' he handed his wallet to Alice, 'look inside.'

Her small hands opened the brown leather slowly and peered in, 'what am I looking at?' her voice trembled.

'The back section,' he nodded for her to continue.

Alice pulled out the small strip of card, two pictures of a younger them, his half of the set she had given him. She studied them for a long time and said nothing. A large tear fell from her cheek onto the well-loved photographs and he nodded.

'Look in the coin bit,' he said then.

She un-popped the soft material and tipped it out onto her open palm.

A small band of gold. A diamond. A question.

'I've had that for fourteen years,' he sighed, 'I wanted to ask you when it would have been so wrong to. All of the nights we were together it was on my mind. Keeping you. Telling you. I wanted to ask a seventeen-year-old girl to marry me and that was the sad and scary truth that ultimately drove me away. But it's yours. Baby, it's always been yours.'

'You've kept this ring with you for that long?' she looked up at him and her eyes were full of tears.

'The same length of time you've kept my heart.'

EPILOGUE

Sometime in the future

June was hot, not that he was complaining. Peter ran out of his front door shortly after supper carrying his army style water bottle filled with orange squash and ice cubes. In his hand he had three homemade shortbread biscuits his mum had given him. One for himself and one each for his two best friends, Luke and Warren. Whom he called for on his way to the back fields.

They often got dubbed the three musketeers by their parents and although they liked it – they didn't really understand what it meant. They were ten-years-old so they would have preferred to be called the three *Power Rangers* or *Ninja Turtles*, something cool like that.

They sprinted to the first stile and vaulted it. Youth allowed them to support their body weight with ease. Luke, who has leading, started coughing some way in front of him. Biscuit crumps flying from his mouth in all directions.

Peter laughed, 'you should have bloody waited,' his strong Irish accent carrying the comment down the dirt track that was edged with lush grass and regiments of wild poppies, towards his friend's ears.

Luke turned around and made some sort of rude hand gesture, smiled and ran on ahead.

They jogged past a few back gardens, turned a sharp corner and up a little hill. They jumped over the small brook that meandered past the bottom of old Mrs Murphy's place and picked up the sticks and rucksack they had stashed there earlier in the day.

Now they had retrieved their kit, they were ready. In the distance he could see their destination beckoning, it was only open fields from here.

Luke and Warren called for him to hurry up when he stopped for a moment to reposition the backpack that kept slipping from his right shoulder as he ran.

He waved back at them, 'I'm coming guys!'

Peter opened the cap on his drink bottle and took a long swig. He grimaced, it was too weak again. He'd have to tell his mum to put more cordial in next time. He pushed the bottle into the bag and ran on.

About fifty yards ahead he glanced to the right. A small white house was visible at the top of a sloping tree lined garden. On the deck he spotted Mr Chambers and waved at him kindly. He was going to be his headmaster next year so needed to stay in his good books.

Mr Chambers waved back, 'Peter,' he shouted in greeting.

Peter waved again before he disappeared out of view.

It was funny, the last time he had passed by he had caught Mr Chambers kissing his girlfriend. The man hadn't noticed him though, and Peter didn't call out or anything. Witnessing any adults 'make out' was a horrible thing, but your parents or a teacher? Well that was emotionally scarring.

He had taken great pleasure in recounting the whole gruesome story to his friends, of course being a young boy he may have added some smutty details plucked from his own imagination to make it sound all the more gag inducing.

He grinned. It was his little bit of security. He was anxious about starting big school and if Mr Chambers ever shouted at him or gave him detention he would take comfort from the knowledge that he knew he wasn't just a scary teacher – he was a real guy too – just like everyone else. A guy who sits in his garden at night, drinking and kissing girls.

'Hi.'

He jumped. A little voice to his right caught him off guard. He looked in the direction of the voice and saw a small blonde girl smiling at him with a wide infectious grin. Her hands were full of the wild flowers that grew at the edge of the garden and her big green eyes studied him intently.

'Hi,' he replied, staring at her for a moment before a high pitched whistle drew his attention and ahead he saw his friends disappear into the cluster of trees.

'Bye,' she smiled again.

'Bye,' he echoed, turning from her slowly and he ran on.

'Luke?' he said as he neared the den and spotted his friends through the thicket.

He quickly put all thoughts of girls, snogging teachers and detentions out of his mind. That was for another day, school was still months away and he had plenty of time to gather more revealing evidence about his future headmaster.

'Bring the bag over here, Peter,' Warren called in a hushed whisper.

'Okay,' he nodded.

He crept towards them unzipping the rucksack as quietly as he could. He pulled out a small net and clean jam jar that his mum had put through the dishwasher for him.

It was darker inside the den and cooler. Luke had the notepad and pen resting on his knee as he jotted down the date and time. Warren was gaffer taping his sister's mobile phone to a nearby tree, so they could record it all on video and upload it to *YouTube* later.

The atmosphere was electric. He could sense it in the very trees that surrounded them. The three boys, the musketeers, were poised on the edge of something massive. It was bigger than all of them, so important that they couldn't speak of it to anyone and it was theirs alone for the taking.

Tonight was the night they had planned and talked about. For weeks they had watched this place, now they were going to prove the legends true… tonight they were catching themselves a fairy.

More Titles by this Author

The Not Gate

53211191R00170

Made in the USA
Charleston, SC
06 March 2016